BLOODLINE

OTHER BOOKS FROM JORDAN L. HAWK:

Hainted

<u>Whyborne & Griffin:</u>
Widdershins
Threshold
Stormhaven
Necropolis
Bloodline

<u>SPECTR</u>
Hunter of Demons
Master of Ghouls
Reaper of Souls
Eater of Lives
Destroyer of Worlds
Summoner of Storms

<u>Short stories:</u>
Heart of the Dragon
After the Fall (in the *Allegories of the Tarot* anthology)
Eidolon (A Whyborne & Griffin short story)
Remnant, written with KJ Charles (A Whyborne & Griffin / Secret Casebook of Simon Feximal story)
Carousel (A Whyborne & Griffin short story) in the Another Place in Time anthology

BLOODLINE

(Whyborne & Griffin No. 5)

JORDAN L. HAWK

Chapter 1

SHARKS SWIRLED AROUND me, waiting only for the scent of blood to attack. One show of weakness and they would close in, dragging their hapless victim down into the depths. Or his reputation, anyway. These sharks glittered not with teeth, but diamonds, gold cufflinks, and gowns from Maison Worth. A bit out of season for a gathering of elite society, as grand balls generally didn't begin until after Thanksgiving, and it was now less than two weeks before Hallowe'en. But no one could pass up the chance to view the triumphant return of my sister Guinevere—or rather, Lady Gravenwold—from England.

Like any minnow, I tried to remain small and still in hopes of going unnoticed. Unfortunately, the enormous ballroom provided little in the way of cover. The best I could do was stand as near as possible to the most hideous portrait of the dozens covering the walls, in the hope its sheer ugliness would frighten anyone else away.

"You must be very pleased with yourself," Stanford growled.

My brother wasn't the biggest shark in these treacherous waters, but he warranted a careful eye nonetheless. "I don't know what you mean," I said truthfully.

Stanford snorted. He'd inherited Father's build, and as a youth, he'd grown brawny from the exercise of chasing and tormenting things smaller than himself. Namely me, but wounded birds and stray dogs would do as well. Over the last few years, he'd run to fat, mainly through excess of drink, but tonight his piggish eyes seemed clear. "Of course you do. How did you convince Father to throw this party for you?"

"It isn't for me." And it wasn't, not really. Although I'd been rather horrified to see my name prominently displayed on the invitations. "It's for Guinevere. I suppose Mother and Father thought they might as well include my birthday, since it's in two weeks."

On Hallowe'en, in fact. The holiday generally marked the beginning of the social season in Widdershins, much as Thanksgiving did in New York. No doubt because the old families wished to gather together to conduct whatever unholy rites they preferred, and an early start to the season gave them perfect cover.

God, these parties had been hideous enough before I'd realized madmen and cultists founded the town, their work continued until this very day. At least I knew now why Father had been absent for all of my childhood birthdays, although the rituals he might have performed with the Brotherhood on those nights didn't bear considering.

"I thought you might have decided to marry," Stanford went on, narrowing his eyes even further as he regarded me. "Make Father happy, and this was your reward. But you haven't danced with anyone. And you brought your—" He caught himself from whatever he meant to say, recalling the crowd around us. *"Companion,"* he finished, the word soaked in scorn and vinegar.

My fingers tightened around my champagne flute. I wouldn't let Stanford make me angry. Not tonight.

Blast it, why had I come here? But I already knew the answer: it presented an excellent opportunity for Griffin to make connections normally out of his reach. True, he'd already handled a case for one of the old families, the Lesters, but this was his chance to establish himself as someone of taste and discretion in the eyes of the Widdershins elite. Even now he chatted with one of the Waite brothers, whose name I could never recall—Fred? Ted?

"I don't know why Father decided to append my birthday to Guinevere's return," I grated out. "I was invited. I agreed to attend. What is it to you?"

His familiar sneer had changed little since we were children. "I know what you're up to."

Was he drunk after all? Before I could even think how to respond, he turned away, tossing back the rest of his champagne as if he'd lost interest in the conversation. A ring set with an enormous diamond flashed on his finger. Mother had mentioned he'd been hard at work changing his fortunes ever since the scandalous divorce from Darla. Father wouldn't have paid for such an ostentatious ring; had he actually earned it himself?

"Percival," a commanding tone barked in my ear.

I started, slopping champagne on my cuff. My ears grew hot, but I struggled to keep any signs of embarrassment off my face as I turned to my father.

More lines showed on the visage glowering at me from beneath a mane of silver hair, but despite his age, the tuxedo he wore showed off a figure that remained firm.

"What are you doing skulking about?" he said, without even giving me the chance to greet him. Sapphires flashed blue fire from his cufflinks. "This is your opportunity to remind those of importance you still exist."

"Mr. Mathison is far more adept than I at soliciting donations for the museum," I said, deliberately misunderstanding Father's intent. "It's why the board made him president of the Ladysmith, after all."

Father's scowl deepened, a reaction to which I was long accustomed. "You're wasting your talents there, Percival. The skills you've picked up recently would be invaluable to our business."

Skills? True, I felt my sojourn in Egypt had sharpened my reading of the hieroglyphs, but...oh. He meant sorcery.

At least now I knew why he'd suddenly deemed my birthday worth mentioning, even if nearly two weeks before the fact. For almost twenty-nine years, he'd scorned my knowledge of languages, my high marks at university, my very existence. But now I'd gained a small amount of arcane power and suddenly warranted his attention.

My right arm ached, the lacework of scars pulling at the skin. At least the formality of the evening gave me an excuse to wear gloves, so no one would ask about the startling pattern of reddened flesh, which decorated the back of my hand since my return from Egypt.

"I'm sure they would," I managed to say, half shocked my voice remained neutrally calm. "But you cut me off from the business when I left for Miskatonic."

He made an impatient gesture. Dismissing the pain of our arguments, sweeping away everything my defiance had cost me, as if it were nothing. "Water over the dam. There's a place for you at Whyborne Railroad and Industries."

So I could be used and then discarded once again? My gloves kept the nails of my left hand from biting into my palm, but my right hand shook around the champagne flute. "I'm quite happy at the museum."

He shook his head, clearly despairing over my obstinacy. How dare I live my own life instead of the one he'd planned for me? "I don't suppose you've even danced with anyone. As I said, this is your chance to remind those of importance you exist, including a number of heiresses."

Was the man completely insane? "Griffin is here on *your* invitation," I said in a low voice, even though it was impossible to hear us over the string quartet playing nearby, not to mention the general chatter.

Father shrugged. "He seems a practical sort. Clever enough to know securing your friendship would give him access to a better sort of client, but not so foolhardy as to make inadvisable demands from me. I'm sure he would be perfectly happy to step back and agree to a different arrangement."

Because, of course, there could be no possible reason for Griffin to be with me other than advancing his own business. "You've never been in love in your entire life, have you?" Except perhaps with power.

"Love won't get you anywhere in this world." His brows drew down in a deeper scowl. "You must be willing to do whatever is necessary. General Sherman understood that."

"This is business, Father, not a battlefield."

"It's survival. One way or another."

Thankfully, one of the other guests caught Father's attention. "Think on what I've said," he ordered. "And for God's sake, at least find some young lady to dance with. Try Helmina Fisk—her father has inquired about you several times. If he thinks there's a possibility of a union, he'll sell his steel shares to me at a lower price."

Father departed before I could formulate any objection. Damn the man, he hadn't changed a whit in twenty years.

"Percival!" my sister called.

Oh dear lord, how many family members did I have at this wretched affair? And why must they all want to speak to me at once?

"Guinevere," I said, giving her a nod.

As befit the wife of an English nobleman, Guinevere blazed with gold and gems. Her dark hair piled high on her head, captured with a delicate net of gold and pearls, and diamonds dripped from her fingers and encircled her neck. Her gown was of pale yellow silk, cut to make the most of her figure, the sleeves and bodice swathed with lace. Tiny mirrors set on the lace reflected back the light of the chandelier. She had our mother's slender build and eyes, traits I also shared.

"A pleasure to see you again, Guinevere," I said, not because it was true, but because propriety demanded it. She'd behaved like imperious nobility even as a small girl, and marriage to Earl Gravenwold had only exacerbated the condition. "I trust your journey proved uneventful?"

Before she could reply, two other individuals appeared on her heels. They were perhaps thirty years of age, a man and woman who closely resembled one another, with hair the color of straw and blue eyes. The man's tuxedo was finely cut, and the woman wore a gown of crimson silk, the skirt embroidered with silver stars. Although not as bejeweled as Guinevere, they certainly looked as if they belonged amidst this crowd. Who were they, that I hadn't met them before?

"Guinevere, will you not introduce us?" the man asked in an English accent, his gaze fixed on me.

Guinevere's mouth thinned slightly in annoyance at the interruption, but she could hardly refuse. "Of course. Percival, I'm sure Mother mentioned our Endicott cousins to you?"

"Ah! Yes!" Guinevere and I didn't exchange letters, but she dutifully wrote Mother long missives each month, detailing her life in England. Mother passed along anything of interest, including Guinevere's unexpected discovery of distant relations in Cornwall.

"Dr. Percival Whyborne, may I present our cousins, Mr. Theodore Endicott and his sister, Miss Fiona Endicott," Guinevere said.

I bowed over Miss Endicott's hand, mouthing some polite words. God, just what I needed the least—more family.

When I extended my hand to her brother, he startled me by grasping it warmly with both of his. "Dr. Whyborne! It is truly an honor to meet you, sir." He wore a pair of small, round-lensed spectacles, which did nothing to diminish the gleam of real pleasure in his eyes. "When we met Guinevere, I couldn't believe you were our cousin, however distant. I'm something of a student of languages myself, and I read the treatise on Aklo you published last year. At the time, I'd assumed your middle name to be a coincidence, rather than an indication of relation. Your paper was very impressive, sir, very impressive."

"Oh! Er, thank you." I'd certainly not expected to meet someone who knew of my work at this gathering. Comparative philology remained an obscure science at best, and a paper concerning the roots of an esoteric medieval language used only by certain cults even more so. "Are you a philologist yourself?"

"I fear I'm but a dilettante." He gave my hand one last squeeze, then let go. "Forgive my enthusiasm, but I greatly admire your work."

I hadn't the slightest idea how to respond. Thank God my gloves had at least concealed any sweat from my palms. "Er, thank you, Mr. Endicott." I probably sounded like a fool. "You're very kind."

"Please, call me Theo." He glanced down, then back up at me. My height had always been something of a curse, forcing me to stand out when I would rather have hidden. "I don't wish to seem forward, but I would greatly appreciate the chance to converse later, at a time of your convenience."

People didn't seek out my company. Well, other than Griffin and

Christine, of course, but one was my lover and the other my best friend. They were rather obligated to do so. It felt strange to have someone I'd just met wish to speak to me again.

And it might be a good excuse to stop pretending to socialize with everyone else. I had to show good hospitality to our guest from abroad, didn't I? I glanced about—perhaps there was some secluded nook where Mr. Endicott and I might continue our conversation now, away from the noise and dancing.

As if my hopes had summoned an evil spirit to dash them, Father appeared at Mr. Endicott's elbow. "Theodore, Fiona—what do you think of American entertainments?" he asked. No doubt making certain they were suitably impressed by the ostentatious display of power and wealth.

Or, for all I knew, he'd somehow sensed someone paying me a compliment and felt the need to put a stop to it immediately. At any rate, I wouldn't be speaking privately with Mr. Endicott tonight, so I bowed to the group and took my leave.

I made my way along the outskirts of the room, staying well clear of the dancing and nodding distractedly to the ladies who sought to catch my attention. Where had Griffin slipped off to? The dazzling glitter of gemstones and fine silk confused my eyes, making it difficult to pick one person out of the crowd. I did spot Stanford, but fortunately, he was deep in conversation with Thomas Abbott, whose father had been part of the evil society known as the Brotherhood. The elder Abbott's death cleared the way for Thomas to take over the family fortunes and promptly fritter a good deal of them away, if rumor was to be believed.

At the moment, he wore a faint smile on his face. Stanford's, in contrast, flushed red with anger. Whatever they spoke of, I wished Abbott luck.

I finally glimpsed Griffin, not far from the doors, and my heartbeat immediately calmed. He conversed with Miss Lester, whom he'd previously worked for on a case involving a somewhat sinister family heirloom gone missing.

To see Griffin in this setting, an outside observer would have thought him born to high society, rather than an Irish orphan raised by Kansas farmers. He appeared entirely comfortable, charming his conversational partner as if he attended such gatherings every day. But he had a natural talent to mimic those around him and put them at ease. The confidence he displayed in nearly any situation had been one of the things that had both drawn me, and—were I to be entirely honest—put me on my guard when we first met.

My experience of confident men included my father and brother. Men so certain of their place in the world they viewed anyone less certain as inferior, to be used or crushed as circumstances dictated.

Not Griffin. His kindness ran deep, and it was what I loved most about him.

Well, along with his handsome face and devilish smile. And the way his form filled his tuxedo. I'd had the pleasure of watching him put it on earlier in the evening, and although the tails currently obscured his backside, I could attest to the fit of the trousers beneath.

I approached just close enough to pick out Miss Lester's voice from the hum of the crowd. "Of course Lady Gravenwold returned," she told Griffin. "They always do, you know."

He sipped his champagne. "I'm not certain what you mean."

"This town knows who belongs and who does not." Her black eyes glittered like anthracite. "Those whom Widdershins claims can never leave for long."

"I don't believe the countess intends to return permanently."

"It hardly matters what she intends." Miss Lester tugged one of her opera gloves higher on her arm. "Just as it does not matter whether you believe or not. Facts do not change to suit one's fancy. Now, if you will excuse me, I see someone I wish to avoid."

As Miss Lester departed, Griffin met my eye, a grin curving the corners of his mouth. I could not help but return it.

"Are you enjoying yourself?" he asked.

"Not in the slightest," I confessed. "You?"

He cast a look about the room before answering. "It is...a bit more rarified atmosphere than I'm accustomed to."

I snorted inelegantly. "To be fair, it's better than a family dinner. At least not everyone present is utterly obnoxious."

He laughed, green eyes flashing, and it lightened my heart further. "I hope I am one of the exceptions."

I made a show of considering the matter. "Hmm...you can be a bit trying at times."

He moved closer. No one else was near, so he lowered his voice and said, "I have always been quite happy to try you, it's true."

I pretended to observe the nearest painting, to hide my blush from the gathering. Griffin had been my lover for close to two years now, yet our flirtations still brought heat easily to my face. "We have put in our appearance. Shall we leave?"

He frowned slightly. "No one will miss you? You are one of the guests of honor, after all."

"I don't give a fig for any of them." Although Mr. Endicott had seemed interesting. "Besides, everyone here is curious about

Guinevere. Most of the old families have remained in Widdershins for generations, and having one of our own relocate to England seems far more exotic here than it would in New York or Newport."

"So I hear," he murmured, glancing in the direction Miss Lester had gone. "How long is your sister visiting?"

"I've no idea." I shrugged. "No doubt she will want to visit New York at some point, and socialize there. I'd expect her to return to England before Christmas, however, for appearance's sake if nothing else."

"And not because she misses her husband and child?" Griffin asked.

I remembered what Father had said. The sharp line he'd drawn between duty and love. One was of great consequence, and the other something frivolous, the sort of thing to be dreamed of by shop girls and readers of bad novels. And me, apparently.

"She will want to do right by them," I said quietly. "Beyond that, I can't say."

His eyes crinkled slightly at the corners when he frowned, hinting at the first touch of crow's feet, even though he was only thirty. Then his expression cleared. "I've never had a chance to tour the house," he mused.

Now it was my turn to frown. "I suppose not. You've seen most of the downstairs, though."

"Still, this seems a good opportunity to see more."

I couldn't imagine why he'd want to view the blasted place, but if it got us away from the party, I would agree to it. "Of course. Come with me."

CHAPTER 2

WE SLIPPED THROUGH the open doors, past the stairs, and into the grand foyer. The chandelier high above blazed with newly installed electric lights, the shadows far more sharp-edged than those I remembered.

"What do you want to see?" I asked. Griffin had been invited into the private parlor, the dining room, and Father's study on previous occasions. "Or do you wish a general tour?"

He leaned against the balustrade and cast his eyes to the upper floors. "What of your room? The one you had growing up. I assume you weren't forced to share with Stanford?"

"No, of course not."

Griffin grinned. "Very few could say the same. Had I not been the only child—adopted or otherwise—I would have shared with all of my siblings. Our neighbor had seven children, all packed into one bed."

"One bed?" I asked skeptically.

"Perhaps two." He nudged me with his shoulder. "So is your old room given over to a guest, do you think? Can we have a little glimpse?"

I hadn't the slightest idea why such a thing would be of interest to him. "It will be empty. Father was so convinced I would fail at Miskatonic, he ordered my room untouched after I left." Because, clearly, I would never accomplish anything without his direction and support.

Griffin frowned. "But surely, after so long...?"

"That would require Father to admit he'd been wrong in the first place."

He shook his head, laughing softly, as if to himself. "Of course."

"At least my family amuses someone," I muttered. "If my old room is what you wish to see, come along."

I led the way up the grand staircase to the third floor. As we emerged onto the landing, I caught a glimpse of dark skirts and a familiar silhouette leaving one of the rooms. "Miss Emily!"

She turned to me with a bright smile on her face. "Master Percival!"

I embraced her gladly. As my mother had been confined to her room for as long as I could remember, often too ill to venture forth, Miss Emily had helped raise me. Some of my happiest memories were of nights when Father was out of town, freeing Miss Emily to take me into the servants' quarters to eat dinner at their simple table.

"This is my friend, Mr. Griffin Flaherty," I said. She hesitated at being introduced to a guest, but Griffin gave her a small bow.

"Whyborne has spoken quite warmly of you," he said. It was the truth, but delivered with his characteristic smile, it could not help but win her over.

"You're very kind, sir," she said demurely, but with a decided blush. I withheld my sigh. Griffin could charm anyone of either sex. "Mrs. Whyborne says you're very good for Master Percival, if you don't my mind saying so. I don't mean to pry, of course, but raising Master Percival from a babe, I can't help but worry."

"How is Mother?" I asked. She'd been too ill to make public—or semi-public—appearances for my entire life. But she doted on Griffin, and I thought she would like to see him.

Miss Emily's face fell. "Not feeling herself tonight, the poor thing. I left her sleeping not fifteen minutes ago."

Griffin nodded his understanding. "Then please, give Heliabel my regards. I hope to see her again soon."

"Yes, sir."

I had no wish to detain Miss Emily from any duty she might have, so kissed her lightly and promised to return soon. As she hurried away, Griffin leaned against my shoulder. "Another piece to the puzzle that is you."

"I'm no cipher," I objected.

"I disagree." A slight frown creased his brow. "I've never though to ask before, but why has your mother remained here, rather than retire to a sanitarium in hopes of improving her health? I understand why she would have stayed when you were younger, but after her children were grown, why didn't she seek out a more congenial climate?"

"Because Widdershins wouldn't let her leave," I intoned, mimicking Miss Lester's voice.

Griffin chuckled. "I'd wondered if you'd heard that. So you don't think there's anything to it?"

"Of course not! It's superstitious bunkum, and I'm appalled someone with Miss Lester's education would believe such nonsense."

Griffin looked less convinced than I. But after a moment, he merely nudged my arm. "Your old room?"

In all truth, I never wanted to lay eyes on the place again. But I understood his curiosity. I would have felt the same about the farmhouse where he'd been raised. "This way."

A part of me hoped the door would be locked. But the knob turned easily under my hand, and I flung it open.

"Here," I said, not bothering to hide my resignation from him.

He stepped just inside, found the light, then waited for me to join him. I brushed past him with a sigh. The air held a certain musty smell, but the servants cleaned often enough it wasn't overwhelming. "Father chose the decorations," I said, gesturing to the bloody hunt scenes depicted on the tapestries, the battles woven into the rugs, the swords carved into the mantelpiece. "That's my paternal grandfather," I added, indicating the massive portrait facing the bed. As a youth, I'd drawn the bed curtains against the censure of his gaze, while I laid hand to my length at the thought of handsome men.

At least until Leander had died. The boy I'd loved as a youth myself; the guilt of having survived when he died convinced me desire was poison. After, this bed had truly been a prison, a struggle between grief and horror and guilt and longing.

"Not many good memories then?" Griffin asked quietly from behind me.

"No," I said, grateful not to have to explain. He understood me so well.

The lock on the door clicked sharply.

I turned. He leaned back against the door, a knowing smile on his face. "Then perhaps we should make a better one."

My heart beat faster. But... "This is my parents' house!"

He stalked toward me. "It is."

I swallowed. "Th-there are people here. Downstairs. I mean..."

He reached me and pressed close, so his breath stirred the small hairs beside my ear—and stirred something else, as well. "Yes. The elite of Widdershins, who won't have the slightest idea I'm sucking you just two floors above their heads."

Clearly, everything I found to be an objection, he considered a benefit. Desire fogged my thoughts. "A-all right."

He mouth turned up into a triumphant grin, green eyes flashing at me from under his lashes. "Lie down on the bed."

My clothes would be in danger of becoming creased—but to the devil with it. We'd sneak down the back stair and leave that way if we ended looking too disreputable. I tugged off my gloves and shed my tailed coat to keep it in decent form, and he did the same.

I pulled him close, kissing him. He tasted of champagne and chocolate cake, mingled with warm male. Griffin returned the kiss, plundering my mouth with his tongue even as he gripped my hips and pulled me tight against him.

"Father thinks you'd be perfectly happy if I were to marry some heiress," I mumbled against his lips.

Griffin snorted. "Then your father doesn't know either of us very well, does he?"

Griffin had been with women in the past. Mainly men, but he was not entirely unmoved by the feminine form. I lacked even an aesthetic appreciation, a fact on which my dear friend Christine occasionally teased me.

"No, but I thought he'd entirely washed his hands of me." And his talk about how sorcery might assist Whyborne Railroad and Industries...what the devil was the man about?

Griffin caught my chin gently in his fingers. "Shh. Quiet your busy mind, Ival."

The pet name always brought warmth to my chest. "Perhaps you'd best offer it a distraction."

He laughed and pushed me back, until my legs met the edge of the bed. I reclined on the eiderdown quilt, the rich brown satin soft under my fingers. The canopy loomed above, familiar from a thousand sleepless nights. Griffin settled between my thighs, his hands already working on the buttons of my trousers.

His touch through the cloth hardened me in anticipation of such a touch against skin. I'd not spent a single moment in this bed for over a decade now, since the morning I packed my things and went down to Father's study to inform him I was leaving for Arkham, to study at a university of my choosing rather than his. He'd known nothing of it— Mother had sold her own jewelry in secret to fund my scholarship— and nerves had kept me awake the entire night beforehand.

If only there were some way to whisper back through the years to that frightened boy. To tell him his life would become immeasurably better in every way imaginable.

I gasped softly at the brush of Griffin's mouth against my member, his tongue tracing a slow path up and down its length.

Teasing with little jabs at the slit then edging the hood. I let him know my pleasure with encouraging sighs, bunching my fingers in the blanket to keep from reaching for his hair. Later, I would disarrange his curls and make a mess of his clothing, but for now, I did nothing to cause undue comment, should anyone see us leaving afterward.

He took me in his mouth, all the way to the root, his throat working around my length. I bit my lip against a groan, hips quivering with the need to thrust against the hot wetness engulfing me. But I let him set the pace, my hands clenching and releasing the satin bedding.

My eyes fluttered closed. I forced them open, glaring at the canopy and all the memories that had collected like dust in the heavy folds of its curtains. Letting the rising tide of pleasure sweep them away. "Griffin," I whispered, like a charm. I loved him. And, no matter how impossible it might have seemed to the achingly lonely boy who'd slept in this bed—how impossible it seemed to me sometimes even now—this man loved me in return with a fierceness which stole my breath away.

He moaned in response, hungry and wanting, the sound muffled by my cock in his throat. And God, it was too much: hot and wet and oh so good. I thrust uncontrollably against him, thought and memory unraveling before the cresting wave of ecstasy.

I blinked at the canopy, dazed and drained. Just a moment, to gather my breath and my wits, so I could return the favor and do the same for him.

Someone knocked firmly on the door.

I jerked up onto my elbows, met Griffin's alarmed gaze where he still sprawled between my legs, my softening cock in his hand and his lips flushed from the act he'd just performed.

"A-a moment!" I stammered. Thank heavens Griffin had thought to lock the door. I rolled off the bed, hastily putting myself back into order even as my mind raced. My eye fell on the door to the dressing room, and I grabbed his arm and steered him toward it.

The barren closet was musty and filled with cobwebs—apparently, the servants felt no need to keep this room up. Griffin's face had gone white, and fear flickered in his eyes, although whether from the close darkness of the dressing room or the chance of discovery, I didn't know. He went willingly enough, though, and I shut the door on him as quietly as I could, the sound covered by another knock.

"I'm coming!" I exclaimed crossly. Damn it, whoever was on the other side of the door would have a great deal of explaining to do. If a guest, I could act suitably offended at their intrusion. If a servant...I couldn't imagine Father would send any of them to spy on me, as he would doubtless prefer not to know what I got up to out of his sight and hearing.

I slid my coat back on—and spotted Griffin's lying draped over the back of the desk chair where he'd left it. Blast! With no better idea what to do, I stuffed it hastily beneath the somewhat disarranged blanket, smoothed out what wrinkles I could, and opened the door.

Guinevere stood on the other side, her hand raised to knock yet again.

I gaped at her. Had she ever come to my room, even when we were children? I certainly couldn't recall it.

"Shouldn't you be downstairs with the guests?" I demanded, a bit more roughly than I intended. Why had I ever let Griffin talk me into this?

"I could ask the same of you." She scowled and pushed past me into the room. "Good, you're alone."

"Yes," I said, more firmly than the situation called for had it been true. "Why are you here?"

"Why are *you* here?" she countered. "Stanford says you rent a room in some awful shack."

"I thought to remind myself why I'd never return to this house," I snapped. "And it isn't a shack, but a very nice home, thank you."

She walked to the window, dangerously near the dressing room door concealing Griffin. "God, Stanford was right—you *are* turning into quite the little prick these days."

The tightening of the scar-laced skin on my right hand made me conscious of my clenched fists. Fighting not to grind my teeth as well, I said, "Exactly. So I suggest you return to the more congenial company downstairs and leave me to my business."

"Congenial—ha. At least Thomas Abbott won't follow me in here. Ordinarily, I pity the poor English girls, chaperoned every instant of the day until they're finally married off. No wonder their men prefer us American females to those dull things. But at least they don't have to put up with old lovers hanging about."

"Did you want something?" I asked. "Because if not, surely your room will provide adequate refuge from Mr. Abbott."

She turned from the window, the train of her skirt wrapped dramatically around her legs, her dark eyes flashing. She'd always cultivated the regal attitude and bearing of her namesake. "Close the door," she ordered.

Despite my misgivings, I obeyed. "What is this about?"

"I've been hoping for an opportunity to speak with you privately." She glanced around, as if suspecting spies in the draperies. At least she didn't think to check the dressing room for anyone lurking.

No doubt Griffin had his ear pressed to the door, listening to every word. But as far as I was concerned, anything she had to say to me, she could say to him. Even if she didn't know it. "About what?"

She started to gnaw on her lip, a nervous habit from childhood, then caught herself. She must be truly worried about something, having been cured of the gesture by the censure of Father and various tutors by the time she was ten. "First, tell me the truth. I've heard... rumors...about you."

Heat scalded my face and tightened my chest, although whether from shame or fury even I couldn't tell. "My private life is none of your concern," I said, tucking my shaking hands behind my back. "I have done far less to bring scandal on this family than Stanford. Given that, I do not see what business it is of yours how I conduct my affairs."

Her eyes widened—then narrowed. "I'm talking about sorcery, you idiot!"

Sorcery? How did Guinevere know about sorcery? The Brotherhood Father and Stanford had belonged to would never have allowed a woman into their ranks. Had Mother brought it up, shown Guinevere one of the spells I'd taught her?

It hurt, to think she might have. I'd believed the magic was something between just the two of us, something I could give back to Mother in return for all she'd given me.

Embarrassment deepened my flush, and I straightened my spine. "Father doesn't *allow* me anything. I make my own decisions."

She snorted. "Please. According to Stanford, you're Father's favorite now, just like you were always Mother's little pet."

What game was Stanford playing, to make such a patently untrue claim? "Father loathes my very existence."

She rolled her eyes. "Just tell me—are you a sorcerer or not?"

At least she was asking me about sorcery and not Griffin. Although God only knew what Stanford might have said to her on that front. "Yes. Shall I light the house on fire and prove it?"

She folded her hands in front of her. "Don't be foolish, Percival. And stop acting so offended by my questions. If anyone in this family would dabble in the black arts, it would be you."

"What do you mean?" I'd never wanted anything but a quiet, scholarly life.

She sat on the edge of the bed. Right where I'd put Griffin's coat. With a frown, she shifted. "This mattress is lumpy."

"The servants have become terribly neglectful," I agreed. "I'm sure Father will be happy to flog them later. But I thought you wished to discuss sorcery, not the state of the furniture."

"I don't want to talk about sorcery. Precisely." She rose from the bed and went to the writing desk. Locating a pen and paper, she scribbled something down and held it out to me. "Meet me at this address tomorrow at midnight."

The devil? I glanced at the address; it was on a street somewhere in the more disreputable part of town. Surely Guinevere wouldn't even consider setting foot in such a place. "Is this some sort of childish prank? I would have thought you had more to occupy your time."

Her lips thinned in anger. "Just meet me there."

"Don't be absurd." Why had I actually bothered to engage her in conversation? I should have shoved her out the door. Or not answered in the first place. "This would have been beneath you when you were a child. Did Stanford—"

Her fingers closed hard on my arm, rings of jewel-studded gold digging in even through my sleeves. Startled, I met her gaze, read a look of determination mingled with fear on her face. "This isn't a joke. This is deadly serious. Do you know of the derelict ship found last week?"

"Of course. The papers have been full of nothing else." The *Norfolk Siren* was found adrift just off the coast, the crew gone and all the lifeboats still in place. Hysterical headlines proclaimed it "THE NEW *MARY CELESTE*" in huge type, accompanied by articles speculating on the fate of the crew. "The harbormaster had to put a guard on it, to keep souvenir hunters away. Why?"

"Don't ask. Not here." She released my arm and took a step back. The shadow of the bed's canopy fell over her face, hiding her expression. But it couldn't conceal the note of worry in her voice. *"Please, Percival."*

Had Guinevere ever asked me for anything, in our entire lives? Most of my memories of our youth consisted of her sweeping past, a small coterie of giggling girls trailing on her heels, like courtiers after a queen. They'd worn the same fashions, agreed with whatever opinion she put forth, and laughed at her every joke.

Of course, most of those jokes—at least the ones made in my hearing—had me as butt of them. *"That was my sister Percival,"* had been a favorite, but she'd found shaper barbs for her arsenal as she grew older. No one had been happier about her departure to Europe than I had.

I could deny her. I owed her nothing.

Griffin stood just on the other side of the dressing room door, listening to every word. He'd spent the last year searching for his brothers, adopted separately off the orphan train. What would he think if I turned down a sibling's plea for help?

"Very well," I said grudgingly.

Her shoulders went back. "Thank you." She took a step toward the door. "I should return to the party, before anyone wonders where we've gone. Will you come down as well?"

"In a moment."

She left. I waited until the sound of her footsteps faded, then opened the dressing room door. "I'm so sorry—are you well?" I asked even before it was entirely open.

Griffin was pale, but not unduly so. I brushed ineffectually at the cobwebs in his hair as he stepped out. "Blast—I'm sorry," I said. "I couldn't think what else to do. My family..." My words trailed off into a helpless sigh.

"I'm fine, my dear." Griffin took my hands to still them, but his eyes remained on the door. "Your conversation provided a welcome distraction. I hope you don't mind my eavesdropping."

"I assumed you would."

"What do you make of it?"

"Devil if I know." I shrugged then freed myself to retrieve his coat from the bed. Of course, it had become horribly wrinkled. "Presumably she'll tell us tomorrow night."

"Us?"

I showed him the address she'd written down. "I'm not foolish enough to venture into that part of Widdershins without someone who knows how to safely navigate the area."

"I see why you thought it a prank." He frowned as he pulled on his coat.

"What do you think?" I asked. "Your instincts are seldom wrong."

"I'm not certain. It seems an odd location for a woman of your sister's status to visit. Stanford, yes—slumming is hardly unusual, and he seems the type. But Guinevere is married to an earl. Surely if someone were to recognize her, the scandal could be considerable."

"So it must be her idea of a bad joke." Acid stung the back of my throat. "She thinks to send me somewhere to be propositioned, while I wait for an appointment she has no intention to keep. Probably the address belongs to a brothel. Or a bathhouse."

"No," Griffin said absently.

"You would know," I muttered.

"It's something of my job to know these things," he said with a small smile. "Especially the locations of houses of prostitution, saloons, and other places people routinely get themselves into trouble. And if the bathhouse addresses once held a special interest, I didn't have the chance to visit before *someone* seduced me too thoroughly for them to hold any allure."

I snorted. "How terrible of me."

"Quite." He leaned against me, hip touching my thigh. We both knew it was something of a lie—the cruel abuse of the attendants at the lunatic asylum, where he'd been unjustly confined, had naturally made him reluctant to submit to the touch of another. Until, apparently, me. "But no. I don't think it a trick. I may not know Guinevere, but I detected honest worry in her voice. I think she's afraid."

"Of what?"

"That, only she can tell us." Griffin turned to me. "You should probably return to the guests. I can slip out on my own easily enough."

"No." I slid an arm around his waist, pulling him closer. "I'd rather make my escape with you. Let them wonder where I went. Besides, I believe I owe you something in return for all you gave me earlier."

His pupils dilated, and his mouth curved in a hungry smile. "Hmm. Then by all means, let's hurry home."

Chapter 3

THE NEXT MORNING, I sat in the largest of the meeting rooms of the Nathaniel R. Ladysmith Museum, trying to pay attention to the droning of the museum director and having little success.

Dr. Hart frequently called all-staff meetings, which, despite the name, excluded the secretaries, janitorial staff, and librarians. Unfortunately, the rest of us were condemned to attend, even when the matter had little to do with our particular jobs. Usually the subject was some sort of scheme meant to elicit more money from the donors.

Today's was no different. Dr. Hart paced back and forth at the front of the room, his enthusiasm combining with his mustache to make him look like an overly excited walrus. "Private tours," he said. "Just the thing for Hallowe'en. We will sell tickets at a price that will ensure exclusivity and, of course, offer first choice to our most generous donors."

I sat beside my colleague—and, other than Griffin, best friend—Dr. Christine Putnam. We each had a notepad in front of us and a pen in hand, in order to appear to be taking notes.

How is Iskander? I wrote on my paper.

She glanced at my notepad, then wrote: *Still languishing in Kent, attempting to get the estate in order before coming here.*

I suppose he anticipates a prolonged stay in America, then.

She smiled rather smugly at her paper. *No doubt. How was the party last night?*

Abominable.

"There will be special displays," Dr. Hart went on in the background.

That goes without saying, she wrote back. *And your magical research?*

Griffin disapproved of my dabbling in sorcery. So I hadn't yet told him I'd decided to make it a serious study. Christine had fewer concerns, and I felt a bit freer to discuss the details with her. *Do you recall the line of arcane power in the earth, which led us to the Fane of Nyarlathotep in Egypt?*

Of course I do—don't be absurd.

"The Ladysmith has the largest collection of cursed items of any museum in America," Dr. Hart declared with pride.

Griffin asked if Widdershins was a place of power, like the fane. So I decided to find out if I could sense any lines of power here.

Can you without the wand?

"Tour groups of four or five persons, led through the museum by a personal guide, with only a few judiciously placed candles to highlight the cursed objects. Of course, since these tickets will be expensive, all tours will be given by our expert staff members."

Yes, I wrote. *It took me some time, and I have to concentrate, but I learned to do it. I've decided to map all the lines of power in Widdershins.*

"And finishing in the grand foyer, where there will be a buffet and string quartet, along with a few more cursed objects to serve as conversation pieces."

Have you found any interesting patterns? she scribbled.

I have. The line in the desert was straight. These seem to curve. I'm not yet sure if they meet at a single point, or if they form a web.

"Now all we need," Dr. Hart said, rubbing his hands together, "is a few volunteers to select the appropriate items, write up the descriptions to be used by the guides, and tend to the decorations."

"It seems to me," drawled Bradley Osborne, "Miss Putnam is the obvious choice. It isn't as if she has anything else to do."

We both looked up from our notepads at the sound of Christine's name, to find Bradley smirking at us. Christine's face went utterly white. "Nothing to do? I'm working on *the* definitive book about Egypt's Old Kingdom!"

"Which has been dust for four thousand years," Bradley said. "Hardly any rush." He glanced at me. "Old Percy can help you. It isn't as if he'll have anything better to do either."

"Hallowe'en is my birthday," I objected.

Bradley gave me a vicious smile. "And you've already had your party, haven't you?"

Curse the man. Bradley had always aspired to high society, and no doubt the newspaper reports of last night's party had stung his pride. Despite the delusions he entertained, none of the old families would even consider putting such a newcomer on a guest list.

I longed to lay claim to prior arrangements. But I could hardly say I'd already made plans to spend the evening in the company of my lover.

So I could only sit and fume while the director beamed. "Excellent suggestions, Dr. Osborne! The entire country is in the grips of this Egyptomania, as the presses call it, thanks to our Nephren-ka exhibit. We'll be able to charge twice the admission if Dr. Putnam's name is associated with the event."

Christine's teeth ground together. "Be that as it may, isn't this a job for the curators?"

"That's what will make this exhibit so special—headed up by our own experts," Dr. Hart enthused. "Dr. Putnam, Dr. Whyborne, I expect a full report on your progress sometime in the next three days. Meeting adjourned!"

I sat still amidst the rustle of papers and gathering of hats, feeling rather as if I'd been run over by one of Father's trains. "But it's my birthday," I repeated.

"Sorry, old fellow," Christine said, collecting her half of our notes. "So much for your Hallowe'en plans of bobbing for Griffin's apples."

I broke the news to Griffin that night, as we strolled through town on the way to meet Guinevere. According to Griffin, the address she'd given us belonged to one of the many saloons thronging the area closest to the docks. The streets in this part of town lay dark, with only a few gaslights to puncture the blackness of the night, and we'd never have found our way without a lantern. The moon had already set, a wrack of clouds blocking out most of the stars. Even the saloons seemed subdued tonight, only the occasional burst of light and song from open doors, to vanish again when they shut. The autumnal chill forced Griffin and me to huddle deeper into our coats and blunted the edge of the fishy reek hanging over the docks.

"Don't worry, my dear," Griffin said. "We'll celebrate your birthday afterward. I'll have cake and wine waiting for your return."

At least he understood the interruption to our plans. "Thank you. I can't believe the director is forcing Christine and me to do this."

"These cursed items...are they actually cursed?"

"No idea," I said glumly. "I suppose I should try to find out before we put them on display. Maybe I'll discover one to make the director's mustache fall out."

He laughed. "Perhaps." Then he grew sober. "Just please be—"

"Careful," I finished for him. "I know, I know." How could I not? It was all he ever said concerning sorcery. I'd even kept my investigation into the lines of arcane power a secret from him, because he'd surely find some way to construe it as dangerous.

"Your sister," he said. "What can you tell me about her?"

I was grateful for the change of subject, although uncertain what to say. "She's a year my senior," I began. "But she always seemed much older."

"Was she close to Heliabel?"

"No." I shook my head. "Mother never regained her health after I was born. Many society ladies attend closely to their daughters' upbringing, in hopes of making a good match later. Mother lacked the strength to do so. Ordinarily, I suppose Guinevere would have been the one expected remain with Mother and keep her company when the family went on holiday, or to church, or outings at the park. But as Guinevere was the picture of health, and I the sickly child, it fell to me instead."

"I'm having trouble picturing Niles raising a daughter," Griffin admitted.

I shrugged. "He bought her whatever clothing or jewelry she wished, arranged respectable company whenever she wanted to go visiting her friends, and made certain she had the best tutors available. Even from childhood, she always had a crowd of other society daughters around her. Emulating her, for the most part. She was always the fashionable one, the beautiful one, and all the other girls wanted her favor."

"I see." A saloon door opened, the scarf of light spilling out to touch Griffin's face, revealing a thoughtful look.

I eyed him uncertainly. "Do you find her beautiful?"

Griffin's mouth shifted into a grin. "She looks a great deal like you, actually. You both have Heliabel's eyes and mouth. Although your hair is entirely your own."

I scowled and automatically touched my hair, which generally stood up in spikes and refused to be tamed by any hair tonic created by man. "How lucky for me," I muttered.

"And for me." He shot me a wink.

My cheeks warmed. He did rather enjoy running his fingers through it, or clutching at the short locks while beneath me.

I hastily diverted my thoughts, before my trousers grew too tight. "I don't know how Guinevere will react to your presence," I cautioned him. "I assume she's taken a private room. If so, I'll go in and speak to her first. If she truly wishes my help, she'll just have to accept you are part of the agreement."

Griffin nodded. "This saloon...is it the sort of place she would know about?"

"*I* wouldn't have known about it, at least not while I lived in Whyborne House," I said ruefully. "Although Guinevere wasn't as sheltered as everyone thought—I once found a book of, er, etchings a friend had lent her."

"Rather explicit, I take it?" Griffin asked with a chuckle.

"To say the least." At the time, I'd been half shocked and half aroused. "But youthful curiosity is entirely different from being familiar with the less savory parts of town. Enjoying unchaperoned outings with youths of the same social standing while in Newport is one thing. Consorting with the sorts of persons we're like to find near the docks is quite another. Stanford might have come slumming, though. Perhaps she asked him?"

"Perhaps," Griffin murmured, but I could tell the detail still troubled him.

The saloon was indeed ramshackle, even for its kind. Close to the wharf, it mainly served sailors and fishermen, and appeared every bit as weather-beaten and rough as its clientele. Grime coated its windows so thoroughly it was impossible to see inside. Only a faint glow escaped to show there was any life within at all.

The door hinges shrieked, apparently never having had oil set to them. The architecture suggested it dated from the end of the last century. It had probably never seen a coat of fresh paint or even a mop in all the time since.

Thankfully, only a few drunkards lolled amidst the long tables, either half asleep in puddles of spilled beer, or else conversing in low voices. Nets decorated the walls. Glass fishing weights added the only spots of color. Everything else, including the people, was the same gray as the weathered boards.

The bartender gave us an unfriendly look. Clearly neither Griffin nor I was a seaman of any stripe, and although we'd deliberately worn our oldest suits, we still appeared better off than any of the other customers.

Had my first instinct—that it was all some sort of silly joke—been correct? Because surely Guinevere would never come to such a place willingly.

Still, I had to find out. I crossed to the bar and cleared my throat. "Excuse me. I'm looking for a woman."

"Brothel's down the street."

"Oh!" My cheeks burned. "No. That isn't what I meant. A lady— my sister—arranged to meet me here tonight. She may have taken a private room?"

"Your sister, eh?" The barman looked uncertain for a moment, then shrugged. "Ain't no gals here right now. Wait for her if you want, so long as you buy a drink while you're at it."

"An excellent suggestion," Griffin agreed.

The barman seemed slightly mollified, even though he kept a close eye on both of us as he poured a pair of whiskeys. Griffin drank his with aplomb; I barely touched my lips to my glass. The fumes alone were enough to make my eyes water.

I checked my pocket watch every few minutes. The watch had been a gift from Griffin; one side of the case opened to reveal the clock face, and the other held a photograph of the two of us together. The photograph and the declaration of love, which had accompanied the gift, made the watch one of my most cherished possessions

When the minute hand showed it to be a quarter after midnight, I put it away. "She's not coming," I said, half-shocked at the bitterness in my own voice. "Of course it was nothing but a stupid joke. No doubt she and Stanford are having quite the laugh at my expense."

"Perhaps," Griffin allowed. "She sounded sincere last night, but I suppose she may simply be an excellent actress. Be that as it may, let's walk back along the route she would have taken from Whyborne House, just in case."

"If you like." Surely she wouldn't have walked, though, not through streets such as these. She would have hired a cab, at the very least.

No, Guinevere was safe and sound at home, probably asleep in her bed. While Griffin and I tromped about in the freezing cold, because she still found it fun to mock her little brother, as though we were both children.

We abandoned the saloon to its dreary inhabitants. Stuffing my hands in my pockets, I hunched my shoulders against the icy bite of the wind. Damn Guinevere. I'd make certain not to cross paths with her again for the duration of her stay. England could have her.

A soft moan caught my attention, barely audible above the keening wind blowing around the cornices. Griffin came to a halt, casting about. "I heard something."

"So did I." The wind's chill seemed to touch me within now.

The cry came again, almost breathless. A name.

My name.

"Guinevere?" I called in alarm, while Griffin swung the beam of his police lantern to and fro. Oh God—had she been attacked? "Where are you?"

"There!" Griffin cried. The lantern's beam penetrated the shadows of a narrow alley, no more than a slot between two crumbling brick buildings. Dark liquid glistened near the entrance, and the stench of blood overrode even the reek of fish.

Guinevere lay just inside, half propped against the wall, her head lolling to one side. Her arms hung limp, and her legs bent at uncomfortable angles. Blood soaked the bodice of her dress, a shabby brown frock, which might have belonged to any woman of the working class.

"Guinevere!" I ran to her, falling to my knees. Cooling blood soaked my trousers, but I didn't care. I touched her face, tilting her head back to see her better. Her skin was like ice under my fingers.

Her pupils were blown wide, only a thin ring of brown iris showing. "Percival," she mumbled.

Griffin tore off his coat and pressed it to her chest, trying to keep what little blood remained inside her. "Go for a doctor, Whyborne—I'll stay with her."

"No," she gasped. Her hand groped blindly for me. Cuts lacerated her fingers all the way to the bone. "I'm sorry." Her voice was faint. "Randolph, please forgive me."

"Your husband will forgive you," I assured her, although I hadn't the slightest idea what she asked forgiveness for. Twisting about, I called out to the street behind us. "Help! Police! We need a doctor!"

Her poor fingers closed on mine. "Listen...have to tell you..." She swallowed convulsively. "Persephone...one for the sea..."

"It's going to be all right," I said frantically. "Griffin, go for the doctor." I reached for his coat, intending to hold it in place, but to my surprise, he sat back and let it fall. "What are you doing?"

"It's too late."

"No, it..." But her eyes had gone glassy, and her fingers slowly uncurled, gravity tugging them away from mine. No breath stirred the bloody bodice.

"No," I said again, like an idiot. "Guinevere? This is all some foolish trick, isn't it? Isn't it?"

"She's dead, Ival." Griffin's bloodstained hand rested on my shoulder. "I'm so sorry."

Tears burned my eyes. Despite all of our animosity, she had still been my sister. I couldn't seem to let go of her hand. "S-send for Father," I managed to say.

Griffin nodded and slipped away. I sat alone in the freezing alley with Guinevere's body and tried not to cry.

CHAPTER 4

HOURS LATER, I sat in the drawing room of Whyborne House, my elbows resting on my knees, hands clasped in front of me, and my gaze directed to the Persian carpet beneath my feet. Despite the warmth of the fire crackling in the enormous hearth, the freezing cold of the night still clung to my bones.

Griffin's shoes appeared at the corner of my vision. He'd gone home, changed, and brought a suit for me as well. The one I'd worn earlier was too soaked in blood to be fit for anything other than burning.

I lifted my gaze sluggishly, and discovered he held a tumbler of brandy out to me. I took it with an automatic murmur of thanks. The burn of alcohol restored a tiny amount of warmth to my core and gave me the courage to look around.

Father stood by the ornate liquor cabinet, one hand holding a brandy, the other thrust into his pocket. His gaze seemed locked on some far-off place only he could see. Stanford slumped in a chair. He'd been drunk when Father, the butler Fenton, and I brought Guinevere's body back to the house. Father had ordered her laid in the cellar where the most expensive wine was kept, a room to which only Fenton had a key.

God. Guinevere. The entire time I'd been sitting in the dreadful saloon, cursing her, she'd been dying in an alley only a block away. Why hadn't I worried more? Why hadn't I insisted we search for her immediately? She would have still been alive if I'd only *done* something.

All of my sorcery, and yet it had been my indecision that cost my sister her life.

Mother sat in a chair beside me, her back very straight. Her eyes were reddened, as if she'd wept before joining us, but no tears showed on her cheeks now. I'd never seen her cry in all of my life. It wasn't the sort of thing our family did in front of each other.

Father tossed back his brandy and set the empty tumbler on a small table. The loud clack of glass against the marble top made everyone jump, including him. Folding his hands at the small of his back, he went to stand before the fire.

"The circumstances of Guinevere's death cannot go beyond this group," he said. Taking charge, just as he'd no doubt taken charge after the carnage of battle, during the war between the states. "If word got out she visited such an unsavory part of town, there would be scandal. There could also be ramifications for her son back in England."

In other words, if the earl's wife was prone to going to low places, perhaps she consorted there with low men. Doubt would be thrown on my nephew's paternity. My gut clenched at the thought, and I took another sip of brandy, hoping it would settle my stomach.

While Father spoke, Griffin moved quietly from his position against the wall to stand in front of the door, head cocked. Listening for any potential eavesdroppers, no doubt.

Thank God he was here. I didn't know how I would have faced this otherwise.

"Percival." Father's voice fell across me like a heavy weight. "You said Guinevere arranged to meet you at this saloon. Why?"

"I don't know." I wanted to bury my face in my hands, but it would show too much weakness, so I forced myself to meet his gaze instead. "She asked if I was a sorcerer. She asked if I'd heard of the *Norfolk Siren*. When I said yes to both, she pleaded with me to meet her. She wouldn't tell me anything more."

"Fuckin' useless," Stanford slurred.

"Language, Stanford!" Father shot him a glare.

My right hand curled into a fist, the scars tugging. How could Stanford, no matter how drunk, turn this moment to our old rivalry? Had he no consideration for our parents?

I took a deep breath and willed my hand to unclench. "She said..." God, how could I say this? How could I speak my sister's last words aloud to Mother and Father? "She asked her husband to forgive her."

"She wasn't entirely lucid," Griffin said gently, from his post near the door.

No doubt, but if the newspapers heard of it...well, they wouldn't. No one here would repeat such a thing. "Yes. And then she said something strange. 'Persephone. One for the sea.'"

Stanford glared blearily at me. Did he blame me for Guinevere's death? "It doesn't mean anything. Just a dying woman's babbling."

Mother flinched. Damn Stanford...but attacking him wouldn't improve the situation. I returned his glare, but moved my left hand to rest on Mother's.

"Persephone...it sounds like a name?" Griffin suggested.

"Yes." I sometimes forgot Griffin didn't have a classical education. "From Greek legend. Her mother, Demeter, was an earth goddess. The god of the underworld carried Persephone away. From then on, she could only visit the upper world for half a year. Spring and summer. The other half of the year, Demeter mourned her lost daughter, thus bringing about fall and winter. But her legend has no connection with the sea. Probably it doesn't mean anything." Just the last thoughts flitting through a dying brain.

"Did she say anything else?" Mother's voice trembled, but didn't break on the question.

I shook my head. "No."

Silence fell over us like a burial shroud. After a few minutes, Father's shoulders straightened. I hadn't even noticed when he slumped.

"We shall put about Guinevere was suddenly taken ill," he said in a tone brooking no argument. "Not even the servants will know, save Fenton, of course. Due to the severity of the illness, we sent for a doctor, who immediately ordered her to a sanitarium in New York to recuperate. Naturally, the name of this sanitarium will not be given out, in order to protect her privacy from nosy journalists. I will send a telegram stating as much to her husband tomorrow morning. After... after two weeks, I will send a second telegram, saying she s-succumbed to her illness."

I stared at Father, who still stood with his back to us. Did those small stumbles in his speech mean he actually felt grief? I wouldn't have thought him capable.

"I must impress upon you all," he went on, "this is not to be spoken of to anyone outside of immediate family. Ever."

"Well then," Stanford said, flashing me a nasty sort of look, "I suppose Mr. Flaherty's trip to the bottom of the bay will be quick?"

I stiffened sharply. Curse it—if Father meant to harm Griffin in order to preserve our family's wretched secrets, I'd...

I'd pull the very house down around us and not give a damn. The air roused in response to my anger, rustling the heavy curtains and sending a stream of sparks up the chimney.

"Don't be a fool," Father growled at Stanford. "Percival has been obstinate since the day he was born, and there is no changing it. The rest of us must live with his ways, no matter how unconventional."

The wind died away. I blinked. Father...defending me? From Stanford?

"And, in this case at least, his notions will prove useful," Father added. "Mr. Flaherty?"

Griffin raised a brow, calm and collected as if they hadn't just been discussing whether or not to murder him in cold blood. "Sir?"

"Someone killed my daughter. I intend to discover who. To that end, I find myself in need of your detective's skills yet again. I believe I can adequately compensate you for your time." He named a sum far in excess of what Griffin might hope to earn in a year.

Griffin's shoulders stiffened, and his brows drew down sharply. "I did not think to find myself so insulted tonight, sir."

Father glared at him. "I'm not in a dickering mood. Name your fee and be done with it."

"You mistake me. To suggest I would enrich myself by this family's suffering is a slight against my character," Griffin replied coolly. "I will excuse it due to your grief, however."

Father's mouth worked, but no sound came out. He looked rather like a landed fish; I would have laughed, had the circumstances been different.

"I will do everything in my power to find Lady Gravenwold's killer," Griffin went on. "Should I require some unforeseen expense beyond our ordinary budget, I will of course request assistance, in order to further the investigation. Otherwise, keep your damned money."

Father stared at him for a long moment, as if wondering what ulterior motive Griffin might possibly have. Then he nodded. "Yes," he said gruffly. "Forgive me. I recall from our earlier conversation, when I asked you to look into Threshold Mine, you have certain principles. Thank you, er, Griffin."

I bristled slightly—Griffin certainly hadn't given Father permission to use his name. But Griffin only nodded back. "Think nothing of it, Niles."

Touché.

Mother rose to her feet, and Stanford and I hurriedly did so as well. She held out her hands to Griffin, and he crossed the room and took them. "I know you and Percival will find justice for my poor Guinevere." Her voice threatened to crack, and she closed her eyes briefly.

Griffin clasped her hands. "We will, Heliabel. I swear it."

Their hands parted, and she turned to the door. Her step stumbled, and Father hurried to support her. "Lean against me," he said.

But she didn't. "I'm fine. Summon Emily—she'll help me upstairs."

I watched my parents depart, Father offering his shoulder, Mother refusing to lean against it. "Come," Griffin murmured, touching my arm. "We should go home."

I nodded. "Yes. Thank you."

As we left, I glanced over my shoulder at Stanford, who had returned to his chair. His eyes fixed on me, contempt and hatred in their depths. For a moment, I would have sworn he wasn't as drunk as he'd seemed. Then he slumped back, eyes closed, and I decided I'd been wrong after all.

The early gray light of dawn touched the eastern sky when we arrived home. Saul, our marmalade cat, ran to greet us as soon as we entered the yard. Perhaps sensing my mood, he clung tight to my legs all the way up the walk, not even scratching impatiently at the door while Griffin unlocked it.

"Is there anything I can get for you?" Griffin asked, putting his hand to my shoulder as I stepped past him.

I shook my head. Everything felt very far away at the moment, obscured by a haze of exhaustion and numbness. "No. I'm for bed. I'll send my excuses to the museum later."

"Let me lock up, and I'll join you."

I carried Saul upstairs, soothed by his rumbling purr. Griffin and I alternated the bed we slept in, in order to have two sets of soiled sheets to present to our cleaning woman each week. Which one had we slept in last night? I couldn't recall, so I chose Griffin's. We'd spent our first night together there, and it always seemed more inviting than my own.

Putting Saul on the bed, I stripped off my clothes. Griffin slipped in just as I crawled under the covers. Instead of lying down, I remained sitting up, my arms wrapped around my knees while he undressed.

"Your family seems to be taking Guinevere's death in stride," he said tactfully as he unknotted his tie.

I shook my head. "No. Tears are a weakness. And not just in the men. Mother never cried in front of me."

He set aside his tie and began to remove his vest. "No doubt she feels she has to remain strong for her children."

"Probably." I closed my eyes and rested my forehead against my arms. "I don't think she ever knew how Stanford and Guinevere treated me. I couldn't bring myself to tell her."

"To show weakness." Soft slithers of cloth marked the removal of more clothing.

"Yes. Maybe. I don't know. She was always so sick, I couldn't bear to add to her burdens. So I kept it all to myself."

The bed dipped beneath his weight. "But you've cried in front of Christine and me."

"I trust you."

His arm slipped around my shoulders, and I leaned into him gratefully. "Then tell me how you're really faring."

I kept my eyes closed, unable to bring myself to look at him. "My sister is dead, and it's all my fault. How do you think?"

"What?" Griffin turned me to face him. "Ival, look at me, please. You aren't responsible for Guinevere's death."

I opened my eyes, because he'd asked it. He gazed back at me with a stricken expression. "Of course I am," I replied. "When she didn't appear promptly at midnight, I should have insisted on searching for her. Instead, I convinced myself she was playing some stupid prank, and dawdled at the saloon while sh-she bled to d-death —"

Griffin pulled me to him, his arms strong and sure around me. "You couldn't have known, my dear. Why would you think she'd be on foot, alone? It seems impossible..." He trailed off, then shook his head. "You had no reason to believe anything had happened to her."

"You did. You're the one who suggested we retrace the path she would have taken from Whyborne House."

Griffin sighed, his shoulder dipping beneath my cheek. "It was merely a precaution. I didn't want to think I'd completely misjudged her earlier, when she had sounded so desperate to meet you. If I'd truly thought anything was wrong, I would have suggested leaving earlier. So if you are to blame for her death, then I am as well, in equal measure."

"No!" I tried to pull free from him, but he refused to let go. Defeated, I slumped into his arms, pressing my face against his over-long hair. "You trusted my assessment of the situation."

"Of course, but I also think for myself." He stroked my back soothingly. "The only person responsible for her death is the one who murdered her."

I didn't want to cry. I didn't. But she was my *sister,* and she'd died in my arms, and...

Griffin only held me quietly, his hands stroking my back. Once, he pressed his lips against my temple.

"Thank you," I whispered, when I could speak again.

"For what?"

"Everything. Going with me tonight. Fetching me a suit to change into, and pouring me brandy, and making sure none of the servants were listening in, and putting up with my awful family, and this..."

"I love you." He kissed me softly, once on each eyelid. "Whatever family you claim is mine as well. I'm with you no matter what."

I spoke thirteen languages, and yet I had no words to express what his presence meant to me. Griffin seemed to understand anyway. Wrapping me tight in his arms, he held me until sleep took us both.

The next morning found us on the sidewalk of Whyborne House once again.

Had it been an ordinary house in mourning, there would have been black crape tied with a white ribbon onto the doorknob, to warn away any callers. But of course such a display was out of the question, so long as we maintained our fiction of a sudden illness.

Fenton answered our knock without his usual supercilious sneer. He looked not to have slept any better than me, the lines around his eyes more pronounced than usual and a certain weariness around his mouth. But his collar was starched and his suit as crisp as ever. "Allow me to take your coats."

A maid appeared a moment later, silently taking our coats from Fenton and vanishing again. "Your father is in his study," Fenton said to me. "This way."

The ordinary sounds of the servants going about their duties echoed from various rooms, but they seemed muffled this morning, as if the house was indeed in mourning. Our shoes tapped unnaturally loud against the marble floors. As we crossed the foyer, the rustle of skirts sounded from the stairs. Mother descended slowly, leaning on the arm of a maid.

"Mother?" I asked in surprise.

Her face was pale, but she had dressed and had the maid arrange her hair. "I kept watch out the window," she said. "I didn't wish to miss you."

In case Father decided she had no place in this. But Guinevere had been her daughter as much as his. "Of course."

Griffin hastened to offer her his arm. "Thank you, Griffin," she said, and I suspected she meant for more than just the support.

Fenton's lips thinned slightly, but he made no comment, only led us the rest of the way to the study. "Mrs. Whyborne, Master Percival, and Mr. Flaherty here to see you, sir," he said, and took his leave.

Father sat behind his massive mahogany desk, papers spread before him. He looked to have aged a decade in a single night, the lines more deeply graven on his face, the set of his jaw less firm. "Heliabel? What are you doing?"

"I assume Percival and Griffin are here to begin their investigation," she replied, taking the seat Griffin guided her to. I quietly fetched a third chair from the corner. "I've come to hear what they intend to do."

Father scowled. "Bel, this is too upsetting for you. Return to your room and I'll come later to tell you—"

"What you wish me to know?" she cut in. "My daughter is dead, Niles. What could be more upsetting than that?"

"Forgive me, Heliabel," Griffin said. "Ordinarily, I would agree. But murder investigations are never pleasant even when one doesn't know the victim. This will be very difficult for everyone."

Mother's shoulders went back, and she gazed coolly on Griffin. "Do not speak to me of difficulties, Mr. Flaherty. I could count myself fortunate to have mourned only two children. Many women face far worse."

"Of course," he said, before I could protest her harsh words to him. "I didn't mean to imply otherwise. Please, take my desire to spare you any pain as an indication of affection rather than contempt."

No one pointed out he hadn't protested so with Father. Then again, none of us were under the illusion he felt any affection for Father, either.

Her expression softened. "Yes. Forgive me, Griffin—my weariness has made me ill-tempered."

"If my wife insists on staying," Father growled, "then let us get on with it."

Griffin nodded. "Yes, sir. I apologize for the indelicacy, but...has anyone made a close examination of Lady Gravenwold's body?"

She'd been so limp in my arms. So pale.

Father's lips pressed tightly together, then relaxed. "No. She has remained undisturbed. Unwashed."

"A closer examination might tell us something about the murder," Griffin said apologetically.

Mother turned her face away from us, as if to hide her expression. "Then I-I shall do it."

"Bel—" Father began.

"Who else is there?" she asked fiercely. "The servants can't know."

"I must ask your forgiveness again, Heliabel." Griffin bowed his head slightly. "But in a case such as this, the painful emotions such an examination would bring up in a family member might lead to important details being missed. I know this is a matter for utmost discretion, but I would like to bring Dr. Putnam here to make the examination."

"Christine, of course," I said, feeling sudden relief. "I don't know why I didn't think of it."

Father's brows drew down. "No. This cannot go beyond the family!"

"Christine is—" I started hotly, then caught myself. *My sister,* I'd been about to say, because she was closer to my heart than either of my true siblings. But it would be too cruel a truth to speak aloud under these circumstances.

"Christine has already proved her discretion," Griffin said, unruffled by Father's anger. "The business with the Brotherhood and in Threshold should have proved it to your satisfaction."

"Percival holds Dr. Putnam in high regard," Mother said. "I trust his judgment."

Father sat back with an angry frown. "Very well. I'll have Fenton fetch her in the motor car."

"Allow me to write a note for him to take," Griffin said. "Otherwise, he'll have a hard time convincing her to come."

"Yes. She's one of those obstinate modern women, isn't she?"

"Be glad of it. Otherwise your son and I would be dead several times over."

I doubted saving my life was much of a recommendation in Father's eyes, but he only passed paper and pen to Griffin. Fenton answered the bell and took the note, along with instructions to bring Christine as quickly as possible.

Once Fenton departed, Griffin sat back and folded his hands in his lap. "It seems to me there are two possibilities. Either Lady Gravenwold was the victim of opportunity—that is, someone saw her walking alone and attacked her—or she was murdered to prevent her from talking to Percival."

It was strange to hear my first name from Griffin. Ordinarily he called me Whyborne, but I supposed in this case it might seem a bit odd. And Ival was certainly too private to use in front of my parents.

"I don't understand why she would walk alone." I'd been so sure she wouldn't, I'd never seriously entertained the idea something might befall her on the way to the saloon.

And the whole time, she'd been lying the alleyway, alone and cold and dying...

"Either way, whatever she had to say was important enough for her to risk being seen in an unsavory part of town," Griffin went on. "Even wearing the clothing of a laboring woman, she couldn't be certain no one would recognize her likeness from the newspapers."

"Who gave her the clothes?" I asked.

Father glanced at me. "Fenton is making discreet enquiries among the staff. We'll find out."

Griffin nodded. "Good. In the meantime, I'd like permission to search her room. Perhaps she left something behind that will tell us what she no longer can. A diary, or some other clue."

"Very well," Father said. "We'll await Dr. Putnam's arrival, then I'll take you there."

Chapter 5

CHRISTINE ARRIVED SOON thereafter. Griffin, Father, and I met her in the foyer. "Whyborne," she said, crossing directly to me with her hand out. "I'm so terribly sorry."

She clasped my hand—then pulled me into an awkward embrace. I hugged her back, my relief at her presence startling. Of course, she'd lost her own sister under circumstances even more horrible just a few months back. But beyond her sympathy, I was simply glad to have her here with me. "Thank you for coming."

She let go of me. "Never fear," she said a bit gruffly. "We'll get to the bottom of this. Just tell me what I can do."

Griffin took her aside and spoke quietly for a few moments. She nodded her understanding. Fenton indicated she should follow him, and they disappeared in the direction of the kitchens, where the door to the lower cellars lay.

"What terrible manners," Father growled.

I shrugged. Christine didn't give a fig for Father, and had no qualms when it came to making her opinion clear.

"She'll do the job," Griffin said. "It calls only for respect for the dead, not manners for the living."

Father didn't look particularly mollified, but led the way up the stairs to the third floor. Guinevere had stayed in the room she'd lived in as a young woman, once she outgrew the nursery. Stopping at the door, Father took a key from his pocket. "I've kept it locked since last night. Just as a precaution."

"Won't the servants wonder?" Griffin asked in a low voice. "First she takes suddenly ill and is whisked away in the dead of night. Now her door is locked and everyone forbidden to enter. Surely it must seem suspicious at the least."

Father unlocked the door. "All who serve in this house have been with the family for a long time. Many, like Fenton, have a parent who served in the same position. They know not to ask questions. Any who have ever attempted to betray the family in the past have been dealt with swiftly."

And probably fatally, especially if intruding on the Brotherhood's secrets. I kept the opinion to myself, however, instead adding, "And Miss Emily has been with Mother since they were both girls."

"Indeed." Father reached for the door to open it, then hesitated. For an instant, the stern expression on his face wavered. Handing the key to me, he said, "Lock up when you're done. I'll return to the study and keep your mother company."

I listened to his footsteps retreat quickly along the hall. When I turned back to Griffin, he gave me a sad half smile. "I know I shouldn't feel sorry for Niles, not after everything he's done. But still, losing a daughter must be a blow to anyone."

I opened the door and gestured for Griffin to precede me. The room was decorated in blue and gold, every surface ornamented and gilded, from the delicate legs of a small table, to the bedposts. Fine carpets muffled our steps on the floor, and blue satin covered the walls.

The bedcovers lay thrown back, waiting for a return which would never come. The ghost of Guinevere's lilac perfume lingered, as if she'd stepped out only a little while earlier and might return at any instant. Her nightdress and dressing gown lay carelessly tossed across a chair, and the door to the dressing room stood open.

"Would you prefer the dressing room or the bedroom itself?" Griffin asked. "Or, if this is too difficult..."

"No." I took a deep breath, seeking to dislodge the weight pressing against my chest. "I owe it to her." Ignoring his worried glance, I added, "The bedroom, I think. What am I looking for?"

"Correspondence. Her diary. Anything out of the ordinary, which might give us some hint as to what had her so concerned."

I went to the writing desk, and Griffin vanished into the dressing room. A neat stack of letters lay there, and I began to rifle through them, hoping for some clue, however small.

The desk yielded nothing—just the ordinary correspondence between friends and family members. The letters she'd never had a chance to post were all written in a light, airy style, save for the occasional cutting remark, usually aimed at someone's sense of fashion or behavior. There was no hint anything troubled her. None of the letters mentioned sorcery or the derelict ship, or anything else suspicious.

I moved on, examining every piece of furniture, opening every drawer. I even looked under the bed, but found nothing.

Curse it all. Why couldn't she just have told me what was wrong the night of the party? Was she afraid of being overheard? But by whom? The servants? One of the guests? Father? If a guest, then why hadn't she just asked me to return here the next night, rather than meet in some wretched saloon?

I picked up the dressing gown, intending to make certain it and the nightgown weren't draped on top of a book or diary left on the chair. Something crinkled under my hand. Paper?

The dressing gown possessed a small pocket, inside of which I found a sheet of paper, folded into a small square. I opened it to reveal a terse note, without either address or signature.

Dismiss me to your own peril. Your family won't be able to save you, should I choose to act.

I stared at the unfamiliar handwriting. Was this why Guinevere had wished to speak to me—because someone was threatening her? But why? And what did it have to do with the *Norfolk Siren?*

I hurried to the dressing room door. The room was a confusion of silk, satin, and lace, dominated by a vanity with legs carved into the shapes of swans. Griffin crouched in front of a trunk. A second, smaller one sat beside it.

"I found something," I said, holding out the note.

He took it from me, reading the words with a frown, then carefully inspecting the paper. "Do you recognize the handwriting?"

"No."

"The paper is of good quality. No letterhead or crest, but I recognize the stationer's watermark. Where did you find it?"

I told him. With a frown, he handed it back to me. "Keep it for now, and we'll show it to your father when we're done. Perhaps he'll recognize the handwriting."

"Have you discovered anything in here?" I asked.

"Not so far. There's nothing concealed behind her clothes. And none of her jewelry chests have a false bottom or back."

"Oh." It wouldn't have occurred to me to look for such a thing.

Griffin lifted the lid of the larger trunk, revealing an interior filled with books. "Help me sort through these—perhaps her diary is in here, as you didn't come across it in her bedroom."

The top layer of books consisted mainly of the most tedious sort imaginable: histories drained of all the blood and passion that might have made them interesting, advice to wives on the proper running of a household, and a collection of the most patronizing sort of sermons. Beneath those, however, lay a wide assortment of fiction, from Dickens to the sorts of dime novels no respectable lady would ever admit to reading. As for the bottommost layer...

"I thought this had been banned, and every copy seized and destroyed," Griffin remarked, flipping through the pages of one of the books.

I picked up another, opened to a random page, and flinched at the illustration thereon. "Dear heavens! This is pornography!"

"But very artistically rendered." He reached over my shoulder and turned the page. "Although I'm not certain how comfortable the position could be for either participant."

I shut the book firmly, my face on fire. "It's clear there's nothing of interest here. I mean, to our case. I mean...blast it."

As we were alone, he leaned over and kissed my burning cheek. "Let's see what the last trunk holds."

Griffin examined the smaller trunk while I put the books back, careful to keep the respectable ones on top. "Locked," he murmured. "But not for long."

He drew a slim leather case from his inside pocket, which he unrolled to expose a set of lock picks. Within a matter of moments, there came a soft click, and he withdrew the picks and tucked them back away. "Given what we've already seen, there may be some very personal items in here. Would you prefer to examine the contents without me?"

"Rather the other way around," I said wryly. "But no, we'll sort through them together."

Various keepsakes greeted us when I swung open the lid. A picture of her husband, Earl Randolph Gravenwold, and another of a baby in an enormous christening gown, which I assumed must be her young son.

Had Father sent word to England already, telling the earl of Guinevere's fictional sickness? Was the man even now worrying over the health of a wife who would never return to him? And what of her son, doomed to grow up motherless? Would the earl find a second wife, and if so, would she care at all for the child of her predecessor?

How would I feel if Griffin died, alone and far away from my side? If never got to see his face again?

"How are you managing, my dear?" Griffin asked softly.

The scars on my right hand pulled, and the pictures frames cut into my fingers. I'd been clutching them, one in each hand, staring blankly down at the sepia figures. I forced myself to set them aside. "I don't know."

"We're almost done," he said gently. Reaching into the trunk, he took out a small object wrapped in cloth. As the cloth fell away, the electric lights caught the gleam of gold.

It was a bracelet, or perhaps an armband, but of no style I'd never seen before. Fully revealed, I reassessed my earlier impression: perhaps it was a gold alloy of some kind, for the luster brought forth by the light struck me as not quite right. Some incredibly skilled artisan had cast it, and high reliefs showed all along the outside. Most consisted of geometrical shapes, but others clearly represented marine animals, although the stylized fashion depicting them came from no tradition I recognized. Large black pearls had been set into the bracelet at regular intervals, interspersed with smaller white ones.

"It looks old," I said, turning it over in my hands. "But I'm no expert on jewelry."

"I wonder why it was in the trunk, instead of with her other ornaments," Griffin mused.

I snorted. "Because it's...well, not hideous, but utterly outside of today's fashions. She wouldn't have been caught dead wearing it."

"Then why bring it with her?"

That was the question, wasn't it? "A memento? Or perhaps she didn't bring it. Maybe she obtained it after returning to America." I set it aside with the photographs. "Is there anything else?"

"One more item." Griffin drew out another object wrapped in black silk. A corner of the cloth fell away, and I heard...singing.

I blinked and shook my head. No. I didn't hear singing. And yet the song was still in my mind. Too distant to make the words out, but there. "Griffin..." I said, but it came out a whisper of breath.

"What the devil?" he murmured, pulling aside the silk. A small black stone lay in his palm, a design carved into its surface.

The song swelled into a command. I had to touch it. Had to trace the design and find its beginning and end. Had to.

I reached for it. The man—what was his name?—holding it pulled it away irritably. "Hold up, I'm trying to see—"

"*No!*" I shouted, and lunged for the stone, knocking us both to the floor.

"Whyborne! What are you doing?"

The words were meaningless—I had to get to the stone, had to touch it, had to, had to, but he kept it from me. I tore at his clenched fingers, snarling like an animal.

"Ival!"

No. Something was wrong. *I* was wrong.

I took a deep breath, even though the need to touch the stone crushed the air from my lungs. For a moment, my brain spun like a machine with a slipped cog, frantically going nowhere. The words, what were the words?

"Griffin," I whispered, and concentrated on the word. The name. Yes.

What came next? Griffin meant love. Safety.

Safety. Home.

I closed my eyes, clung to the vision of slamming shut a door and locking it, drawing the curtains over the windows. Nothing could come through. Nothing could get to me now.

The unearthly song faded away. I sat back, scrubbing at my face. To my horror, I saw I'd wrestled Griffin in my inexplicable frenzy to reach the stone. We'd made quite a mess, knocking over a chair and pulling down several dresses.

I didn't remember any of it.

"Oh. Oh God." I clasped my hands in front of my mouth. "I-I'm sorry. You didn't...you didn't hear it?"

Griffin sat up, watching me warily. Retrieving the black silk, he hurriedly rewrapped the stone. I didn't dare watch, but instead focused on his face. Thank heavens he didn't seem hurt.

When he was done, he put the stone aside and crouched in front of me. "Whyborne?"

I nodded mutely.

He touched my hands, tugging them down. His thumb ran over the scars on the right, a soothing gesture. "What happened?"

"There was...singing. Coming from the stone."

Griffin frowned. "Singing? In your mind? As with the dweller in the deeps?"

Ice crystals grew in my veins. "God, I hope not. But it is magical, whatever it is. It...it didn't affect you at all?"

Griffin shook his head grimly. "No. Not in the slightest. Are you all right?"

"Yes." I swallowed. "Once I realized what was happening, I managed to strengthen my mind against it. What *is* it?"

"I don't know." Griffin let go of my hands and sat back, staring at the silk wrapping as if it concealed a dangerous spider. "Nor do I know what such a thing was doing in your sister's possession. But I rather think we'd best find out."

~ * ~

Griffin tucked the stone and bracelet into his coat pocket, and we both set the dressing room back to rights. "You don't have to worry," I told him, shame-faced. "It only caught me by surprise."

"As you caught *me* by surprise," he said with a wry twist of his lips. "It's rather startling to have one's ordinarily mannerly companion suddenly hurl himself on one like a wild animal. Had it been in the service of passion, of course, that would be another matter."

Now I flushed for reasons other than shame. "I've never attacked you like a wild animal," I protested.

"No." He glanced up at me through his lashes. "But should you choose to do so, I have no objections."

"Scoundrel." But I felt a little better. Well enough to face Father, at any rate.

We retreated downstairs to the study, making certain to lock the door. As we passed the second floor landing, Christine called to us. "Wait up a moment, gents, and I'll walk down with you."

She strode up the hall from the guest rooms. I frowned in puzzlement. "What are you doing up here?"

"I rather needed to wash up somewhere, didn't I?"

Guinevere's blood had been cold under my knees when it soaked through my trousers. Even colder later, on the ride back to Whyborne House, despite the blanket thrown over my legs so her body could rest across the seat in our laps.

I must have blanched, because Christine winced. "Damn it—I'm sorry, old fellow. I'm an insensitive clod."

I dredged up a weak smile. "Yes, well, it's part of your charm."

We trooped the rest of the way down to the study. A fourth chair had appeared across from Father's seat in our absence, accompanied by three glasses of whiskey, as Mother didn't drink, on the advice of her doctors. Ordinarily, I would have thought it far too early in the day to indulge, but at the moment, I was rather glad for something to brace me.

Mother rose to greet us. "You must be Dr. Putnam," she said.

"I am," Christine said, before I could make proper introductions. "A pleasure, Mrs. Whyborne. I assume it's you I have to thank for your son not treating me like a brainless fritter head due to my sex?"

Father frowned, and I suppressed a sigh. But Mother only smiled ruefully. "I would like to think I had some influence on him, yes."

"Let's get on with this," Father growled, resuming his place behind the desk. A whiskey of his own sat in front of him.

We seated ourselves, and I glanced at Christine. She shifted uncomfortably. "My condolences on your loss," she said abruptly, with a nod first to Mother then to Father. "I lost a family member of my own recently, in rather awful circumstances, and...well, it's never easy. I'm terribly sorry this happened."

Father's eyes darkened. "I don't require your sympathy, Dr. Putnam. Nor does any one else in this house. Now tell me what you found."

Curse the man. He'd seen Christine's display of concern in the foyer, and now sought to remind me how unmanly it was to ever show emotion.

Mother ignored him. "Thank you, Dr. Putnam. I, for one, appreciate the sentiment."

"Usually the bodies I examine are far older," Christine said, "but I imagine I did as well as some of the medical examiners might. Lady Gravenwold was stabbed six times in the chest. She had defensive wounds on her hands and forearms. It was a savage attack, but there were no bruises or broken bones. Her underthings were still in place, and she carried this." Christine put a small pouch on the desk, spilling a few coins out as she did so.

Stabbed six times. A savage attack. Defensive wounds...her poor fingers had been slashed so deep I could see the bones.

"Oh," Mother said in a small voice, and put a hand to her mouth.

I felt faint myself, but I forced myself to stand up and go to her. Kneeling before her chair, I took her hands. They were icy cold.

"Mother, please," I said. She'd turned her face away, striving for some semblance of control, but the dampness on her eyelashes proclaimed it a losing battle. "You've done so much for me. Let me do this for you."

I wanted to take this cup from her, but no one can swallow the dregs of another's grief. At least I could give her the space to mourn, if she would only let me. She wouldn't weep in company, but Griffin and Christine had already seen me at my worst, and Father didn't give a damn.

She took a deep, shaky breath. "I owe it to her."

"Not this. Not making yourself suffer to no purpose." How would the loss affect her health? And God, how selfish was I, to worry it would take her from us sooner? "Needing to rest, to grieve, isn't weakness."

"I suppose you're right." Her hands tightened on mine, then released. "Niles, would you ring the bell for someone to assist me?"

He did so. We all stood as one of the maids escorted her out. She looked so frail, so hurt, and I wanted desperately to do something, anything, to make it all right again. But I couldn't.

Griffin looked equally unhappy, as if he wished to run after her and offer some solace but had none to give. Christine only seemed sad; perhaps she was remembering her own dead sister and how her mother blamed her for everything Daphne had suffered.

"Well," Father said, once Mother departed, "what do you make of this, Griffin?"

"It seems clear neither rape nor robbery were the motive," Griffin said. His eyes took on the far-off expression they held when he was deep in thought. "Whoever killed her meant murder from the start. Unless we've some sort of lunatic like the Whitechapel killer on our hands, it seems likely the motive was related to whatever she meant to tell Percival."

"Who else knew she was meeting you?" Christine asked me.

"The maid who brought her plain clothing to wear?" I suggested. "Perhaps the maid then told someone else...whoever Guinevere feared would overhear the night of the party?"

"Perhaps." Griffin reached into his coat pocket and took out the jewelry and the silk-wrapped stone. He glanced at me, and I nodded my readiness. My mental walls were strong.

I hoped.

Griffin tossed aside the silk. Neither Christine nor Father reacted, save to lean in more closely to see the stone. "What the devil is it?" Christine asked.

"We found it in Guinevere's things," Griffin replied, but his eyes were on Father. "Do you recognize it?"

Father shook his head. "No."

"What about this?" He set the bracelet down beside the stone.

"Never seen it before," Father said impatiently. "Some woman's trinket, I expect."

Christine's mouth turned down in to a thoughtful frown. "I can't say as I've ever seen designs like those before. Clearly they belong to some artistic tradition, but blast if I know what."

Griffin took them both back and put them away. Thankfully, I'd sensed nothing further from the stone...but I had no desire to put it to the test by exposing myself to its influence for a moment longer than necessary. "Show your father the note," he prompted me.

"I found this in the pocket of her dressing gown." I passed the note to Father.

As he read the terse lines, his face grew dark with anger. "When I find out who wrote this, they'll wish they'd never picked up a pen in their life," he growled.

"You don't recognize the handwriting?" Griffin asked.

"No."

Curse it. There went our last hope for a quick solution. Griffin clearly thought the same, because he said, "I believe we've done all we can today. Give our regards to Heliabel."

"I'll come by as soon as I can to see her. Once she's up to it," I said.

Father nodded. "Very well. Stay in touch, Griffin."

"I shall."

A few minutes later, we stepped into the frosty air of an October morning. I tipped my head back and breathed deeply, letting the chill sear my nostrils. I always felt like I couldn't breathe inside Whyborne House, as if the air grew heavier and heavier, so gradually I didn't even notice until I was gasping my life out, like a fish stranded by the tide.

"Honestly, Whyborne, are you certain you're related to that man?" Christine asked. "I don't mean to cast aspersions on your mother, of course, but perhaps the fairies left you as a changeling."

"I wish they had sometimes." We turned our steps away from the house. "But no, I'm afraid there's no question about it."

Christine patted me on the shoulder, then directed her gaze at Griffin. "What next?"

Griffin's curls tumbled over the collar of his coat as he hunched his shoulders for warmth. "Guinevere mentioned the derelict ship to Whyborne, the night she asked him to meet her."

"What, the *Norfolk Siren?*"

"Unless Widdershins has been visited by another ghost ship in the last few days. Although, given this town, it very well might have."

Christine snorted. "If such were the case, the newspapers would be up to twelve special editions a day."

"And all of them filled with speculation and outright lies," Griffin agreed. "I mean to find whatever actual facts I can about the ship."

He took the jewelry from his pocket and passed it to me. "Whyborne, I'd like you to take this to the museum. Discover what you can about it."

"Of course."

"And what about me?" Christine asked.

Griffin smiled, but there was no humor to it. "Make certain your rifle and pistol are loaded and ready. I have the feeling we'll need both before this is over."

CHAPTER 6

IN THE EARLY hours just past midnight, Father, Griffin, and I slipped through the iron gates of Kings Hill Cemetery. Behind us, Fenton waited in the motor car, alert for anyone who might disturb our grim work. Mother said her goodbyes earlier, alone in the wine cellar of Whyborne House.

Griffin picked the lock by the light of our lantern. Father led the way through the low, stone wall, past the lines of weathered tombstones. Griffin and I followed, bearing between us a solid wooden plank. Guinevere's body, shrouded in spare linens, lay atop it.

The autumn wind rattled in the branches of the great oak trees, which in the summer months provided shade for mourners. Leaves swirled down around us with dry whispers, brief flashes of red or orange or fiery yellow in the lantern's beam. The air smelled of smoke and the earthiness of decaying leaves.

There was no moon, but the stars spangled the sky in their multitudes. The black bulk of the Draakenwood stood out against them atop the hill. As we climbed toward it, the sound of branches rubbing against one another came on the wind: creaks and groans and whispers, as if the trees communed with each other.

Perhaps they did. I'd only been past the forest verge once, and it was not a place recommended for hikes or bird watching. Casual visitors had a nasty habit of vanishing within its dark tangle of limbs. Surely the lines of arcane energy laced throughout Widdershins must run through the wood. Perhaps I'd return one day soon and map them.

Guinevere had shared Mother's slender build, but the edge of the board dug into my shoulder, even through my coat, as if weighed down by stones. Stanford should have been with us, should have been the one to bear the other end of the makeshift bier. But when Griffin and I returned to Whyborne House in the evening, we'd found my brother too drunk to be of any use. Was he taking Guinevere's death hard? Or did he simply use it as an excuse to fall back into the bad habits that had cost him his marriage and his place in New York?

I didn't give a damn. He'd left this task to us, not even caring enough for Guinevere's memory to stay sober long enough to honor her. Thank heavens for Griffin.

We reached the hilltop. A row of family crypts surrounded an inner wheel of headstones marking the oldest burials in Widdershins. At the hub of the wheel lay the ostentatious tomb of the town's founder, Theron Blackbyrne. A necromancer of the worst sort, he'd ultimately vanished screaming through a portal to the Outside, after the Brotherhood ill advisedly resurrected him almost two years ago.

I felt a little flicker across my skin, like a faint electrical charge. So the lines of arcane energy did cross the cemetery to the wood. This one likely ran directly over Blackbyrne's grave. No wonder he'd chosen to be buried here.

The first generation of Whybornes lay among Blackbyrne's inner circle, but we'd gained enough prestige afterward to build a crypt. No one could know Guinevere had died, but keeping her body in the wine cellar was out of the question. Quietly—and temporarily—interring her in the family crypt seemed the best solution. Whenever Father decided to declare her dead at the sanitarium, an empty coffin could easily be brought in with a public ceremony. Until then, she would at least rest peacefully among the bones of our ancestors.

We reached the family crypt. Carved faces stared solemnly at us from above the door. Presumably, they were meant to be angels, but their expressions seemed a bit sinister for servants of heaven. A rusted chain and padlock held the heavy stone door closed. I'd seen it open only once before, when my grandmother had been interred. I'd been quite young then, and barely remembered anything about the funeral, save for the terrible creak of the hinges and the thud as the crypt slammed shut once more.

Griffin and I waited in silence while Father fought with the lock. The limbs of the Draakenwood whispered, perilously close. The spot between my shoulder blades itched, and the small hairs on the back of my neck prickled.

Was someone watching us?

I glanced apprehensively back over my shoulder. The wan circle of lantern light showed only Griffin, dressed in his most sober suit.

Who could be observing us, in a cemetery long before dawn? Surely, no one would choose this hour to clamber over the low wall and visit a family member's grave. Resurrection men, then? Griffin had once remarked on the startling amount of grave robbing in Widdershins, considering the university lacked a medical school. But even the most foolhardy resurrectionist would avoid disturbing the rest of any of the old families.

Wouldn't they?

Griffin cocked his head; I'd stared too long. Clearly, he didn't feel anything amiss. It was just my nerves.

The lock clicked so loudly I would have jumped, save for the weight resting on my shoulder. The chain rattled loose, and the door opened with the same agonized shriek of hinges I recalled from my grandmother's funeral.

A whiff of damp came from within the crypt: old wood and even older stone, all returning to the dust from which it had come. Father led the way inside, and we followed.

The space within was cramped. Two large tombs took up most of the floor space, but the walls were lined with shelves. Many already contained moldering coffins, but there were several empty places yet awaiting new generations of Whybornes.

Would I join them some day? The way my life had gone the last two years, it seemed more likely I'd end up in the gullet of some monstrous horror, or else buried in a shallow grave. Whatever happened, I certainly didn't want to spend eternity here.

Had Griffin made arrangements? Perhaps I ought to make a will specifying I be buried with him, just in case. Father wouldn't protest; no doubt he'd be glad to put as much distance as possible between his corpse and mine.

"Here." It was the first word Father had spoken since we'd left the motor car. He indicated one of the empty shelves, and Griffin and I dutifully shifted our burden to it

Goodbye, Guinevere.

Griffin bowed his head, his lips moving in silent prayer. Father looked faintly surprised, but then bowed his head as well. I stared straight ahead, reading the small plaques beneath the shelves identifying those interred above. One in particular caught my attention. *Infant daughter, October 31, 1870.*

My twin sister. Our birth, two weeks before expected, had ruined Mother's health. My twin died shortly thereafter, and I'd been expected to join her for some time. What would my life have been like had everything gone differently, and we'd been born hale and hearty, in the proper time? Or would nothing have changed at all?

Mostly likely the latter. It would not have altered my nature, after all.

Griffin's prayer ended, and he lifted his head. Father cleared his throat and indicated the door. "We should go."

We stepped back outside. A bird roosting at the edge of the Draakenwood flushed, its wings fluttering frantically in the dark. Had we disturbed it, or had I been right all along, and we weren't alone? I stared fixedly into the night, but nothing appeared beyond the circle of lantern light save for indistinct shadows.

The door thudded closed behind me. I took a few steps forward while Father fiddled with the chain and lock. The weathered headstones looked like crouching figures. The wind gusted in my face, bringing with it the earthy smell of the wood, along with something else. A scent of salt and the sea, clean and crisp.

And utterly wrong. The wind blew from the landward side, not the ocean.

I snatched up the lantern. Ignoring Father's indignant shout, I lifted it high, casting a wider pool of light.

Something broke cover, darting from behind one of the nearest headstones. I glimpsed sleek skin the color of pearl, mottled with dark gray. Gold and jewels flashed, a confusing dazzle, like a cloud of minnows.

It fled down the hill. With a shout, I gave chase.

The creature seemed humanoid, but ran with a curious, loping gait. It darted around the headstones, heading for the east side of the cemetery. I couldn't make out anything but the pale patches of its skin, so I focused intently on them, determined not to lose it.

And tripped over a footstone.

My hands scraped over leaves and soft earth, and I felt the knee of my trousers rip. The lantern flickered madly but, fortunately, didn't go out. Griffin and Father called behind me. I ignored them, rolling to my feet and running in the direction I'd last seen the creature. Where the devil had it gone?

Another flash of white and gold, this time against the stones of the low wall demarcating the cemetery's edge. "Stop!" I shouted.

It didn't, of course. I had the confused impression of an almost-human silhouette as it balanced for an instant atop the wall, then dropped to the other side.

The wall was low enough for me to scramble over. On the other side, a long slope ran down to the bank of the Cranch River, interrupted briefly by the road encircling the hill. The creature made for the bank, and I followed. Surely, it would turn at bay when it reached the river.

Instead, it dove in, body cutting the water so smoothly there was barely a splash. A moment later, a set of fins broke the water, then vanished.

I stumbled to a halt. As the excitement of the chase drained away, I became aware of my pulse fluttering in my throat, my breath wheezing in my lungs.

Footsteps pounded down the slope behind me. "What happened?" Griffin asked as he joined me.

"It went into the water. Where's Father?"

"I left him at the crypt. You ran off with our only light."

"Oh." I hadn't even thought. "I didn't want it to get away."

"Understandable." He frowned at the restless water of the river. "Did you see what it was?"

"No. Just a few confused glimpses." I peered up the hill at the cemetery. "I think it was watching us the entire time. What do you imagine it was after?"

Griffin shook his head slowly. "I've no idea. I suppose it could have been a coincidence, unrelated to our mission tonight."

It was possible. For all we knew, the thing might crawl out of the river and sit in the cemetery every night of year. And yet... "You don't think so."

"No. Call it instinct, or a simple mistrust of anything appearing to be a coincidence." Griffin took the lantern from me. "Come on. Let's retrieve your father and leave."

The next morning found me struggling not to fall asleep at my desk in the museum. Our late excursion would have stolen enough sleep as it was, but the mysterious creature I'd chased occupied my thoughts and kept me awake until my alarm clock rang.

Griffin, on the other hand, woke just long enough to give me a sleepy kiss. I left him curled beneath the covers, Saul purring on his feet.

Now I took yet another sip of coffee and checked the clock on the wall. Only ten. I'd never make it through the day without a nap.

In an attempt at wakefulness, I drew out the bracelet we'd found amidst Guinevere's things and stared at it. Perhaps a visit to another department would wake me. I'd contemplated whom to approach about the bracelet. Christine would have recognized anything of Oriental origin, and I felt certain it didn't belong to any European tradition. Perhaps Oceania?

I tucked it in my pocket and set off for the Department of Ethnology. Due to the eccentric nature of the museum's architecture, this was easier said than done. I went down several corridors, cut through the taxidermy room—then rather wished I hadn't—passed the director's office, ducked into a public wing, then back through a staff door, and finally reached my goal.

The plaque on the office door read *Dr. J. Gerritson*. I knocked politely.

"Who is it?" Dr. Gerritson called through the door.

"Percival Whyborne. I need to speak with you a moment, if you're, er, available."

The lock on the door clicked open. "Oh, of course, Dr. Whyborne. Come in!"

I slipped inside and suppressed a sigh when I saw what Dr. Gerritson wore. The floor plan was far from the only eccentric thing about the museum, and the director had been forced to insist Gerritson remain in his office with the door locked while "indisposed." Which was a polite way of saying the doctor's preferred work attire consisted of women's underthings.

Considering I'd fought off a mad cult while wearing a feminine dressing gown, I could hardly disapprove. But I did feel a corset and stockings were not precisely professional enough to wear to one's office.

"What can I do for you?" he asked, thrusting out a massive hand to me. I shook it, trying to keep my eyes on his bearded face and away from the thickly furred chest peeking above a rather frilly corset.

"Dr. Gerritson," I said. "I need a bit of a favor, if you have a moment."

"Of course." He gestured to one of the chairs, and I sat in it. Gerritson perched on the edge of his desk, casually crossing his legs. Where did he even find silk stockings in his size? "Is this about the Hallowe'en tours? I'm pretty sure we've got a cursed pearl around here somewhere. Supposedly wiped out a whole line of Polynesian chiefs."

"Er, no, not today. Although I'll keep your pearl in mind." I took the bracelet out of my pocket and passed it to him. "I'm attempting to discover the origin of this jewelry. I didn't recognize the artistic tradition, and so thought it might come from your part of the globe?"

He uncrossed his legs. The silk underthings didn't go far toward concealing the attributes beneath them. I looked away quickly, feeling my face heat. Gerritson wasn't really my sort, but judging from the view, his wife must be very pleased.

"Quite striking," he murmured. He went around his desk and removed a magnifying glass from a drawer, in order to study the bracelet more closely.

"Do you recognize it?" I asked hopefully.

"Yes and no."

Well, that was spectacularly unhelpful. "Whatever do you mean?"

"I've no idea what part of the world it comes from. But I have seen something like it before." He put the glass away. "A few years ago, I visited a colleague who works for the art museum in Boston. A donor had recently died and left his collection to the museum. A necklace very much like this one was among the pieces. Like you, he hoped to learn its origins. Very disappointed when I couldn't tell him—made me pay for dinner." He handed the bracelet back to me.

"Do you know if he ever discovered its provenance?"

"No idea." Gerritson shrugged his massive shoulders. "I can write him, if you'd like."

"Thank you. It's very kind of you to offer."

"Any time." He smiled broadly. "Now, is there anything else I can help with?"

"No." I shook his hand. "Thank you again."

"Anything for a colleague," he assured me. "I'll pop round to your office as soon as I hear something. And don't forget about the pearl!"

Chapter 7

I SPENT THE afternoon napping fitfully in my office, blunting my weariness but gaining a sore neck in return. Griffin sent word for Christine and I to meet him later, so the two of us stopped at Marsh's Diner after leaving the museum. While we ate, I told her about the strange creature I'd seen at the cemetery the night before.

"Interesting," she mused as she consumed her sandwich. "And you're certain it wasn't a ghūl?"

"Certain," I agreed emphatically. "Whatever else it might have been, it had nothing of the jackal about it. Quite the opposite."

"There's that, at least. Although I suppose the idea of unknown monsters is hardly comforting."

After, we visited her boarding house, so she could change clothes and retrieve her pistol. I waited for her in the parlor, under the disapproving glare of the landlady, who seemed to think I'd sneak away for an assignation with one of her tenants if not watched constantly.

Griffin awaited us at the corner of River Street and Blackstrap Lane. He stood beneath a streetlight, carpetbag in hand, bundled up in dark clothing with a heavy scarf against the chill.

"There you are," he said with a quick smile for us. "Christine, you have your pistol?"

"Yes." She patted her purse. "Poor Whyborne had to face my landlady for me to retrieve it."

"Next time I'll wait on the sidewalk," I said with a shudder.

"I'm going to have to find somewhere else to live," Christine said. Griffin began to walk, and we fell in beside him. "I'll never have a moment's privacy with Kander, otherwise. I have some savings put away—perhaps I should consider renting a house."

"I think there may be one vacant in our neighborhood," Griffin said.

What? Had he lost his mind? I tried to catch his eye, but he either didn't notice or chose to ignore me.

"Really?" Christine perked up. "Do find out if it's for rent, won't you?"

Perhaps I could claim the place to be a vermin-infested hellhole. But no, Griffin would just contradict me, and they'd both think I'd gone mad. I loved Christine dearly, but I had enough of her barging into my office whenever she pleased. I certainly didn't want her doing the same at home. What if Griffin and I were making love in the study, and she started banging on the door demanding to be let in?

Maybe Iskander would keep her occupied. I could only hope the man had stamina.

"How is Iskander?" Griffin asked. "Has he set an arrival date yet?"

"No, he's still settling the estate in Kent. There are lawyers involved, so even the simplest matters immediately become complicated. He did an initial survey of a barrow on the property, though," she added more cheerfully. "He suggested we might excavate it together, some day."

"How romantic," I muttered.

"I know," she sighed happily.

I rolled my eyes, but she didn't notice. "What do you have planned for us this evening?" I asked Griffin. "I see you brought your tools."

"I spent the afternoon loitering about the docks in disguise," he replied. "The *Norfolk Siren* is berthed at the farthest end of the harbor. I take it no other ships wanted to dock near her, sailors being a superstitious lot. There is a guard on the dock, to keep away curiosity-seekers until her owners decide what to do with her. The man on duty earlier was more than happy to talk in exchange for a few nips from a flask. He didn't know anything of note, but imagined his job would be done soon, since the newspapers have lost interest in the story. Oh, and he doesn't like the night guard, who's a notorious drunkard."

"How convenient," I said.

"Not as convenient as the whiskey bottle I have in my bag. We'll get by him one way or another." Griffin glanced at me. "But first things first, I'd like to stop by the saloon where Guinevere intended to meet us."

The air grew thick in my lungs. How could I go back in there? The place where I'd sat and drank bad whiskey, while my sister was being set upon only a short distance away, stabbed again and again. Had she screamed for help? God, why hadn't I insisted we leave earlier?

I trapped the words behind my teeth. Griffin would only say I couldn't have known, and Christine would agree with him. They loved me; of course they would try to reassure me.

"Why?" Christine asked with a small frown.

Griffin pursed his lips. "Guinevere asked Whyborne to meet her at that particular saloon for a reason. I want to know what it is. Interrogating the bartender seems like a good first step."

"Perhaps it was the only saloon she knew of," Christine countered.

"Or Stanford might have mentioned it to her, if he'd ever gone there," I added.

"Surely, he would have said so the other night." Griffin paused to let a group of women pass by along the sidewalk. Their dresses were cut low and their faces heavily painted. "He was drunk, but not so intoxicated he couldn't follow the conversation."

I scowled, remembering his threat against Griffin. "True. Mother said he'd ceased to rely on drink over the summer. I suppose Guinevere's death was as good an excuse as any to turn back to the bottle."

"There is another thing." Griffin unbuttoned the top few fastenings on his coat to draw out a folded bit of newspaper. "I don't know if either of you read the paper today?"

"I didn't," I admitted. I'd been too cursed tired to read anything with any amount of comprehension. Christine, however, nodded.

Griffin passed the clipped article to me. "Perhaps, Christine, you noticed the article about the horse and cab found wandering driverless not far from here?"

"Yes. The driver's body was found in the river, wasn't it? The police think he was robbed and...oh." She trailed off, eyes going wide.

I handed the article back without more than a glance. "Guinevere wouldn't have walked here," I said numbly. "You think this cab brought her from Whyborne House."

Griffin accepted the paper, his fingers brushing mine a bit more than strictly necessary to take it back. Even in the dimness of the ill-lit streets, I could see the sympathy in his eyes. "Yes, my dear. It's not certain, but it seems an unlikely coincidence for a cab to be found empty and the driver murdered the same night Guinevere died, and in the same part of town."

"Yes," I agreed.

"Which means either someone is keeping watch on Whyborne House and followed her from there, in a conveyance themselves, as they couldn't have kept up on foot. Or they knew her destination and prepared an ambush."

"And if she had some reason to choose the saloon, someone else might have known it, and thus been able to lie in wait."

Griffin nodded. "Will you be all right to go inside?"

With a start, I realized we'd reached our destination. Griffin had brought us a different way, no doubt to keep us from having to walk past the alley where Guinevere had died. The quiet kindness of his choice lessened the pressure on my heart a bit. "Yes. Thank you."

Griffin led the way inside. Nothing had changed since our last visit, save different faces on the clientele. And on the barkeep.

Damn. But perhaps this one might still be of help.

Griffin clearly thought so, as he sauntered up to the bar and took a seat, thankfully at the opposite end from where we'd sat the other night. Even so, my nerves drew tight as I settled beside him. What disasters might befall while I sat here tonight?

No, that was absurd. I was over-tired and not thinking clearly.

The bartender glanced at us, but didn't seem to find anything objectionable about Christine's presence. Given the area, he probably saw any number of women drinking in the establishment. "What can I get you?"

"Three whiskeys," Griffin said.

The barkeep poured and set them in front of us. Before he could turn away, Griffin added, "My friend and I were in here the night before last. I need to talk to the man who tended bar. Do you know when he'll be working again?"

The current bartender scowled. "Never. Left me in a damned bind, he did."

Griffin looked sympathetic. "Oh? How so?"

"I'm the owner." The man poured himself a shot, and tossed it back neatly. "That bastard Jerry sent a note around yesterday morning, saying he wasn't coming back. Now I've got to run the place and keep the bar all by myself until I can hire someone else as won't steal from the till. He just better not come slinking back looking for pay, I don't care if he *did* work three days this week."

Griffin casually slipped a dollar bill from his pocket and laid it on the bar beside his whiskey. "If you have any idea of where Jerry might be found, it would be of a great help to us."

The bartender looked disappointed. "I wish I did, sir. But I didn't inquire as to his living arrangements. One of the tenements around here, I'd expect, but I couldn't tell you which one." He started to turn away, then stopped and thrust one meaty hand into his pocket. "There is something, though. Don't know if it's of any value to you or not, but I've the one apron for me and whoever works the bar when I ain't here. Found this note in the pocket the next morning; figure Jerry must have left it there by accident. Damned if I know what it means, though."

The folded paper the man handed Griffin looked to have been written on good stationary, even though it was now covered with grime. As the barkeep turned away, Griffin unfolded the note. Christine and I both leaned in to read over his shoulder.

Midnight tonight. Meeting others. One wet, one dry. Prepare the back room.
"One for the land, and one for the sea."

I stared at the paper, unable to look away. "The handwriting," I said. "It's Guinevere's."

We left the bar soon after and made for the wharfs. My head spun with questions, none of which had answers. How on earth had someone like Guinevere met a lowly barkeep? What did her note to him mean? Had he disappeared of his own volition, or had the same hand that struck down the cab driver and Guinevere done away with him as well?

And what did any of it have to do with the creature from the cemetery? The thing had taken to the water like a dolphin. Guinevere's references to the sea seemed to suggest there was indeed a connection.

What was it? What had it wanted? Were there more of its kind lurking about? Perhaps clinging even now to the barnacle-encrusted pilings beneath our very feet? I shuddered at the thought.

If only I'd gotten a better look at the thing. While possessed by the dweller, I'd seen terrifying shark-men accompanying the creature. There had been statues of such things at the awful temple deep under the sea. The whole thing seemed a dream now, though, the memories fading and fragmenting as time passed. I couldn't be sure if the monster I'd glimpsed was one of those which worshipped the dweller, or some new aquatic horror.

Other than the light we carried, the only illumination along the wharfs came from the occasional lantern of a night watch aboard the ships, the harbormaster's quarters, and a lone lamp at the farthest end of the docks, where the *Norfolk Siren's* guardian kept watch. Thin clouds shrouded the stars. The waves shifted restlessly, causing the ships to creak and groan like restless sleepers. The scents of salt, pitch, and fish filled the air, and I breathed deep. After the time spent in the sandy wastes of Egypt, so far from the sea, I found the sounds and smells of the ocean more soothing than I ever had before.

Griffin halted. "Wait here," he murmured to Christine and me. "I'll see to the guard."

Placing his carpetbag on the rough wood of the dock at our feet, he drew out a half-filled bottle of cheap whiskey. He uncapped it, swished a mouthful around with his tongue, then spat it out into the ocean. His breath suitably reeking, he clutched the bottle in one hand and the lantern in the other, and staggered toward the guard.

The distance was too great for us to hear their voices. In the faint light of the lanterns, I saw the guard rise to his feet. Griffin waved the bottle and shouted something distorted by the sigh of the waves. Within moments, both men were laughing, and the guard now held the bottle. He gestured for Griffin to join him in his makeshift driftwood shelter, to get out of the wind and cold.

As he turned away, Griffin delivered a single, sharp blow to the back of his head. The guard crumpled like a sack of wet laundry.

I picked up the carpetbag. "Give me a hand," Griffin ordered as we drew closer. Christine obliged, and between the two of them, they shifted the guard into his shelter.

"With any luck, he'll be out for a bit," Griffin murmured. "But we'd best not linger."

He splashed some of the whiskey on the guard, perhaps in hopes the man would think he'd passed out from drink. Or did he mean to rouse suspicion in anyone the guard might go to for help, should he recover too soon?

Griffin took back his carpetbag, and Christine shuttered the lantern until only a single, strong beam cut through the gloom. The black bulk of the cargo ship loomed above us, its single stack pointing at the sky like an accusing finger. The lines protested as low waves shifted her bulk; without any cargo, she rode high in the water. Thank heavens the gangplank was still in place. Griffin and Christine might be up to climbing the ropes like a pair of monkeys, but I certainly couldn't have managed it.

"What exactly are we looking for here?" Christine asked in a low voice as we stepped onto the deck.

"Anything out of the ordinary." Griffin took the lantern from her and swept its beam slowly about us. To the fore lay the crew quarters; midships was the chart house and galley. In between lurked coils of rope, cleats, and equipment lockers, all of which threw odd shadows, amidst which anything might lurk.

"Out of the ordinary?" Christine asked skeptically. "On a boat found adrift, its crew missing to the last man? All lifeboats still in place, and the captain's pipe laying beside his logbook, as if he meant to return any moment? Blood everywhere, but no bodies and no signs of piracy? What could possibly be out of the ordinary here?"

"Point taken. Anything that might explain why Guinevere saw fit to mention it to Whyborne, then." Griffin made for the door leading to the crew quarters.

"What happened to the logbook?" I watched my step, but the deck was mainly clear of any unexpected obstructions. If there had been any cargo stored outside the holds, it had been removed already.

"Seized as part of the investigation into what happened. Probably in the hands of the insurers at the moment." Griffin made a face. "Everything in the refrigerated holds spoiled by the time the ship was spotted. If the insurance company can prove the loss due to some sort of mutiny, they'll escape a rather large payout. Needless to say, the owners are equally desperate to prove it an act of piracy or foul weather, so as not to take a total loss."

Griffin opened the door to the crew's quarters. Inside, the room was utterly black. Cold air flowed out over us, bringing with it the reek of old blood.

A small shape darted from inside.

I leapt back, a startled cry escaping my lips. It ran over my foot, and I shouted again, springing out of the way.

"Honestly, Whyborne, it's just a rat." Christine shoved me from behind—I'd almost trodden on her. "No need to leap about shrieking like a maid."

"I didn't shriek." My heart seemed reluctant to leave its new abode in my throat. "It was an exclamation of surprise."

"Very manful," Griffin agreed, but I thought his lips twitched in an effort to suppress a smile.

I glared at him. "Are we going to look inside, or stand about all night?"

Griffin obliged by shining the light within. The crew quarters were small, and looked to have been left exactly as they'd been found. Any trunks with personal effects had been removed, but the sheets still lay rumpled on the bunks. Blood stained most of them, and dried blood formed a crust on much of the floor. The place must have been awash with it.

"Ghastly," Christine murmured.

"Some of the men were sleeping," I said. "Whatever happened must have occurred during the night."

"Agreed." Griffin carefully inspected the walls and floor, but found nothing of interest.

We explored the officer's quarters, chart house, and galley with no more luck. Clearly something terrible had befallen the crew. But as to what, or what Guinevere's interest might have been, there was no clue.

"Do you think we'll have to go into the holds?" I asked as we crossed the expanse of the deck, making for the rear of the ship. The idea of poking around dank holds made me shudder, but if Griffin thought it necessary, then we had no choice.

"I certainly hope not, but it might come to that," Griffin replied.

Blast.

The ship's saloon lay at the rear of the ship. Cards still scattered across a table and the floor, as if a game had been in progress when disaster had befallen. An empty tumbler and bottle lay fetched up against a couch built against the wall. A faint, fishy odor clung to the room, which was to be expected.

The door to the head stood open. Griffin aimed the lantern beam within. "Look. On the wall."

A fine spray of dark spots clung to the wall, just inside the door. "Blood," Griffin judged. "See the way it splashed? Not from a gunshot, at least I don't think so. A slash with a knife would do it."

Had some terrified crewman hidden in here? Waiting in the dark for...what? Pirates? Monsters from the sea? Deadly spirits inhabiting a bank of fog? A lunatic among his fellow crew who'd somehow managed to murder everyone else?

Griffin went to his hand and knees. I hoped the sailors had been scrupulous about cleaning the floor.

"Here!" He scrambled back up and held his hand out. On his palm lay a small golden plaque, attached to a scrap of what appeared to be fine gold mesh. A geometric design stood in high relief on the outer surface of the plaque. It matched the designs on the bracelet from Guinevere's trunk.

I started to ask what the devil was going on. But the words died in my throat when the sound of voices drifted from outside, a beam of lantern light reflecting from the windows of the chart house.

CHAPTER 8

THE THREE OF us froze, listening intently.

"Damn it," Christine murmured.

"Quick." Griffin shuttered the lantern, plunging us into darkness. "Find a place to hide. If it's the police, surrender—safer to concoct a story about being curiosity seekers and let Niles bribe our way out of jail."

"And if it isn't?" I asked.

"Stay hidden. If they go past us, or down into the holds, we might be able to sneak off behind them with no one the wiser. Now go!"

How he expected us to navigate in the gloom, I hadn't the slightest idea. The low clouds reflected just enough light to show the outline of the ship, nothing more. The lockers for stowing equipment were near each rail, weren't they? I made blindly for the port side, tripping over a line, before my groping hands found the square shapes of steel welded to the deck.

I flattened myself against the side of the locker. As plans went, this certainly wasn't one of Griffin's best.

Lantern beams cut across the ship's deck. "Come out," called a deep male voice. "We won't hurt you."

One of his companions guffawed. No doubt the remark passed as wit among them.

Not the police, then. They would have identified themselves as such. Just as clearly, these men had come searching for intruders, rather than seeking loot or souvenirs. Had the guard summoned them? Or had someone else put a watch on the ship? Did they—whoever they might be—know Guinevere had mentioned the *Norfolk Siren* to me, and now took action to keep us from discovering any clue as to what she had known?

If so, they probably meant to kill us as well.

I tried to make myself as small as possible against the locker. Given my absurd height, it wasn't very small at all. Was there any sorcery I could use against them? Fire only worked if they had something easily flammable on them already. Lightning would only kill us all, considering we sat on a metal-plated deck. Water...

I could summon a wave. Sweep it over the deck.

Capsize the boat and kill us all. As high as the cargo-free ship rode, it would take an immense wave indeed, and we'd drown alongside the men stalking us.

There had to be something, though. There—

A hand closed around my arm.

"Got one!" a man shouted, hauling me out from behind the locker. I hadn't even heard him come up—he must possess the eyes of a cat to have found me in the dark.

I struggled, but his grip only tightened. The lantern beams cut over us, and the dull gleam of his knife caught the light.

The other men drew near, laughing. "Cut 'im!" one shouted. "Cut —"

Griffin rose up from alongside the rail. There came a soft whistle, and the man holding me jerked, gurgling. He let go of both me and the knife, took a step forward, then collapsed dead at my feet, blood spreading across his back where Griffin had stabbed him with his sword cane.

Christine's pistol let out a sharp crack, and another man went down. Then everything was chaos—men running, Griffin shoving me aside so he could engage another. Fire flashed from a revolver's muzzle as one of our attackers shot at Christine.

No! Anger roared through me. They would not hurt her. They would not hurt Griffin.

They would not.

I shouted the secret name of fire, setting flame to the powder within the weapon. The gun exploded in the ruffian's hand, the stink of scorched flesh and hot blood mingling with burning powder. His lantern hit the deck and guttered madly as he screamed.

The water of the bay heaved beneath us in response to my anger, and the wind came up, hurling foam scraped from the white caps over the deck. One of the remaining two men stumbled at the sudden surge of the ship under our feet. Another shot rang out from Christine, tearing a hole through the sleeve of his shirt. Bright blood followed, but not enough for a serious hit. The movement of the ship must have fouled her shot, for Christine seldom missed.

The dropped lantern rolled toward me, trailing fire. I snatched it up and threw it at the man as hard as I could.

He shrieked, batting at the oil coating his clothes even as it ignited. With a wild howl, he ran for the side and flung himself over, plunging like a flaming star into the ocean.

The final man had cornered Griffin against the rail. Griffin must have wounded him—blood dripped freely from a shallow cut on his face. Now wary of the sword cane, he'd snatched up a long cargo hook. Christine couldn't fire without risk of hitting Griffin, so I started forward, shouting to distract the attacker.

A swipe of the cargo hook caught Griffin's slim blade, wrenching it from his hand. I ran, arm out flung, as if to put a stop to the inevitable. The man grinned horribly, raising the hook and preparing to impale Griffin on it.

A man's voice called out, chanting in Aklo. The air around us grew suddenly cold, and frost coalesced on the ruffian's skin. He let out a startled cry of shock and pain.

In the moment of inattention, Griffin dove for his sword cane. A quick slash across the throat, and our attacker slumped to the deck, his blood steaming where it met the layer of frost that had formed around him.

The chanting ended. Light from a lantern bloomed, blinding after the dimness, and two figures made their way toward us.

"There you chaps are," exclaimed Theodore Endicott. "We've been looking for you, cousin."

I gaped at him and his companion. "Th-theodore? Fiona? What are you doing here?"

"Saving your friend's life," Fiona said. "Now let's get away from here, in case anyone heard the noise or saw the lights on board. We have a great deal to talk about."

"We've been hoping to speak to you," Theodore said an hour later as he handed me a glass of brandy.

We'd left the *Norfolk Siren* as quickly as possible, retreating as a group to the house Theo and Fiona rented on Wyrm Lane, near River Street. It was an old pile dating from the colonial era, two stories tall with what must be a cramped attic beneath a steeply pitched roof.

"Of course your father offered to let us stay at Whyborne House with the rest of the family," Theo had reassured me during our walk over. "But we wished privacy, for...well, you've seen some of it."

The sorcery, he meant. I'd nodded, but Griffin had only glared. "And the rest?" he asked.

"Not on the streets, Theo," Fiona ordered.

Theo rolled his eyes behind her back and gave me a wink. "Sisters. Always so bossy."

Theo didn't know Guinevere was dead. He couldn't have realized his remark would be in any way painful. So I summoned up a faint smile. "Er, yes. Quite."

Now I sat on a couch upholstered in red velvet, across from a blazing fire. Griffin sat beside me, still glowering from under his brows. Christine occupied one of the chairs, and Fiona another. The room was nicely appointed, if a bit dusty: a pleasant landscape above the hearth, thick drapes to keep out the cold drafts seeping through the windows, a rather nice grandfather clock ticking away in the corner.

"I thought you English preferred a cup of tea after a fright," Christine said, downing her brandy with gusto. "Not to suggest I'm complaining, mind you."

"Tea? How bloody *boring*," Fiona said with a roll of the eyes. Like her brother, she'd dressed in dark clothing for the expedition to the ship. It leached the color from her face and pale hair. "Besides, tonight barely qualified as a bit of light exercise, let alone a fright."

What did she mean? She sounded as if they were used to fighting for their lives. And given their use of sorcery...

It seemed there was a great deal more to my cousins than I'd guessed.

"Fiona and I wished to offer our congratulations on your destruction of the Eyes of Nodens last year." Theo's blue eyes crinkled in a rueful smile. "Of course, the subject isn't one we could have brought up over champagne and cake at the party the other night."

I sat up straighter. "You know about the Eyes of Nodens?"

"Not all of the cultists died. Those who escaped, talked," Fiona replied.

"I ran out of bullets," Christine said. "Otherwise, I assure you, they wouldn't have."

"Well done anyway," Theo said. Then he turned his smile on me. "The arcane world has been abuzz ever since over the Yankee sorcerer. Where did he come from? Who is he? Who trained him?"

The knowledge others had been speaking about me brought a flush to my cheeks. "Er, no one. There's a book—"

Griffin shot me a hard glare. "Perhaps this should wait until we're better acquainted."

What on earth was wrong with the man? They'd saved his life on the *Norfolk Siren*.

Using sorcery, of which Griffin didn't approve.

Theo didn't seem at all offended by Griffin's rudeness, however. "Quite so, Mr. Flaherty," he agreed. Taking a sip of his brandy, he leaned against the hearth. I couldn't help but note his clothing had clearly been tailored to flatter his long legs and lean torso. "But are you saying no one trained you, Percival? How extraordinary! You must be a prodigy."

"Oh, er, no," I mumbled, putting my brandy down. "I can only do some very simple spells. Call fire, summon wind, manipulate water, shatter stone. Oh, and lightning," I added, displaying the scars on my hand ruefully.

"Extraordinary," Fiona said. "Even those with mentors seldom proceed so quickly. You have a great gift, cousin."

Warmth flooded my chest. I'd grown so used to arguing with Griffin, it had never occurred to me others might regard my sorcery as something worthy of praise. But before I could gather the words to thank them, Griffin cut in.

"Who are you?" he asked coldly. "Really? And why were you on the *Norfolk Siren?*"

Fiona frowned at his tone. Even Christine seemed taken aback. "They saved your life, man," she reminded him.

"I haven't forgotten." His gaze remained trained on the Endicotts. "Forgive me, but our prior experience with sorcerers has been unpleasant."

"Ah." Theodore and Fiona exchanged a knowing look. "Of that I'm quite certain. Bloody sods are always summoning abominations, or sea gods, or things from the Outside."

Griffin blinked, obviously taken aback. "Well...yes."

"It's our duty to stop such nonsense." Fiona lounged back in her chair with a grin. "Our family has dedicated itself to keeping other sorcerers in line, and destroying any monsters we come across."

"Which hasn't made us very popular with the rest of the arcane community," Theodore added. "You should hear the names they call us."

Christine sat forward in her chair, her eyes sparkling with interest. "You hunt monsters? One of our, ah, friends," her cheeks pinked slightly, "is half Egyptian. His mother's family fight ghūls. Although they aren't sorcerers themselves."

"At the family estate, we've records going back to the twelfth century," Theo said. "From what little I know, there used to be many such bloodlines. Most of them are gone now, either stamped out by the forces of darkness, or else lost their purpose to the mists of history. But the Endicotts persevere."

My heart beat quickly. To think, I had family who had accomplished heroic deeds, things of which I could justly be proud. "We've been doing our part," I said, gesturing to Christine and Griffin. "The Eyes of Nodens, as you said—we kept them from enslaving the dweller in the deeps and decimating the land."

"A shame you couldn't have done in the dweller as well," Fiona said. "But we do what we can."

"And we prevented an undead necromancer from opening a gateway to the Outside, and other creatures from destroying a town in West Virginia." I wanted to mention our adventures in Egypt, but given Christine's sister had been the one trying to annihilate the world, I didn't feel I could without causing her undue pain at the reminder.

Theo beamed at me. "You *have* been busy," he said. "The Endicott blood runs true in you, it's clear."

"We were rather worried when we first learned a heretofore unknown sorcerer had defeated the Eyes." Fiona finished her brandy and set the glass aside. "When we heard the name Percival *Endicott* Whyborne, we had to find out if it was a coincidence or not."

"Imagine our delight when we learned not only you were our cousin, but your sister Guinevere had returned home to England." Theo made it sound as if we'd all been languishing in exile for generations, longing for repatriation.

The warm glow in my chest died away. I had to tell them. "Guinevere..."

I trailed off, staring at my brandy. I sensed Fiona leaning forward. "Is she all right? We'd heard she was taken ill, when we went to visit earlier today."

I swallowed hard. "No. She's dead. Murdered."

Fiona let out a small gasp. "Oh no. Poor Guinevere."

Theo crossed the room. A moment later, I felt his hand settle on my shoulder. On my other side, Griffin stiffened sharply.

"I'm so sorry." Theo's fingers tightened. "If there's anything we can do, anything at all, don't hesitate to ask."

"There isn't," Griffin said. "But we'll inform you if the situation changes."

What on earth was wrong with the man? I looked up from my drink, intending to thank Theo, but he'd gracefully retreated.

"Then you must be desperate to know why we were on the *Norfolk Siren*," Fiona said. If she'd noticed the interplay between Griffin and her brother, she gave no sign. "As we've said, we do our best to hold back the things that mean no good to mankind. We watch for portents and anomalies, anything unexplained which might be the first sign of evil. In this modern age of swift communication, our task has become much easier. Late in the summer, we noticed a series of ship disappearances stretching back through the spring. All of them American, most out of New England, involved in the Transatlantic trade."

"Those bloody refrigerated ships," Theo muttered angrily. When Christine gave him a curious look, he flushed pink. "Forgive my language, Dr. Putnam."

"Not at all," she responded drily. Christine could swear a sailor into the ground in both English and Arabic. "I only wondered at your grudge against refrigerated ships."

"They've destroyed the economy in England. At least for the old estates." Fiona answered for her brother. "One of the reasons so many of the nobility find themselves looking abroad for rich wives."

"Ah, yes, Kander mentioned it," Christine said. A tiny smile touched the corner of her mouth, and her eyes went unfocused. "I confess I was too distracted at the time to pay much attention."

"The missing ships?" Griffin prompted.

Fiona inclined her head to him. "Ships vanish all the time, of course. The ocean is still a vast place, even if now we can cross back and forth in a matter of days rather than months. The number was unusually high, however, and uncorrelated with any reports of storms or other natural phenomena to account for their loss. When Guinevere announced her plans to return to America for a visit, it seemed the perfect opportunity to investigate more closely. We'd met socially a few times, and so it was easy enough to convince her to allow us to accompany her, under the guise of wishing to meet our other distant cousins."

"The mystery of the *Norfolk Siren* seemed to confirm our worst suspicions of the involvement of otherworldly forces," Theo finished. "And now you say poor Guinevere is dead, and it has something to do with the ship?"

"Yes," Griffin cut in. "But we vowed to Niles we'd tell no one of it without his permission." He shot me a dark look.

"Griffin, you're being terribly unfair," I protested.

"I'm being honest." Griffin turned to Theo and Fiona. "Word of her death must *not* go beyond you two. Do you understand?"

"Of course," Theo said immediately.

"We won't tell a soul." Fiona caught my eye and offered a smile. "After all, we're used to keeping family secrets."

CHAPTER 9

I SPENT THE next morning listening to Christine complain about the director, from whose office she had just come.

"The man has done some appallingly stupid things before," she said. "I pointed out, tactfully, this Hallowe'en nonsense was a job for the curators and having two senior staff members work on it was absurd."

I suspected her idea of tact simply meant she hadn't yelled at him. Or not yelled at him much. "And what did he say?"

"He said we would assemble the list of objects and give orders to the curators, but my experience with the Egyptian Gala meant I was the perfect person to arrange the private showings." Her teeth ground together alarmingly. "I told he him was quite right, if he meant the gathering would be attacked by thieves and madmen halfway through the evening."

I suppressed a sigh. "I imagine that went over well."

"The man is impervious to logic. And to spring this on us with no warning, and barely a week to work on it! Bah!"

"Dr. Gerritson has a cursed pearl we can use," I offered. "Kills Polynesian chieftains, or something."

"Hmph. A good thing *some* of our colleagues can be called upon to help." She rose to her feet. "With any luck, the thing really is cursed and will do in Dr. Hart."

Once she had departed, I downed another cup of coffee, splashed some water on my face, and checked the clock. Close enough to lunch.

The omnibus took me to High Street and let me off a short walk from Whyborne House. Fenton looked unusually pale when he answered the door, and dark circles showed under his eyes. The sight shocked me, almost as badly as if he'd been naked. Fenton's job was to represent the dignity of the Whyborne family, and it was a charge he took with great seriousness. To see him display human frailty...I couldn't recall such a thing ever happening in my lifetime.

"Your father and Stanford are in the study, Master Percival," he informed me as he led the way inside.

In truth, I'd hoped to avoid both of them. "I'll speak to Mother, first. Is Miss Emily in?"

"No. She has the day off. I believe she went to visit family."

Before I could turn my steps toward the stairs, the sound of raised voices echoed from the direction of the study. "That is my final word, Stanford." Father's voice drew steadily closer, and a moment later he crossed into the foyer. "Fenton! Bring around the motor car."

"I won't be dismissed like this!" Stanford shouted. His face was flushed scarlet, and his eyes narrowed into slits.

"I have other things to attend to," Father snapped back over his shoulder.

Stanford stopped, hands clenching into fists. "Go on, then. Make whatever paltry deals you want. But remember today, when I've taken Whyborne Railroad to heights you can only dream about."

Stanford spun on his heel and stalked away. Catching sight of me, Father stopped. "Percival. Mr. Flaherty was already here this morning. Is there some new development?"

"No." I considered asking what he and Stanford argued over, but from the sound of things, it was some business affair of which I had no interest. "I've come to see Mother."

"I see." Father left without saying anything further. Relieved at my escape, I hurried up the stair.

Mother's chambers lay on the uppermost floor of the house, away from the hustle and bustle of daily life. Bookcases lined the walls, save where enormous windows let in light. A cheerful fire crackled in the hearth. Above the mantel hung a portrait of the Lady of Shalott, painted using Mother as a model long ago in the days of her youth.

Mother sat at a table, holding herself rigidly in her chair. On the table lay a large crystal bowl filled with water and a leather-bound book. The book I recognized, as she'd read it to me many times in my childhood: Wolfram von Eschenbach's *Parzival*. *Percival*, in English.

As I entered, she spoke a word, and the candles set about the room leapt into flame. The light guttered wildly for a moment before settling into a soft glow, which helped alleviate the October gloom.

"Mother," I said by way of greeting. "How are you?"

She didn't look at me, only stared at the bowl in front of her. Her face was haggard, even beyond the ordinary ravages of her long illness. Had she slept at all since Guinevere's death?

"I've been practicing." She indicated the bowl, the candles. "Every spell you taught me. It makes me feel a little less useless."

The grief in her voice wrung my heart. "You aren't—"

"Yes, I am!" The crystal bowl chimed in response to her anger. "I want to be out there, looking for whoever murdered my daughter. Instead, I must sit here and wait for news, while others do the work."

What could I say? Even if she'd had her health, society would never have allowed her to investigate Guinevere's death. She would still be here, waiting for someone else to either capture the killer or fail.

Doubtless, she knew the bitter truth better than I. So I only said, "I'm sorry."

She rose from her chair and went to stand at the window. One hand lifted, resting on the cold glass, as if she longed to touch the world outside. Did she see this room as her refuge or her prison? Or both?

Griffin's question the night of the party returned to me. "Why did you stay here, once I left? Instead of retiring to a sanitarium?"

"I considered it." She trailed her fingers over the glass panes. "Told myself that once all of my children were grown and gone, I'd depart as well. But when the time came, I couldn't bear to leave. I've lived my entire life near the sea. I know it's near, even if I haven't seen it with my own eyes for twenty years."

"There are health resorts and the like which take advantage of the fresh ocean air," I pointed out.

"Perhaps. But Widdershins suits me, far better than Boston or anywhere else I've ever been." She cast me a rueful smile. "Surely you understand. You might have gone anywhere after university, yet you chose to return here."

"The Ladysmith is a fine museum." And the town was familiar, comfortable. I disliked travel and new things.

That was all. There was no otherworldly reason such as Miss Lester had suggested to Griffin. Widdershins was just a city like any other, even if it had been built over lines of arcane power. To think it could want things or keep people from leaving was the height of absurdity.

"You are my one consolation," Mother said with a small, sad smile. "If I cannot leave this room and bring justice to Guinevere's murderer myself, at least I can send you out in my stead."

"Griffin and I are doing everything possible," I said. "And Christine." Should I tell her of the Endicotts? They'd not sworn me to secrecy, and yet they hadn't given me permission to speak, either. "And others," I finished, a bit lamely.

"I know. But it's still difficult."

Uncertain what else to say, I picked up the book. "Reading an old favorite?"

"Yes." She crossed the room and took the book from me, turning it over in her hands. "Your father meant to name you Ulysses, after President Grant. But when you were born so sickly, he didn't think it appropriate."

I made a face. "It's probably just as well. I can't see myself as a 'Ulysses.'"

"Everyone thought you would die, like your poor sister. The doctors, the midwife, everyone. They were all so certain." A little smile touched her lips. "But you defied them all. So stubborn, to refuse to leave this world once you'd tasted it. This was the first book I ever read to you."

"In German."

"Of course. You weren't even a week old, but I thought it would be a good start on your education." Her smile faded as she stared thoughtfully at the worn leather binding. "I asked Niles for permission to name you. And I chose the best of all Arthur's knights, the one who found both true love and the Grail."

"Until he was replaced in later versions of the story by Galahad, at any rate," I pointed out ruefully.

"I was *not* naming you after some bloodless virgin. I rather hoped you'd have a more interesting life."

"Perhaps I can borrow one of the suits of armor downstairs. And find a white charger somewhere. Griffin would fall down laughing."

"Hmm, I don't know. I think he'd find you quite the striking figure."

"Mother!" The tips of my ears burned with embarrassment.

"It was merely an observation." Her brief smile slipped away. "Thank you, Percival. For coming to see me."

"Of course." I stepped forward and embraced her carefully. She felt painfully delicate, as if her long illness had hollowed out her bones like those of a bird.

I took my leave. As I reached the second floor landing, a voice spoke from the shadows of the corridor.

"If it were up to me, you wouldn't even be allowed to set foot in this house."

I froze, my hand on the bannister. Stanford stepped in front of me, blocking my way forward.

Memories of childhood surged from the dark places to which I usually consigned them. Dangling from the third-story balcony, screaming in terror as Stanford laughed and threatened to drop me to my death on the marble far below. Hiding in a linen closet, only to be dragged out and forced to eat some noxious concoction my brother and his friends had made. Struck about the legs with a stick, until my shins were mottled with bruises.

And when I went to tell Father, to beg him for help, he'd put his hand on Stanford's shoulder and smiled benignly down on my brother. Phrases such as "boyish high spirits" and "you must toughen up" and "no one likes a tattletale" floated past my ears, all of them meaning the same thing.

No one will ever help you. Nothing will ever change.

I swallowed hard against the sudden pounding of my pulse. I was no longer that boy, that youth, weeping into my pillow and praying either Stanford or I would die in the night. "A good thing it isn't up to you," I said coolly. I tried to step around him, but he moved in front of me.

"I could almost tolerate you, before. At least you knew your place."

I wanted to ask "before what," but I already knew the answer. Before sorcery and cults and monsters forced me to act, rather than passively allow life to happen to me.

Before Griffin.

"You think you're so high and mighty," Stanford went on. "Prancing around with your catamite. You think you have Father on a leash, but you're just a disgusting sodomite. Jail is too good for you perverts." The look in his eyes was beyond anger or annoyance, or even disgust at what he saw as my perversions. It was hatred. "They ought to cut your balls off and force you to feed them to each other, before they hang you from the highest tree around."

Bile scalded the back of my throat, and my skin flushed hot. My hands clenched, the scars drawing tight on the right one. The air currents shifted, stirring my hair. "Don't you dare threaten me."

"I didn't. Just said what I thought the law *ought* to be." His lip curled. "Touchy as always."

Arcane words burned on my tongue. I'd read more spells in the *Arcanorum* than Griffin realized, dark things I told myself I'd never actually practice. But at the moment, I longed to unleash them against Stanford, to fill his mind with shadowy horrors and drive him screaming to the madhouse.

"Get the hell out of my way," I said, voice trembling with rage.

His smile told me he'd mistaken anger for fear. "Have it your way." He stepped aside, clearing my path to the stair.

I certainly wasn't going to trust him at my back. I returned his stare, and he retreated just far enough I didn't think he could lunge forward and give me a shove.

I descended the stair with more haste than usual, but he made no move to come after me. Nevertheless, I felt the scorching heat of his gaze on my back, until the door of the house finally shut between us.

An hour later, I sat in my office, still trying to rid myself of the sour taste of the encounter with Stanford. We'd never been friends, quite the opposite. But although he'd always viewed me with contempt, his feelings over the last two years had turned into outright hatred.

Perhaps he'd never before realized my true inclinations toward my own sex. Certainly it was nothing I'd ever spoken of directly to anyone in the family, although Mother had most likely always known, and Father strongly suspected. Did the new intensity of his dislike stem from revulsion toward a love he no doubt considered unnatural?

No matter the cause, how dare he say such things to me? To anyone? Had he no shred of decency left?

A soft knock on my half-open door distracted me from my angry thoughts. "Dr. Whyborne?" Miss Parkhurst asked, peeking around the edge. I forced myself to give her a genial smile, despite my foul mood.

"Yes? What can I do for you?"

Her cheeks pinked and she ducked her head, "Um, there's a Mr. Endicott here to see you, sir."

I couldn't imagine why it would occasion her to blush. Perhaps she found him handsome? "Oh, yes. Please show him in."

A few moments later, Theo strode into my office, hand outstretched. I rose to my feet and shook it. "I must say, the museum is amazing, old chap! Absolutely amazing."

"Shall I bring coffee?" Miss Parkhurst asked from the doorway.

"No thank you." I hoped to go to the library, and Mr. Quinn would probably cut my heart out with a letter opener if I dared bring food or drink within its hallowed walls. Miss Parkhurst departed, looking faintly disappointed at my refusal.

"Fiona sends her regards," Theo said. "She lacks the patience for books, I fear." He hesitated delicately. "We were surprised to receive your note this morning. Mr. Flaherty didn't seem particularly eager for our assistance."

A worm of guilt squirmed unpleasantly in my chest. "Er, Griffin doesn't know I wrote you. He has an irrational fear of sorcery, and...

well."

"Ah." Theo's blue eyes gleamed with amusement. "We shall simply have to be discreet, then."

It sounded as if we were conducting an illicit affair, although of course he meant nothing of the sort. "Y-yes," I stammered. "Would you care to sit down?"

He took the guest chair, leaning forward, folding his hands primly atop one knee. "Now. How can I help?"

I'd brought the odd stone in with me this morning. Griffin had placed it within a locked box at home, just in case. I hadn't felt anything more from it, but there was no sense in taking unnecessary risks.

"We found this in Guinevere's things," I said, unlocking the box. "It seems to have arcane properties—it influenced my mind when first uncovered."

"I will guard myself mentally, then."

I carefully opened the box and unwrapped the stone. I could still hear its siren song, tugging at me on some deep level, but my mental preparation allowed me to disregard it. Theo frowned and picked it up, careful to keep the silk wrapping between his fingers and its surface. "Interesting. It's definitely enchanted."

"Can you guess what it might be?"

"No." He re-wrapped it carefully, and the faint singing vanished from my mind. "I haven't seen anything like it before. If only we were back in England, where I could ask other members of the family, or at least have access to the estate library."

I locked the stone into the box and put it away again, in exchange for the strange bracelet. "What about this?"

"I'm not certain. It seems vaguely familiar, but I can't place it."

"We found the bracelet in Guinevere's possession." I took out the gold plaque and laid it on the desk. "And this aboard the *Norfolk Siren* last night."

"It looks as if it was torn from something," Theo speculated, fingering the bit of gold netting clinging to the back. "And it's clearly of the same design."

"Yes." I hesitated, but if what the twins had told us was true, he ought to be used to the idea of monsters stalking the edges of everyday reality. "There's something else. I saw a creature in the cemetery when we laid Guinevere in the crypt."

I described the thing as best I could, which wasn't very good at all, in truth. I also told him of the note from the bartender, with the strange phrase that echoed Guinevere's final words.

Theo shook his head slowly. "I haven't the slightest idea what it could mean, although the reference to the sea does suggest a connection with the creature you saw." He handed back bracelet and plaque. "I take it from your note the library has a number of books which might be useful for research?"

"Yes. As you know sorcery and languages, I thought you'd be interested in helping?"

A grin stole over his face. "A chance to fondle old books I might never see anywhere else? You'll have to tie me to this chair to stop me."

CHAPTER 10

"THIS IS...HAVE I died and gone to the dark fields?" Theo asked, gazing about the library with wide eyes.

I might not be entirely certain what the dark fields were—my religious education was rather lacking—but there was no mistaking the sentiment in his voice. "Even better—you can visit while still alive," I replied. "And this is only a small portion. The library is a labyrinth of sorts, and just when you think you've reached the end, whole new rooms open up."

We stood at the entrance of the library, not far from the main desk. As usual, Mr. Quinn, the head librarian, lurked about. Upon spotting us, he drifted forward from a space between the nearest stacks. With his black suit and dark hair slicked back with oil, he looked more like an undertaker than a librarian. Silvery eyes peered at us unblinkingly.

"You've brought a guest, Dr. Whyborne," Quinn observed in a sepulchral voice.

"Er, yes." Conversing with Quinn always made me nervous. I felt as if I never knew what he might say next, or what he might expect from me in return. "This is Mr. Theodore Endicott, a distant cousin of mine, visiting from England. He's here to help me with some research. Theo, this is Mr. Quinn, our head librarian."

"A pleasure," Theo said, holding out his hand. Quinn looked at it as if he'd never seen a human appendage before. After a moment, Theo let his drop.

"Can I be of assistance, Dr. Whyborne?" Quinn asked. His spidery fingers flexed and knotted around one another in a disturbing manner.

I gave him a list of books I thought might be useful and told him where in the library to bring them. Theo's eyes grew wide as I named them. Once Mr. Quinn drifted away, summoning an assistant librarian to help with those kept under lock and key, he said, "I recognize some of those titles. Do you mean to say they're just kept here, at the public museum? Where anyone could read them?"

"Not anyone," I assured him hastily. "The staff, yes, but visiting scholars have to offer some evidence they have a serious reason before being allowed access to the library."

"Still, it doesn't seem very safe. What's to stop some nefarious sorcerer from gaining access and using them to his own ends?"

I wanted to reassure Theo such a thing couldn't possibly happen. But a moment's reflection convinced me Mr. Quinn would probably find an interest in the dark arts a compelling reason to allow access to the library, rather than forbid it. "It hasn't been a problem so far," I said lamely. "Would you like to hear the library's history?"

Fortunately, this distracted him. "Please."

"The museum's architect died in a madhouse," I said as I preceded him into the stacks. "It's said the library was the final part of the plan he drew up, and it either reflects his descent into madness, or else drove him to it. At any rate, the librarians are a...well. *Interesting* bunch."

"So I see," he said.

I led the way to one of the smaller rooms within the convoluted maze, which contained several of the volumes I hoped might prove of assistance. "I studied some of these while attempting to identify the Eyes of Nodens and their god," I explained to Theo as we walked. "As we are investigating disappearing ships, I thought they might be a good starting point. There may be relevant lore I either forgot or simply didn't recognize the importance of the first time."

"A good suggestion," he said. "I would have done the—dear heavens! Is this the 1839 edition of *Nameless Cults?*"

I eyed the book, which was chained to a reading desk, with a certain amount of pride. "It is. The Ladysmith spares no expense when it comes to research."

Theo gazed at the books Mr. Quinn's assistant delivered to our table. "The *Al Azif*—and in the original Arabic! I've always wanted to see it."

I couldn't help but grin. "Not even my old university had a copy in anything but Latin. The first time I saw it here in the library..."

"An antiquarian's dream," Theo said, meeting my eyes in perfect understanding. "Our family has what I thought to be an extensive collection of old volumes, but nothing like this."

I gestured at the pile of books. "Then shall we begin?"

"I thought you'd never ask."

I'd expected the afternoon to prove awkward, despite our good beginning. I seldom worked with others, and generally found it not to my taste. Theo, however, turned out to be a boon. He never interrupted my studies for anything other than a find of genuine interest, or an intelligent question. One such led to a spirited debate on medieval Aklo as applied to alchemy, and whether alchemy and sorcery were truly separate or merely two parts of the a whole.

"Not to suggest you need further instruction," Theo said diffidently, "but if you wished to study the arcane with like-minded persons, you could visit Fiona and me. It would truly be our pleasure. And Fiona would love to show off her alchemy laboratory to someone."

I opened my mouth to happily accept his invitation, but the image of Griffin's disapproving glare imposed itself on my mind. What would he say, if I said I'd decided to study sorcery with my cousins?

I could imagine all too easily. "I can't," I said, shoulders slumping in disappointment. "As you gathered last night, Griffin doesn't really approve of sorcery."

Theo cocked his head to the side curiously. "And does his approval matter so much to you?"

How to explain without betraying the true nature of our relationship? "Griffin is my closest companion." That sounded innocent enough, didn't it? "As such, his approval is important to me."

"Not so important it kept you from summoning me here," Theo noted.

Damn the man. "He's also my landlord," I hedged.

"And a comparative philologist at the museum isn't paid well enough to find other lodgings?" he countered.

Had I a wife and children depending on my salary, I might have argued. As it was, I had no real excuse. "I'm sorry. I simply can't."

"Very well. But the invitation remains open." Theo took out his watch. "It's after closing time—I suppose we'd best finish up."

The hour surprised me—the time had flown by in his company. I summoned an assistant, and the books kept locked up were whisked away. Not without a longing look from Theo.

"They'll be here tomorrow," I assured him with a smile as I gathered my notes.

"Then so will I." He made a small bow. "I don't suppose you—"

"Whyborne?" Griffin asked.

I froze guiltily, hands hovering over my papers. Griffin stood in the doorway recently vacated by the assistant, wearing one of his better suits, his silver-headed cane in his hand. His emerald eyes moved from me to Theo and back again.

"Griffin," I said stupidly. "What are you doing here?"

His gaze narrowed. "I came to see if you wished to dine with me. I thought we could discuss the case. But obviously, you've been doing that already."

Theo stepped toward the doorway. "I'll just show myself out, shall I?"

"I'll see you later," I said, but I aimed the words at Griffin.

Theo's hasty footsteps receded. I finished gathering my papers and swept out after him. Griffin followed on my heels.

To his credit, he held his tongue until we reached my office. Then again, it wasn't always wise for us to quarrel in public. As I put the papers down on my desk, he shut the door behind us and threw the lock.

"Are you going to tell me what Mr. Endicott was doing here?"

I turned to face him, leaning back against my desk, arms folded over my chest. "What do you think? He was helping me research the jewelry we found."

"I thought Dr. Gerritson was helping you."

"Given the plaque we discovered last night, I suspected there might be a connection to a sea cult, or something of the sort." As he opened his mouth to object, I let my arms fall to my sides and stood straight. "Curse it, Griffin, my sister is *dead*. If Theodore and Fiona can help us find out who killed her and why, I'm not going to turn them down."

Griffin's expression softened as my words sank in. "I...you're right. I hadn't thought of it in such a way." He shuffled his feet. "Still, I can't say I like how Theodore looks at you."

Looked at me? I hadn't noticed anything amiss. "What do you mean?"

"Like you're a dessert he can't wait to try."

I burst out laughing at the sheer absurdity of it. "Now you're being foolish."

"Am I?"

I moved toward him. He arched a brow, but said nothing as I leaned against him. My greater height allowed me to trap him against the door, pressing him back into the wood. He tilted his head back, and I kissed him.

Lips parted eagerly beneath mine, and I slid my tongue into him. His mouth tasted faintly of mint. He returned the kiss, lips caressing mine, tongues swirling together in a complicated dance of desire. Teeth nipped lightly at my lower lip when I withdrew. "Yes," I murmured. "You are. It's just scholarly zeal."

Griffin's hand slipped between us, fondling me through the cloth of my trousers. "Oh, is that what this is?"

I pushed against him, felt the hard line of his erection against my thigh as I slid it between his. "No," I growled. "This is lust."

A groan of desire escaped him. I captured it with my mouth; even though most of my colleagues had left, there were still guards and janitorial staff about. We fumbled with each other's buttons; I managed to get his free first, and slid my hand down inside his clothing, wrapping my fingers around the hard heat I found there.

Then his hand closed around me, and I was the one whose moans had to be stifled. I leaned against him, pressing him back against the door, as we tugged and jerked and rutted against each other. It was chaotic and messy and incredible, heat building quickly. I couldn't seem to catch enough breath, barely daring to take my mouth from his, lest our gasps be heard. His fingers tightened around my length, and I thrust against his grip until excitement and pleasure turned suddenly into searing ecstasy.

Still half-blind and barely able to think coherently, I dropped to my knees and guided his cock into my mouth. His fingers, slick with my spend, clutched at my hair. I let him use my mouth as he wished, and he thrust deep once, twice, thrice, before stiffening. I swallowed around him, felt him shudder as I sucked everything I could out of him.

He sighed and caressed my hair, then drew his hand back sharply. "Curse it—I've made quite the mess of you."

"Nothing the washroom won't put to rights." I took out a handkerchief and cleaned myself before tucking my clothes back into order. While he did the same, I slipped out to the men's washroom. Fortunately, I didn't encounter anyone on the way there, for the mirror revealed a flushed face and swollen lips. No to mention questionably damp hair.

When I had put myself as much to rights as possible, I stepped out and found him waiting for me in the corridor, a satisfied grin on his mouth. "I had thought to take you to dinner," he said. "Shall we count this as an appetizer?"

"You're terrible." As there was no one else in the hall and no sound of footsteps, I chanced giving him a swift kiss.

We strolled out together, both our moods greatly improved. But as we descended the steps to the sidewalk outside, Father's motor car pulled up to the curb, with Fenton at the wheel.

"Master Percival," he said, clambering out. If anything, he looked even worse than he had before. Dread set my nerves on edge—surely he wouldn't have come here unless something dire had happened.

"Mother?" I blurted out my worst fear.

"No." He shook his head, face gray. "It's Miss Emily. She's been murdered."

A short time later, Fenton stopped the motor car in front of the Widdershins city morgue. The car's seat was too small for three people, so I'd spent the ride over with Griffin balanced on my knees, my mind spinning.

Miss Emily couldn't be dead—there had to be some mistake. What had Fenton said earlier? She'd taken the day off to visit family? Surely she was with them, and this body belonged to some other unfortunate woman.

Griffin climbed out of the motor car and turned to help me down. Our hair was in even more disarray than before from the wind.

"Shall I wait here?" Fenton asked. "I've...already seen the body."

"How was she found?" Griffin asked.

Fenton's mouth tightened slightly, as though he didn't care to be directly addressed by Griffin. But he said, "Her daughter grew worried when she didn't come for a planned visit last night. She waited until this morning, thinking perhaps Miss Emily had been detained by some business at Whyborne House and forgotten to send word. When neither word nor Miss Emily appeared, she came to the house in search of her mother. Mr. Whyborne was concerned, and sent me to the police station with her to make inquiries." He paused, throat working, as if he swallowed against some obstruction. "There we learned a woman fitting Miss Emily's description had been found dead in the early hours of the morning and sent to the morgue."

The words floated past me, almost meaningless. "Wh-why is she still here?"

"Your father thought it might be useful for you to view the body and speak to the medical examiner. She was found not far from where Lady Gravenwold died."

God. I swayed on my feet, and Griffin put his hand to my elbow. "Steady, my dear. I'll go inside, and you wait here with Mr. Fenton."

"No." I'd never forgive my cowardice if I did such a thing. Making an effort to stand straight, I told Fenton, "You may return home. Tell Father we'll send word as soon as we know anything."

Fenton touched his cap. "Very good, Master Percival."

When he was gone, Griffin led me inside the morgue. No doubt he'd been here before; not all of the missing persons cases he took ended happily. The door opened onto a large room, its windows meant to let in daylight for viewing, although now only the darkness of the long, autumn night pressed against the panes. The stone walls and tiled floor seemed to hold a chill. Part of the room had been divided off by a low wall topped with a glass partition.

Bodies lay on the other side of the partition, propped at an angle so as to be easily viewed. All were nude, their clothing hanging above them to help identification. A woman leaned against the glass, sobbing piteously, a small child clinging to her skirts.

An attendant came to greet us. "Mr. Flaherty," he said. So Griffin had been here often enough to be known to the staff. "You're here to see Emily Corbitt?"

"Yes." Griffin introduced us, but such was my state, I couldn't remember the man's name five seconds later. He led us back through a discreet door. This room lay in shadows, and all the terrible scents of death washed over me, rising from the three bodies lying on steel tables.

The attendant went to one and pulled back the shroud, revealing the face beneath. At the sight of the familiar features, I sagged against the wall.

Griffin caught my elbow. "Whyborne! Are you all right?"

"I'll fetch a chair and some smelling salts," the attendant said and scurried off.

"She knitted me a scarf one Christmas." It was a stupid detail, but my mind seized upon it as if it had vast importance.

Griffin's hand rubbed comfortingly on my back. "I remember."

"It was oranges when I was growing up. Always an orange on Christmas. And a little cake for my birthday." Why was I talking about such idiotic, insignificant things? But my mouth ran on as if it had a mind of its own. "She'd let me eat dinner with her in the servants' kitchen, whenever Father was gone. I could actually stand to eat there, you know, not just push the food around the plate."

"She was a kind woman," Griffin said. "I'm so sorry, my dear."

The attendant returned with a doctor, who I gathered must be the medical examiner. When I sat in the chair the attendant brought, the doctor took my pulse without asking permission, then administered the restorative salts himself. I jerked away from the ammonia scent and glared at him.

"What happened to her, Dr. Greene?" Griffin asked the medical examiner, indicating Miss Emily's body.

"Stabbed," the doctor said. "She must have been set on suddenly from behind. The parietal bone of the skull was cracked from a heavy blow. Still, she wasn't knocked completely unconscious—there are defensive wounds on her hands. There was no sign of sexual interference, and given her employment, the police believe it a robbery gone wrong."

"I see. Thank you."

"What will happen to her?" I asked. She couldn't feel the steel table beneath her body, and yet it seemed so wrong to leave her there, with only a thin shroud to keep away the chill. She'd made a scarf to keep me warm. How could I abandon her here so cold?

"Her daughter will take her for burial, once we're done," the attendant offered.

"Are we? Done?" I looked to Griffin.

"Yes." He held out a hand to help me to my feet. "We are. Thank you, gentlemen."

CHAPTER 11

HE KEPT A steadying hand on my elbow all the way back outside. I leaned against the wall, breathing deeply of the crisp October air, struggling to clear the clinging scent of death from my nose.

"Tell me what I can do," he said quietly.

I wanted him to hold me. I wanted to cry into his shoulder. I wanted to scream it wasn't fair, none of this was fair. Miss Emily had been a good, decent woman who had never harmed anyone. The only person besides Mother who'd ever shown me kindness within the walls of the house I'd been born in, and now she was dead, and I didn't even know why.

But society wouldn't let us embrace so on the street. So I forced myself to stand, hands folded tightly in front of me. "Should I call on her daughter, do you think? Or...or go to the funeral?" At least she would have a proper one, unlike Guinevere.

Guinevere. "She was found in the same part of town," I went on. "Do you think...it isn't a coincidence, is it?"

"Doubtful." Griffin looked pensive. "We wondered who had given Guinevere the clothing she used as a disguise. Miss Emily seems the likeliest candidate now."

"No. She would have said something," I protested. "She and Mother were together from childhood—she wouldn't have kept such a secret from her."

"Unless Guinevere swore her to secrecy." Griffin's mouth curled into a frown. "If Miss Emily was drawn into this, whatever *this* is, by

Guinevere, against her will, perhaps she couldn't bring herself to tell Heliabel. When Guinevere was said to suddenly fall ill, Miss Emily must have guessed what had happened, even if Heliabel didn't confide the truth to her. Perhaps she felt she had betrayed Heliabel's trust and was too ashamed to speak."

"Perhaps." I slumped against the stones of the wall, weariness aching in my bones. "I should go to Mother. She must be devastated."

"Of course." Griffin touched my arm. "Give her my condolences."

"I will." I stepped away from the wall. "Don't wait up for me. I have no intention of spending the night there, but it may be late by the time I return." I lowered my voice cautiously, even though no one stood near. "I'll go to my bedroom, so as not to wake you."

"Please don't. I want you to wake me." His eyes darkened to the shade of moss in the dim light. "I want to be here for you."

God, I wanted to kiss him. Not from passion, but from love and companionship, and all the other things I could never find the words to say. But of course I couldn't, at least without being hauled off to jail for indecency. So I only said, "I'll see you later, then," and forced myself to walk away.

Less than a half hour later, I stood in front of the rented house on Wyrm Lane.

The wind kicked up, scattering leaves from a nearby tree across the stoop, then inside as Theo opened the door. His eyes widened at the sight of me. "Percival! I wasn't expecting to see you here. Especially after...well. Mr. Flaherty."

"Griffin thinks I'm at Whyborne House." I ought to feel guilty about lying to Griffin, shouldn't I? But I didn't. I couldn't. Because this was for him as much as—more than—anyone else. "The maid who was like a second mother to me is dead, murdered just like Guinevere. I'm tired of the people I care for dying. I swore last spring I'd do anything it took to keep those I love safe, but I failed to act on that promise. No more. I have to do something, before I lose anyone else."

The words had come out in a confused rush. Theo must have thought me an utter lunatic. But he only looked at me as if he understood. "And you've come to us because...?"

"Because I want to study sorcery with you." I met his eyes and, a bit to my own surprise, found I wasn't at all afraid. "I want your help finding whatever cult or sorcerers or monsters are responsible. And then I want to make them pay."

Theo smiled and stepped back. "Well, then. Come inside."

"My condolences on your loss," Theo said, as Fiona poured me a glass of wine. We stood in their parlor once again, near the fire. "It must be very difficult for you, so close on the heels of Guinevere's death."

"Yes." I took a steadying swallow of wine. The vintage was an excellent one, worth more attention than I was inclined to give it at the moment.

"I'm glad you came to us." Fiona poured glasses for herself and Theo as well, then set the bottle aside. "Of course we'll do everything we can to help."

"Griffin doesn't know I'm here," I admitted. "But I can't just stand by and let this continue."

She watched me over the lip of the wine glass. "It must be difficult having a friend who doesn't appreciate you properly."

"That isn't it—he does—it's just..." I trailed off, heat involuntarily flushing my face. What could I safely say?

Theo chuckled at my discomfiture. "You may speak freely in front of us, Percival. Is Mr. Flaherty your lover? I can't imagine you'd care so much for his opinion otherwise."

My face grew even hotter, to have it stated so baldly. "I..."

"Our family has been sorcerers for eight hundred years," Fiona said with a smile showing teeth. "We don't bend to society's rules, dear cousin. Society bends to us."

"Except in the matter of refrigerated ships," I said, but the strength of my relief took me by surprise.

"Indeed." Theo made a face. "We used to be the power behind the throne—literally, in some cases. But with the nobility itself growing more impoverished, we're having to seek out new avenues of influence."

"Ugh, *boring*," Fiona said. "Percival, would you like to see my laboratory?"

"I told you," Theo said with a grin.

I gave Fiona a small bow. "I'd love to."

She led the way out of the parlor and to the stairs. As we went up, I said, "Speaking of our family, I'm not really clear on how we lost contact. I know my great-great-great-grandfather came to America, but all information was lost when my grandfather died."

"What happened?" Theo asked. The house still relied on gaslight, and its soft illumination reflected in his spectacles when he glanced at me. "Guinevere said something about him dying young, but seemed reluctant to elaborate."

"I'm sure she was. Having a madman in the family probably wasn't conducive to her image as a noblewoman."

"You'd be surprised," Theo assured me.

"So will you tell us the secret, or shall we make up something scandalous?" Fiona asked.

"It's not really a secret," I said. "Isaiah Endicott went insane about a month before Mother was born. She was his first child, and apparently the strain of fatherhood took its toll on a delicate mind. He attacked his pregnant wife with a knife, shrieking he'd cut 'it' out of her. The servants were able to restrain him, thank heavens. Off he went to a madhouse, where he died shortly thereafter."

"How awful!" Fiona exclaimed. We'd reached the attic stair, and she led the way up, to a small door.

"It could have been worse. The servants went with my grandmother to her new marriage in Boston, and took care of her and Mother." I bit my lip. "Miss Emily's mother was among them. She and Mother have been together since they were both girls."

Theo put a steadying hand to my shoulder. "I can't imagine how Heliabel must feel at the moment. To lose a daughter and her oldest companion only a few days apart must be devastating."

I swallowed against the knot in my throat. "Yes."

"But we were going to tell you about the split in our family lines," Fiona said. She laid her palm against the door and whispered a few low words. A moment later, there sounded a distinct click, even though she'd put no key to the lock. "In essence, there was a pair of twins—Zachariah and Jeremiah."

"Zachariah being my great-great-great-grandfather." I at least knew that much.

Theo nodded. "Twins run in our family. Family lore says we're especially attuned to the arcane arts."

"I had a twin," I offered. "She died only a few hours after our birth, though."

"Apparently, Zachariah murdered his." Fiona pushed open the door. "Supposedly, they were both in love with the same woman, but Jeremiah's courtship proved more successful. Zachariah killed his brother only a few months after the wedding, when they were off chasing down cultists in some horrid fen. He concealed Jeremiah's body in the muck and fled England."

"Of course when neither returned, other members of the family went looking for them," Theo said. "They found Jeremiah with his throat cut, and learned Zachariah had left on a ship bound for the newly minted country of America. Fortunately for us, Jeremiah's young bride had already conceived; we're his latest descendants."

"A bit more sordid a history than I'd hoped for," I confessed. The Whybornes were bad enough, having been thieves and whores who fled to the colonies to escape the hangman. Now I found out my maternal line descended from a man guilty of fratricide.

"Every family has its darker moments." Theo offered me a smile. "But I'd say your exploits have more than redeemed the honor of the Yankee branch."

The heat returned to my face. "I'm not—"

"Yes." Theo put his hand to my shoulder. "You are. Stop being so self-deprecating. You're with people who appreciate you now."

"And would appreciate you more if you'd come and look at my lab," Fiona called from inside the room.

I laughed and followed them inside.

Theo joined me again at the museum the next morning.

I'd crept into bed with Griffin in the small hours of the night, tired but exhilarated. All of my study of sorcery until now had been solitary; I'd never had the opportunity to speak freely with other practitioners.

Fiona's lab had been impressive, full of strange chemicals and ingredients, accompanied by the expected foul smells. We'd had a lively discussion about the role of alchemy in sorcery. After all, Blackbyrne wouldn't have been able to practice his necromancy had there not been some method of rendering the bodies into their essential salts. And yet, was it truly part of the sorcery, any more than, say, the manufacture of the chalk used to sketch a sigil?

Our conversation had wandered to other points of theory. Did the words we spoke matter, or did they only serve to shape the sorcerer's will? What were the implications of my being able to summon wind without a sigil now?

I'd never felt so easy in the company of anyone save Christine and Griffin. Never felt so accepted and appreciated for all my talents.

Of course, Griffin inquired after my mother over breakfast. I made some evasive replies, and garnered only sympathy in response. It made me feel a twinge of guilt.

But this was *for* Griffin. I'd faced the possibility of losing him last spring in Egypt, which convinced me I needed to further my arcane studies.

I wanted to protect him. I wanted to keep him safe.

I wanted to grow old at his side, and if he left this world before me, it could only be through the natural consequences of age. Anything else was unbearable to contemplate.

So if I lied, it was only for his good. And Christine's, and Mother's, and that of everyone else I loved. There was no reason to feel guilty. None at all.

I headed straight for the library as soon as I entered the museum, eager to resume our research. When Theo appeared, I did no more than cast him a distracted nod before delving back into the book in front of me. He seemed to understand, and when I glanced up a while later, I found him engrossed in his own reading.

Griffin's suggestion Theo had any interest in me beyond our distant relationship and our shared interests was absurd. I loved Griffin beyond words to express, but the brutal truth was he'd not been exposed to the vagaries of scholarship as I had. His school had been with the Pinkertons, learning to mimic the ways of others. Mine had been in the rarified halls of Miskatonic University. Where I identified an academic's passion for knowledge, he understandably mistook it as passion for me.

Well, not understandably, perhaps. No one had ever shown an interest in me before Griffin. Whatever charms I might have, they seemed apparent only to him.

"Oh! Hello!" Theo exclaimed, breaking our silence.

I looked up from the moldy volume I'd been examining. My neck had developed a painful crick, so I stretched as I asked, "What?"

"I think I've found it. The source of your jewelry."

I hurried around the table to peer over his shoulder. He smelled of cedar, mingled with a faint hint of incense. "Here," he said, tapping a page of the *Unaussprechlichen Kulten*. "See this illustration?"

The entire volume contained fanciful depictions of creatures, most of which I devoutly hoped were figments of the author's imagination. I'd not seen this one before, but I hadn't studied the book with any kind of depth.

The monster shown on one of the illustrated plates was humanoid, its androgynous body long and lean. Dolphin-like fins jutted from its arms and legs, and shark teeth filled its wide mouth. In place of hair, its skull sprouted what appeared to be stinging tentacles, like those of an anemone or a jellyfish. Gill slits showed to either side of its neck.

I let out a gasp of shocked recognition. "This is the same sort of creature that accompanied the dweller in the deeps!" I'd seen their image before, first on a ceremonial bowl, then later in visions, carved upon a blasphemous temple far below the surface of the ocean. And last, as tiny shadows, swimming alongside the vast dweller while it possessed me.

I shuddered at the memory. Although I'd aided the dweller against the Eyes of Nodens, I had no illusions it cared a whit about humanity. No doubt these shark-men who worshipped it had no greater love for our species than the creature they revered.

"Look at the jewelry it's wearing." Theo handed me the magnifying glass he'd been using, and I leaned down even closer.

The shark-man wore something like a ragged loincloth, made of some kind of net and decorated with small plaques. It also sported armbands and ankle bracelets, and a thin circlet adorned its head. The design on the jewelry, although not identical to the pieces we'd seen, was clearly of the same origin.

Good lord, I'd assumed the jewelry to be strange, yes, but not the work of inhuman creatures from beneath the ocean. How on earth had Guinevere come upon the bracelet?

"The plaque we found on the ship—it must have been severed when a crewman tried to fight back." I recalled the splash of blood on the wall and shivered. "These creatures...they must have attacked the ship. Killed everyone aboard. Dragged them down to the watery depths." What must it have been like for the crew, wakened from their sleep to find monsters standing over their beds?

"The question is why? And what did Guinevere know about it? Are they responsible for all of the missing ships?" Theo flipped through the book. "Let me find the page the plate refers to. Ah...here it is. You read German faster than I; would you care to take a look?"

I sank down in the chair beside him, and he pushed the book over to me, the heavy chain scraping against the desk. I scanned the text, trying not to rush in my impatience for answers. "The creatures are called by many names, it seems, but *ketoi* is the one used most commonly. It could be a corruption of the Greek *ketos*, which more or less means 'sea monster.'"

"Perhaps." Theo frowned slightly. "It's also the name of one of the Kuril Islands." When I looked at him in surprise, he shrugged. "You wouldn't believe the things our family keeps track of. Supposedly, the Yezo people perform certain sacrifices there twice a year, on May Day and Hallowe'en. In their language, ketoi means 'bad.' What does the book have to say?"

I glanced over the next paragraph. "Apparently, the ketoi give gold and jewels to willing humans in exchange for...oh dear. How awful."

"What?"

My stomach turned. "Mating with them."

Theo shuddered. "Horrid."

"The hybrids raised as human are used to spread their hold on land." I couldn't help but remember the ghūls in Egypt, who kidnapped human babies and created hybrids of their own. "Apparently, hybrids who serve well are rewarded by being transformed into full ketoi by some sort of spell. They live beneath the water with the other ketoi, cured of disease or any wounds."

"Who the devil would choose such a thing?" Theo's lip curled in disgust. "These hybrids are traitors to the entire human race. Pretending to be human, tricking ordinary people into thinking nothing is amiss, until it's too late."

I sat back in my chair, staring at the words. What did any of this have to do with Guinevere? Had she, too, noticed the pattern of disappearing ships? Had she uncovered some sort of plot between the ketoi and their monstrous offspring to do...what? Why hadn't she dared say anything to me the night of the party?

Unless...what if some of those in attendance, the elite of Widdershins, were hybrids themselves? The threatening note I found in her room had been written on good stationary, even if not marked by a family crest. Was there any way to tell a hybrid simply by looking, or did they mimic human form too well? If so, if she didn't know who sent the note, Guinevere wouldn't have been able to trust anyone outside of our own family.

"This could be terrible," I said, "If attacking ships is only their opening gambit."

"Agreed." Theo rose to his feet, and I followed suit. "I'll go home and find out if Fiona knows anything more about these creatures. I'll stop by the telegraph office first and wire the estate back in Cornwall. If the family has fought these creature before, someone there will know."

"That sounds like a good plan."

He hesitated. The tip of his tongue touched his lower lip. "Will you join us later?"

"Of course. And I'll bring Griffin and Christine—they need to know what we've found."

Theo's look became wry. "Of course. I can't wait to see Mr. Flaherty again."

CHAPTER 12

I SPENT THE afternoon in my office, working on the blasted Hallowe'en tours with Christine. The plans she'd drawn up included using actual shrunken heads for decoration. "Perhaps octopi and hellbenders preserved in jars," she went on. "On the buffet table. What do you think?"

"I think the director wouldn't stand for it." I considered. "But keep the shrunken heads."

She'd compiled a list of cursed artifacts, and I went through it slowly, wondering how many, if any, might actually do harm to someone. While I read, Christine entertained herself by inventing vulgar parodies of party games at my expense.

Shortly before closing, Griffin knocked on the door. I'd sent a note round asking him to join us, accompanied by a brief explanation of what Theo and I had discovered about the nature of the sea creatures.

"I hope I'm not disturbing anything," he said with a smile.

"Just considering what birthday games Whyborne will be missing out on thanks to this wretched idea of the director's," she replied cheerfully. "I've gotten to Blind Man's Duff."

Griffin laughed. "How about Pin the Tail on—"

"Would you two stop?" I asked crossly. "Some of us are trying to do actual work here."

"Don't be absurd," Christine said. "This isn't 'work,' it's fundraising nonsense, and the sort of thing we both abhor. Just pick a few objects and be done with it."

"And if they're truly cursed?"

"It isn't as if the guests are actually going to be touching them," Christine said with a roll of her eyes. "And if they were that deadly, we'd have curators dropping left and right."

"I suppose." I looked at the list dubiously. What would Theo and Fiona make of it?

Given Theo's concerns over access to the books, probably that the artifacts in question were dangerous and needed to be destroyed. Or kept somewhere far safer than the museum, so the unwary couldn't stumble across them.

Griffin perched on the edge of my desk, presenting me with a somewhat distracting view. "I spent the day looking into the ship disappearances."

"Checking up on my cousins' work?" Curse the man.

"Yes." He didn't bother to deny it. "And before you become defensive about it, I would have done the same with anyone who I didn't know as an investigator. People see non-existent patterns all the time."

Having read far too much about strings of coincidences blamed on cursed objects in the last few days, I had to agree. "You have a point."

"Thank you. In this case, the Endicotts are correct. There are more disappearances than usual this season. Furthermore, every ship has some connection to Widdershins, either because of cargo delivery or ownership."

Christine frowned. "That can't be a good sign."

"No." Griffin drew up one knee and laced his hands about it. "My next step is to determine who benefited from their disappearances."

"Whoever sent the threatening note to Guinevere."

"Most likely. *Someone* must be reaping the benefit, either by destroying their competition or by collecting insurance money."

"Unless the motive isn't financial," Christine said. "People will go to extraordinary lengths in the name of revenge."

"I'm keeping every possibility in mind." Griffin glanced at me. "Whatever their motive, this is someone who didn't scruple at murdering a member of the Whyborne family, followed up by one of your servants. Whether their gain is of wealth or revenge, or some other motive, they're likely to be very powerful people."

"One of the old families," I said grimly. My earlier suspicions had been correct, it seemed.

"I hope not. But it does seem likely." He slid from the desk. "Come. Let's see what your cousins have to say about these creatures."

~ * ~

"Welcome back, Mr. Flaherty," Fiona said. She'd taken the same chair she'd sat in the other night, and watched Griffin with a faintly amused expression.

Griffin gave her a small bow. "Thank you for inviting me. I should apologize if I seemed cold to the idea of accepting help from you the other night."

It wasn't the most handsome apology I'd ever heard from him, but it was a start. "We were all short of sleep," Theo said diplomatically. He sat in a large chair beside his sister, a sheaf of telegrams in hand. "What has Percival told you about our research this afternoon?"

"The basics," Christine replied. "We're apparently up against some sort of monsters from the sea and their corrupted offspring."

The Endicotts served wine tonight, of yet another excellent vintage. Griffin sipped his, then set it aside. "Any thoughts on how Guinevere came to know about them? *Is* there a way to reliably identify the hybrids?"

"Not that we're aware of," Theo replied. "Although it seems our family has faced the ketoi before." He held up the stack of telegrams. "It's all a bit terse given the medium of communication, but apparently it happened around thirty years ago. Fiona and I weren't even old enough to walk, and our parents weren't involved. Thank heavens."

I leaned forward. "What do you mean? What happened?"

"The ketoi seem to enjoy living in undersea cities near to land, and had established one just off the coast of Cornwall." Theo scowled. "Of course it wasn't to be tolerated. A group of our older cousins found a ritual they believed could be adapted to kill the ketoi by sorcery."

"And it worked, somewhat." Fiona's skirts rustled as she poured herself another glass of wine. "The ritual required a sacrifice of one of the beasts—the blood was the key used by the magic."

Griffin stirred uncomfortably. "That sounds...unpleasant."

"These are monsters, Mr. Flaherty," Theo said. "Spilling the blood of one to save human lives is a more than acceptable trade."

"It's no different than blowing up the yayhos in the mine, or shooting ghūls," I pointed out. "Please continue, Fiona."

"The spell worked, to an extent. Unfortunately, the only ketoi affected were the most vulnerable. Infants, pregnant females, the elderly. Even worse, there was some sort of magical backlash, and the sorcerers performing the spell died as well."

I shifted to the edge of my chair. "How awful."

"Indeed." Theo seemed to have recovered his good humor. "So we won't be trying that spell again. Not to suggest we aren't willing to die in service to humanity, but we aren't quite so eager to throw our lives away."

"What did you do about the undersea city?" Christine asked.

"I believe there was an attempt at dumping poison into the water. When it didn't work, explosives were used." Fiona shrugged. "If the ketoi didn't disappear altogether, their numbers became much more manageable. We haven't had any further trouble out of them, at least."

"And is that what you suggest in this case?" Griffin asked skeptically.

"As we don't know the exact location of their city, no," Theo replied. "However, there may be arcane methods of discovering it. Possibly, we could take out a small boat to the area of the ship disappearances and use an enchanted pendulum. What do you think, Fiona?"

She considered. "It might work."

"Does anyone here know how to handle a boat?" I asked. "If not, we'd have to hire a pilot."

Theo laughed. "Good heavens, Fiona and I are old hands. I must say, I would have imagined you would be the expert among us, Percival, having grown up in Widdershins. Guinevere spoke often about pleasant yacht excursions."

I shifted uncomfortably. "I don't like water." After Leander had drowned when we were boys, I'd been terrified of boats. The trip on the steamer to and from Egypt had blunted the fear somewhat—but then, the passenger ship was large enough not to feel as though we might capsize and drown at any moment. A smaller boat would be a very different proposition.

"We should all go together," Griffin decided. "Presumably the ketoi aren't targeting every ship that passes through the area, so we shouldn't attract their notice. But better to be on the safe side."

"Right you are," Theo agreed. "Fiona and I will see about renting a small vessel, then."

Griffin nodded. "All right. In the meantime, I'll continue looking into who might benefit from the disappearing ships. And I need to speak with Niles."

"I'm sorry," I said. "Why?"

Griffin cast me a small smile before responding. "Guinevere had only been in Widdershins for a few days. So when did she learn something that alarmed her enough to seek out Whyborne? Percival," he clarified, nodding at me. "How did she come by the bracelet? Who sent her the note?" He glanced at the twins. "I assume she seemed in a normal temper on board the ship which brought you here?"

"Quite," Theo agreed. "Although perhaps she concealed any

concerns she had."

"And she gave no indication to Heliabel that anything troubled her?" Griffin asked me.

"I don't think so."

"So. Let us assume she discovered something disturbing after returning to our shores." Griffin leaned back in his chair. "No doubt she visited old friends, or they visited her. It seems likely one of them might hold the key to whatever is happening."

"And if Father doesn't know who she visited—or who came to Whyborne House to call on her—Fenton certainly will," I said.

"There is one thing to keep in mind," Fiona said. She set her wine glass aside. "We're assuming the ship disappearances are connected to someone on land—a hybrid, calling on his foul kin to further his own aims."

"Or hers," Christine put in.

"Quite right." Fiona gave her an approving smile. "This person may have no sorcerous knowledge, no larger game to play. But if they do...well. Hallowe'en is one of the so-called Witches' Sabbaths for a reason. The walls between this world and the Outside are more easily breached, and arcane energy easier to raise. If they have something sorcerous planned, it would be the day they would act."

"Oh, good gad," Christine groaned. "Isn't the damnable museum event bad enough?"

Before we departed, I discreetly inquired as to whether the Endicotts would be amenable to meeting the following afternoon. Theo indicated they would, and so the next day I knocked once again on their door.

"Cousin!" Fiona hurled her arms about me. I'd always heard of British reserve, but apparently my cousins didn't subscribe to such conventions. "What fun have you planned for us today?"

"I'm not certain about fun," I admitted, although I rather found it enjoyable. "I've been mapping the lines of arcane power in Widdershins, and hoped you might be so good as to help me."

"Ooh, did you hear that, Theo?"

Her brother emerged behind her. "A good thing we're still dressed for walking. We went to the docks earlier and found a launch for rent tomorrow night," he added to me.

I hid my disappointment, having hoped our excursion might take place tonight. "I see. This will occupy a few hours of our time, then."

I'd brought the map on which I'd already marked the lines of power I'd found. "The line in the desert was straight, but these have a curve to them."

"I wonder," Theo murmured, taking the map from me. "There are similar places in England, usually near old stone circles, where the arcane lines come together to form small...one might call them whirlpools, I suppose. It's possible to do a greater enchantment there, drawing on the energy, especially on the days when the veil is thin. The spell against the ketoi was performed at one such place on Hallowe'en."

"Do you think such might be the case here?" I asked. Heavens, it was wonderful to have more knowledgeable sorcerers to talk to. If only they'd been with us in Egypt, perhaps the situation wouldn't have become so desperate. "Griffin thought Blackbyrne must have some reason for founding the town here."

"Blackbyrne?" Theo asked.

"A long story," I said. "I'll tell it as we walk."

We decided to start at the cemetery, as I'd sensed arcane power there the night of Guinevere's interment. On the way, I told them everything I knew about the necromancer who had founded Widdershins, from his escaping the witch-craze in Salem to his resurrection and second death two years ago.

"And the book you've learned sorcery from once belonged to him?" Theo asked. "It's a jolly good thing it ended up in your hands, then. Lord knows what vileness someone outside our family might have perpetrated with it."

"They did before my involvement." I still shuddered to recall the hideous Guardians.

We located the line of power within the cemetery and added a point on the map. "What of the wood there?" Fiona asked.

"Best avoided." I told them of the Draakenwood as we left the cemetery and continued on our way. I took the opportunity to play tour guide, pointing out the island where the Brotherhood had held their accursed ceremonies, the arrangement of streets laid out by Blackbyrne to draw the Brotherhood's symbol on the town itself, and other points of arcane interest.

"Good heavens, what a wretched place!" Theo exclaimed at length.

The sentiment took me aback. Griffin sometimes complained about what he perceived as the town's oddities, although not so much now as he once had. But Theo seemed almost alarmed. "The town is a bit strange, or so I'm told," I said uncertainly. "But it's an excellent place, really. Everyone keeps to themselves and minds their own business."

"Probably because they're busy cooking up evil sorcery in the basement," Theo muttered. "I don't mean to cast aspersions on your home, old chap, but it's a good thing we came here. Surely you must have your hands full, keeping back the forces of darkness which well up in such a place."

"Er…" What could I say? "Only Blackbyrne. And the business at Stormhaven, of course. And one or two smaller cases—a possessed carousel and a strange heirloom. Perhaps some other insignificant matters."

"All of which occurred in just two years?" Fiona laughed. "Face it, cousin—this town is a bloody nightmare. I propose we relocate here and help you scour the place clean."

Did I want that? Their company, certainly. Having other sorcerers about to learn from, to discuss things with, had lightened the last few dark days since Guinevere's death. And certainly Widdershins did have its share of troublesome inhabitants, some of whom were surely behind the high incidence of grave-robbing and missing persons. Until now, I'd only reacted whenever their evil boiled over in such a way as to become unavoidable.

But I could do better. I'd sworn to use my sorcery to protect those I loved—wouldn't my oath be better served by taking action? By hunting down threats before they got out of control, as the Endicotts did?

"It would be a great deal to ask," I said slowly. "But I won't lie. I'd be grateful for your assistance, now and in the future."

"Splendid." Fiona linked arms with Theo and me. "It's getting dark, and we can barely see the map anymore. Let's leave off work and celebrate our decision to move to the colonies!"

"I'm not sure I can. Griffin is expecting me home, and…" I trailed off.

Theo laughed. "And you're not sure he would want to celebrate having us become long-term residents?"

"Send him a note," Fiona suggested. "Tell him you're busy at the museum. Then the three of us can enjoy ourselves without him glowering from across the table."

"Surely our time would be better spent doing research, or…or something," I said uncertainly.

Theo came around my other side and slung his arm across my shoulders. "Life is for living, old chap. In our line of work, we could die any day. If we never take even one evening to enjoy ourselves, then what's the point?"

How different we were! I'd never been one for the usual entertainments…but perhaps it was simply because I'd never had companions such as them.

"Please," Fiona wheedled. "We'll be ever so bored without you."

"Well...all right, then."

"Brilliant!" She hauled on my arm, pulling me toward the nearest cab. "This is going to be fun."

CHAPTER 13

WE DINED AT Le Calmar, even though I wasn't dressed for such an expensive restaurant. But I'd sent Griffin a note claiming I worked late with Christine on the matter of the Hallowe'en tours, so I could hardly go home and change first. Still, Theo lent me a nicer tie and cufflinks, although the coat I tried on at his urging was hopelessly too short in the arms.

The twins' appearances and my name made up for my simple attire, however, and we were soon seated and served. The champagne flowed freely, as did the conversation. The twins had a wealth of stories from their exploits back home in the British Isles.

"...so we entered the cave," Theo said, as we finished up our desert of pumpkin pie, "and see this *hag*—and I mean that literally."

"She had blue skin," Fiona put in, signaling the waiter for more champagne. "Blue! Why would anyone want to turn themselves into something that looks like a walking bruise?"

"I doubt she was as concerned about fashion as *some* people," Theo said. "At any rate, Uncle Ned, the great ox, charges in with his ridiculous ax."

"He cuts her head clean off." Fiona made a gleeful chopping motion with her hand. "But of course it doesn't do any good. You'd think the man had never seen a hag before."

"You're having a joke at my expense," I protested. Some of the champagne's bubbles seemed to have made it into my head, leaving me light and relaxed.

"Not at all. One has to cut out their *hearts*," Theo said. "Decapitation only makes them angry."

Fiona leaned over the table. "So the body is strangling Uncle Ned, and meanwhile the village children the hag hasn't gotten around to eating yet start attacking *us*, the rotten little blighters."

"They were ensorcelled," Theo pointed out.

"Meanwhile, the head is screaming at the top of its lungs."

"Not to suggest it had any lungs attached at the moment."

"And I've got a bloody headache, so I just grabbed the thing and chucked it right out of the cave."

Theo grinned. "I look up, and here goes the head, flying off into the valley below, still screeching away. Well, it made things easier, since the hag couldn't see us anymore, so directing its body to attack didn't work half so well. We got the job done, but I still have a scar where one of the blasted children bit me."

I shook my head in amazement. "You've had such interesting lives. And not just the terrifying bits, but the rest of it. Boating, horseback riding, fencing."

"Well, we're not having an interesting time right now," Fiona said, finishing off her champagne. "I'm bored. Let's go find a proper pub where we can have a bit of fun. Some of the places near the docks looked likely."

"Oh, no, they aren't," I said hastily. "They aren't at all respectable."

Theo winked at me. "Exactly."

A short time later, we stood on the sidewalk outside the restaurant. "I'm not certain you've both thought this course through," I said as Fiona surveyed the street for a cab. "Your reputation, Fiona —"

Theo put a hand to my shoulder. "Percival. If we're to live here for a time, the sooner the inhabitants learn not to play such games with us, the better."

"We aren't high society," Fiona explained. "We're *above* society. Now do stop fretting."

"I'm not sure our Percival knows how to stop fretting." Theo smiled to take the sting from the words. "You need to have balance in your life, old chap. Tell us what you ordinarily do for fun."

"Cryptography. Reading—usually philological journals, of course. Um, bird watching."

"So 'nothing,' then," Fiona said with a grin of her own.

"Hush, Fi. What about when you were a child?" Theo asked.

No one had asked me such personal questions since I'd first met Griffin. At the time, I'd thought him impertinent. "Er...the same," I admitted.

The twins glanced at each other, and their grins grew. "When you were a boy, you never, say, hung onto the back of a coach and laughed when the driver tried to dislodge you from getting a free ride?" Theo asked.

"Certainly not!"

Before I could even think to protest, they each took one of my arms and broke into a run, hauling me with them. To my horror, they made for the back of a moving omnibus. "No, stop!"

"Get ready to grab hold, cousin!" Fiona shouted.

If I didn't leap with them, I'd drag us all down into the street and probably end up run over by one of the cabs racing back and forth. With a strangled cry, I jumped when they did. My hands closed on the rail, and my shoes found purchase on the step.

The wind rushed into our faces, and the other passengers stared in shock, probably wondering what three grown adults in evening dress were doing clinging to the rail like schoolboys. Fiona grabbed her hat to keep it on her head, laughing and holding on to the rail with only one hand. "You're both mad!" I exclaimed, but I couldn't help but laugh as well.

"Indeed we are." Theo agreed. "Uh oh, looks like our ride is at an end!"

Indeed, the conductor stormed toward us with a murderous look. Fiona dropped easily off, and Theo and I followed a moment later. My ears ached from the cold wind, and my blood surged in my veins. "I never thought I'd dare do such a thing!"

Theo put a friendly hand on my arm. "Dare, Percival. We face horrors for the sake of humankind, but during the times between, in the ordinary world, we live without fear."

"Live without fear," I repeated. I nearly couldn't imagine it...and yet in their laughter and joy in life, I felt I could almost see it, spreading out before me, filled with endless possibility. To do whatever I wished, whenever I wished...to not care what the director, or the museum president, or Father, or society thought of me...

"Come." Fiona grasped my hand and tugged impatiently at me. "Let's hail a cab and find a pub. The first round is on me."

An hour later, I sat at one of the tables in the Barndoor Skate saloon, combining several smaller piles of money into a larger one.

Theo shook his head. "Warn a chap next time, won't you? I wouldn't have sat down to play if I'd known you were a master hand."

I smiled smugly. Although Griffin and I sometimes played at cards, it was mainly to keep his skills sharp should he have to visit a gambling hall in the course of his investigations. Christine didn't enjoy cards at all, which meant my only opposition came during my infrequent visits home.

"Mother taught me," I explained.

"Thank you for managing to make my utter defeat even more humiliating," Theo said. "I've been trounced by a man whose invalid mother taught him to play poker."

A bit to my surprise, I'd actually enjoyed the evening. Some of it might have been from the card game, and some from the whiskey currently warming my blood. The other two men playing cards with us didn't look as if they were having a very good time, but I didn't care. I doubted Theo did either.

We'd compromised by coming to a saloon I knew to be respectable enough we wouldn't have to worry about our safety while inside. Fiona had immediately hopped up onto a seat at the bar and challenged the man beside her to buy her a drink. And it had indeed been delivered as a challenge rather than an invitation. The poor fellow had no idea what to do, confronted by a well-dressed Englishwoman demanding whiskey in a saloon, so he'd wisely complied.

Now a burst of laughter and song came from the end of the bar. Theo shook his head in mock despair. "She'll be at it all night if we let her. Best you gather your winnings and we go, before I'm reducing to wagering articles of clothing."

Like an idiot, I blushed, and hoped no one else noticed. "We can't have that," I agreed, and began to pocket my winnings. "Gentlemen, thank you for your time."

One of the men grabbed my wrist. I stilled, the whiskey turning sour in my belly. "You can't leave," he said, and his previously friendly voice now took on a threatening air. "You've got to give us a chance to win some back."

"Those weren't the rules," Theo said. "My friend has to get home soon, or else his excuse of working late will strain credulity."

Thankfully, the man let go of me. His companion leaned over and whispered something in his ear as we made our way to the bar. I hoped it had nothing to do with us.

"Come along, sister mine," Theo said, catching Fiona by the arm.

She hopped off the bar stool with no signs of impairment. "Good night, gentlemen!" she called gaily. One or two began to protest, but she ignored them, and we made our way outside.

"Now wasn't the evening much more interesting?" Theo asked. "And you came out a richer man."

We turned down an alleyway, which would take us back to River

Street. "Yes," I said, and was surprised to find it true. "It was. Thank you."

A dark shape stepped out and blocked our path.

I came to a sharp halt. The sound of footsteps echoed back the way we'd come, and we turned to see a crowd of men making their way toward us. The other two card players were among them, along with some of those who had been flirting with Fiona. The lone man at the other end of the alley must have run out the back of the saloon, to give the others time to come after us.

I swallowed, my gut tightening on the whiskey I'd drunk. "Stay back," I ordered, and hoped I sounded more authoritative than I felt.

The dim light leaking from either end of the alley fell across the bared blade of a knife. "Give us your money and the woman, and maybe we'll let you walk out of here with both your legs in one piece."

"Oh, this will be enjoyable!" Fiona exclaimed in apparent delight. "I want this one, and the cheeky fellow behind him, who tried to get a hand up my skirts in the bar. Which do you want, Percival?"

Before I could even think how to respond, the first man started forward. "That's enough out of your mouth, you filthy whore—"

She spoke a string of words in Aklo.

Frost raced over his skin, and he let out a cry of pain. At the same moment, footsteps sounded behind us. I turned to face the lone man at the end of the alley. Only he wasn't alone any more.

"Sorcery, Percival!" Theo shouted encouragement although, from the sound of it, he had his own enemies to contend with.

I took a deep breath, and the world seemed to slow around me. I felt the whisper of the ocean breeze against my face, sensed a rain barrel filled with water beneath a nearby downspout, tasted the ash of a newly doused fire.

The scars along my arm flared with heat, and a sudden gust knocked the men's hats off and staggered them. I caught a glimpse of a cigar sticking out of one of their pockets, and set fire to it with a word. A moment later, he leapt and shouted, beating at his breast as the heat scorched through to his skin.

I laughed.

Power filled me, thrummed through my veins along with the alcohol I'd drunk. These men had *dared* come against us? I'd saved this wretched town, their worthless lives, twice over. They ought to be thanking me, not attacking me in an alley and threatening my cousin.

The water in the rain barrel responded to my will, bursting out the top like the jet of a fire hose. The stream smashed into the second man, hurling him into the wall.

I turned, just in time to see the cobblestones ripple at Fiona's command, tripping one of our attackers and sending him sprawling. She casually kicked his knife aside and put her foot on his neck, shoving him against the ground.

The other men fled, shouting and crying. "What's your name?" Fiona asked the man under her heel. He started to answer, but she pressed down harder. "I've changed my mind. Your name is now 'messenger boy.' Do you know why?"

He stared up at us as Theo and I closed in. My heart pounded, and I could hear the ocean in the distance, its roar echoing in my blood.

"Please, mistress," the man whimpered.

"Ooh, very good, messenger boy. You're a fast learner." She grinned at him. "Now, you're going to tell all of your little friends things are going to change here in Widdershins. The Endicotts are in town now. Be nice to us, and we can be nice back. Make yourselves our enemies, and...well. It will be the last thing you'll do." She glanced over her shoulder at me. "Am I not right, Percival?"

I could still smell the smoke from charred wool, the water from the rain barrel. The world waited for my command; I could speak and the universe itself would obey.

Why had I ever been afraid of men like this? Or even of the more mannerly serpents among the upper classes, who wielded words in place of knives? All the stupid little rules, all the stupid little fears, and I'd *let* myself be bound by them.

Well. No more.

"Absolutely right, cousin," I agreed. "Absolutely right indeed."

I flung open the door to our house.

"Whyborne? Are you home? I'm in the parlor," Griffin called.

Instead of answering, I locked the door, then went to the parlor, shedding my hat, overcoat, and suit coat onto the floor as I went. Griffin sat at his desk, bent over his account books. When I entered, he looked up, and a puzzled smile crossed his lips. "My dear?"

I seized his shoulders and kissed him. My blood pounded in my veins, and my cock ached from the long journey back from the alleyway. I shoved his chair back and climbed into his lap, never breaking the kiss.

When our lips finally parted, he let out a little, breathless laugh. "You must truly enjoy cataloging cursed objects. Have you been drinking?"

"Christine keeps a bottle of whiskey in her desk," I lied. "Now less talking."

His emerald eyes glittered. "Less talking? But whatever else shall I do with my mouth?"

I stood up and began to unfasten my trousers. Grinning wickedly, Griffin went to his knees, reaching for his own buttons as he did so.

"No," I growled, catching his curls in my hand and forcing him to look at me. "No touching yourself until I tell you to."

His pupils dilated and he licked his lips hungrily. The outline of his hard prick stood out against his trousers, but he obeyed, instead using his hands to grip my buttocks and urge me closer.

I groaned as his mouth closed over me. I'd hailed a cab from the alleyway, my blood thrumming with the aftershock of power and whiskey, my cock half hard from it. I tangled my fingers in his hair as his lips and tongue played with my shaft, the sensation bleeding into the memory of the moment when the entire world had waited for my command.

"I'm going to fuck your mouth," I told him. He moaned his enthusiasm for the idea, so I did, pushing deep, until the muscles of his throat worked around me. His gaze found mine, eyes wide and lips swollen, the glisten of spit on my length as I pulled out and pushed in again.

The tingle in my sack warned me, and I had no wish for things to end so soon. I pulled free. "Get upstairs."

When he gained his feet, he kissed me deep, letting me taste myself in his mouth. His cock felt like an iron bar against my thigh. We stumbled up the stairs together, kissing and caressing, losing clothes along the way.

We entered my bedroom, and I went to the nightstand, retrieving the petroleum jelly in the drawer. Griffin tossed aside his vest, then slipped his suspenders off his shoulders. As his trousers and drawers were already unfastened by now, I shoved the whole lot down to his ankles, turned him around, and bent him over the bed.

His hips shifted, rubbing his erection against the bedding in search of relief. I gripped his hips to still him. "No breaking the rules."

"Mmm, you caught me—ah!" His words turned into a little sound of pleasure as I touched my slick fingers to his fundament. His back arched, and he pushed against me.

Once he was ready, I took him, all at a go. His hands bunched in the bedding and he gasped encouragement. I adjusted my angle, until a groan signaled I'd found just the right spot inside him.

Then I rode him hard, wringing out cry after cry of pleasure. My fingers gripped the bones of his hips, holding him in place while I took him. The world spun around me, and I felt almost as I had in the alley, the universe poised and waiting on my breath. It felt so good to touch the secret fire that lay beneath reality, to shape and bend it, to coax forth magic from what seemed so mundane.

Like this magic of two bodies moving together, the base clay of lust shaped into something else: love and need and a strange sort of power all its own.

A shudder ran through Griffin. "Ival, please, touch me, let me touch myself, I can't stand it."

I could feel the impending wave of my own release, so I gasped, "Do it! Come for me."

He moaned my name when his hand wrapped around his cock, and it was the end of me. I spent myself in him hard, back arching, pressing tight against him until he gasped and spilled a few moments later.

I collapsed against his back, my breathing slowly evening out. When I thought I could move without falling over, I went to the washbasin and retrieved a damp cloth. We cleaned up and shed the last of our clothing, before Griffin pulled me down into the bed by him.

"That was amazing," he murmured, nuzzling my ear. "I love it when you take charge of me."

I rested my head against his shoulder. "I'm glad."

"If preparing for the Hallowe'en tours inspires you so, I hope the director makes them a yearly occurrence."

Guilt squirmed in me, like a worm in an apple. I wanted to tell Griffin. The only thing that would have made tonight better would have been to have him with us.

Perhaps, once he grew used to my cousins and their ways, he might consent to such an outing. But telling the truth tonight would only have led to an argument. The evening would have ended with us lying on opposite sides of the bed, fuming.

No, this was far better. I snuggled more tightly against him, breathing in the scent of his skin. He'd come around eventually. Until then, I simply had to be discreet. What Griffin didn't know couldn't hurt us.

Chapter 14

THE NEXT MORNING found Christine and me in the library. Sadly, not to do research, but as part of the Hallowe'en tours. Christine had already removed a number of shrunken heads from storage, along with preserved spiders of troubling size and the most disturbing mummies she could find. I hoped none of the guests fainted during the tours.

"Cursed books?" Mr. Quinn murmured when we inquired as to whether the library had anything it wished to contribute to the special tours. "Oh, yes, yes. I have just the thing."

He led the way from the desk near the library entrance, deeper into the labyrinth. Sounds echoed strangely here: the rustle of paper, the scuff of a shoe, someone whispering "The words are changing, the words are changing" over and over again to themselves. The scent of old paper and dusty covers hung thick and still in the air, and the irregularly placed lights threw odd shadows.

We penetrated farther into the maze of rooms than I could recall going before. The stacks towered up on every side, filled with volumes bound in cloth and leather, some with stamped titles and others tantalizingly unmarked. The assorted sounds of the library fell away, replaced by a deep silence. The shadows seemed thicker, somehow, almost as if they had substance of their own, rather than merely being the absence of light.

"One could die back here," Mr. Quinn remarked, "and no one else might know for weeks."

I exchanged an alarmed glance with Christine, who looked as if she wished for her pistol. Well, if Mr. Quinn meant to murder us both, I'd simply set fire to a book. That would distract him long enough for us to flee. Assuming I could find a common novel quickly enough, as I'd no wish to destroy a rare tome, no matter the danger. Too bad I didn't have any of Griffin's dime novels in my pocket.

Fortunately, Mr. Quinn didn't follow up his remark with any murderous actions. Instead, he halted before a plinth, bearing on it a locked glass case. "Here we are," he said, unlocking the case and taking out the volume inside. It bore no title. "Note the anthropodermic binding." His pale, spidery hands caressed the tanned skin lovingly. "We call it the Lundsford Codex, after its last owner, who donated it to the museum. If it has a title, no one knows. It is said anyone who reads it will die within the week."

"Perfect," Christine said.

"Christine!" I exclaimed. "We're supposed to entertain the donors, not kill them."

"Then the director should have put someone else in charge, shouldn't he?" Christine sighed at my reproving look. "We'll keep it in the glass case. Will that satisfy you?"

Mr. Quinn tenderly replaced the book within the case. "It is my fondest hope to someday read it," he said dreamily. "Perhaps I will tell everyone of its wonders before I die. Or perhaps I shall keep them to myself."

"What if it's not very good?" Christine asked.

The lock clicked shut. "Be careful carrying the case," Mr. Quinn replied, a bit shortly. Personally, I thought Christine's question a good one. Bad enough to die from reading a gorgeously written book, but what if it turned out to be rubbish? Being killed by bad prose would only add insult to injury.

He swept out, leaving us alone. "I'll take one side, and you take the other," she said, indicating the glass case. "And if we run into Bradley on the way, we'll stop and offer him a bit of light reading."

During lunch, I slipped away from the museum yet again. It had occurred to me that I knew one other who might be able to shed some light on the ketoi. To that end, I sent a letter with the early post requesting a brief meeting. The response surprised me with its promptness, but the moment I could, I set out for a boarding house on Merry Cat Lane, not far from my old apartment.

Amelie Bisset answered the door almost before I could finish knocking. Neatly dressed, her skin clean and her red-gold hair pulled back into a bun, she seemed a far cry from the madwoman I'd met at

Stormhaven Lunatic Asylum.

She offered me a dazzling smile and clasped my hands with the familiarity of an old friend. She'd saved my life, and possibly the world, that night at the asylum. And seen me naked, a thought I tried to put out of my mind.

"Dr. Whyborne, I was so happy to get your letter." She drew me inside after her. The boarding house had a small parlor, the furniture worn but still in good condition. "Would you like coffee? Tea?"

"No, thank you, Miss Bisset." I settled myself in a chair covered with a hideous floral print, and she sat opposite me on the small couch. "You seem to be doing well."

She laughed ruefully. "Better than one might expect from a raving madwoman, at least."

"I've followed your work for reform."

"I rather fear you're the only one who has." She rested her hands on her knees. "Your letter was rather unexpected—what do you need from me?"

I wished I'd asked for coffee after all, if only to have something to do with my hands. "I fear I must bring back bad memories. Last year, you seemed to hear the dweller rather clearly, even without Dr. Zeiler's drugs." Indeed, the god's telepathic calls had been what sent Amelie to the madhouse in the first place. When we'd met, she'd been too lost in visions to communicate with any coherency.

She nodded slowly, her eyes grave. "Yes. I did. But the god has slept since then."

Thank goodness for that. "There were other, smaller creatures which worshipped it. I recall their appearance, but learned nothing else about them while the dweller possessed me. I wondered if you might have gleaned anything more."

A frown line creased her brow. "Such as?"

I spread my hands helplessly apart. "Anything at all. Their motives, or their weakness, or anything."

She stared at a framed print on the wall, which showed a pastoral landscape complete with shepherd and gamboling lambs. I suspect she didn't actually see the banal scene before her, but something far darker.

"No," she said at last. "I'm sorry, Dr. Whyborne. Most of the visions I saw were of the dweller, and the temple, and you."

"Me?"

"The dweller needed your help." Amelie smiled. "We all did."

Blast. Well, it had been rather a long shot. "I'm glad to see you're doing well," I said, rising to my feet.

"And you." She glanced down, then back up again. "You can call upon me any time."

"Oh." I struggled to keep heat from my face. "That's, er, very kind." I started for the door, then paused. "I don't suppose the words 'one for the land, and one for the sea' mean anything to you?"

Amelie laughed, and for a moment, I was reminded of the gleeful madwoman. How much remained beneath the carefully civilized persona she cultivated now? "You mean the old poem?"

"Poem?" I repeated blankly.

"I don't suppose you'd know of it. It's not the sort of thing the old families would care for. They don't like to be reminded there are powers that do not bow to them." She offered me a secretive smile. "It belongs to those of us who slipped in later, called by the town."

Called by the town? She sounded uncomfortably like Miss Lester. "Do you remember this poem?" I asked.

"Oh yes. My mother used to recite it to me." She turned in the direction of the unseen ocean. "She's gone now."

"I'm sorry."

"That's all right." Amelie smiled again. "It goes like this:

"Listen up little fish, little fish,
Let's make a wish, make a wish,
For a time not come but yet to be,
One for the land, and one for the sea.

"When enemies arrive to dig our grave,
Tear down the bridge between earth and wave,
Then the town will rise to his hand,
One for the sea, and one for the land.

"A new queen shall rule beneath the flood,
Down with the sharks and the crabs and the mud.
Strike sharp and hard, in triumph free,
One for the land, and one for the sea.

"For Widdershins always knows its own,
In blood and spirit, breath and bone,
The time will come for one to rise,
To ride the foam and touch the skies.

"Listen up little fish, little fish,
Let's make a wish, make a wish,
For a time not come but yet to be,
One for the land, and one for the sea."

Dear lord, what awful doggerel. The meter was terrible, the rhymes uninspired, the final line didn't resonate throughout, and... well, no wonder I'd never heard it. "What does it mean?" I asked.

Amelie looked at me as if I were a complete fool. "It's a prophecy. No one knows what it means until after it's already happened."

"Thank you. Most enlightening." But despite my words, my heart beat faster. The poem—prophecy?—obviously had some meaning to Guinevere and Jerry the bartender. But what? "Truly, you've been most helpful. Can you write it down for me?"

She grinned slyly. "Do I get a kiss?" At my expression, she burst out laughing. "Just recalling old times," she said, as she went to the writing desk for pen and paper. She copied the poem quickly and handed it to me. "I hope it helps."

"As do I." I leaned in and, very quickly, brushed my lips across her cheek. "Take care, Miss Bisset."

Griffin met Christine and me for dinner at Marsh's. "I assume you heard from the twins?" he asked as he slid into the booth beside me. Under the cover of the table, he gave my hand a welcoming squeeze.

"Yes." I discreetly shifted my foot so my ankle rested against his. "They've secured a launch for the evening, and will meet us at its berth."

The waiter came to take Griffin's order. "I have news," I said, once the waiter departed. I quickly outlined my conversation with Amelie, and passed the poem around for them both to read.

"A prophecy?" Christine exclaimed. "Good gad, this is becoming absurd. Your sister wasn't involved with spiritualism or some such, was she?"

"I don't know." I shrugged. "But it obviously meant something to her."

"Not just to her," Griffin said with a frown. "Or the bartender. But allow me to start in order. I met with Niles this morning. Guinevere visited—or was called upon—by only three families before the night of the party."

"Which ones?" I asked.

"The Lesters, the Waites, and the Abbotts."

"The Lesters certainly are odd enough," I said with a shiver. One of Griffin's cases had involved the retrieval of a sinister family heirloom for them. The chances of them practicing dark magic seemed rather high. "And Miss Lester spoke of Widdershins as though it had a will of its own. It ties into the prophecy."

Christine made a rude sound at the word "prophecy." Griffin and

I ignored her. "True, but recognizing there is something odd about this town and ascribing it to some sort of sentient force...well, I'd be shocked if she was the only one."

I held my tongue. Griffin had once asked me if I believed some greater power had brought us together. I didn't, but I understood he found the idea attractive, whether due to divine providence or some other force.

Our conversation paused while Griffin's meal of fish soup was served. Once the waiter had left again, he said, "I had to ask your father...how did he put it? Impertinent questions."

"I fear to ask what," I said.

Griffin sighed and swirled his spoon in the soup. "There is one family far more obvious than the Lesters, Waites, or Abbotts to be hybrids, although not to have murdered Guinevere and Miss Emily."

I stared at him blankly. "Well? Who?"

"Don't be absurd," Christine said. "He's talking about the Whybornes, of course."

"My family?" Shock gave way to annoyance. "This is about what Daphne said, isn't it? When we were inside the lightless pyramid in Egypt, and she accused me of not being human."

Griffin had the grace to look guilty. "Yes."

"Are you daft? These—these ketoi are animals! Monsters! To suggest someone in my family *mated* with them is preposterous." I swallowed back my revulsion. "The Whybornes are scoundrels who fled the hangman in England, not supernatural monsters."

"Scoundrels who helped Blackbyrne found this town," Griffin countered.

"And the Endicotts *fight* these creatures, have done so for centuries!"

"Don't be angry, my dear," Griffin said to me. "I didn't think it true, but I had to ask. Your father was as offended as you."

"With every right! Not only did you say we have the blood of monsters in our veins, but you all but accused him of killing his own daughter." Father and I might never have gotten along, but he would never murder a family member. Not even me. "And then hired you to, what, uncover the truth? What a ridiculous notion!"

"All right, all right." Griffin scowled at me. "You've made your opinion very clear. As I said, I couldn't imagine it to be true, but I had to ask for the sake of thoroughness. Your father's answer was as vehement as your own. How did he put it? 'The Brotherhood was founded to *control* otherworldly forces, not *breed* with them.'"

Christine snorted at his rather eerie imitation of Father's most supercilious tones. As, for once, I agreed with Father, I glared in

Griffin's direction. "Was there anything else?"

"Yes." Griffin sobered. "I also requested to see Miss Emily's room, in case some clue of her involvement with Guinevere's trip to the dock might be found."

The sharp sting of grief punctured my anger. I sank back in the booth. "Did you find anything?"

"I wasn't certain at the time, but now that I've heard the prophecy...well, I'm afraid so."

"What on earth do you mean, man?" Christine prompted.

Griffin took a slow sip of his coffee before answering. "Miss Emily's diary was missing, and none of the other servants seemed to have any idea where it might have gone. According to Niles, her possessions will be delivered to her daughter—the woman hasn't been allowed in to take or see them."

"Oh." I'd almost forgotten Miss Emily's daughter would naturally want her things. Had Father kept them for Griffin to look through, or simply because he refused to let anything out of the house if he could at all help it?

"Nothing else seemed out of the ordinary in her room," Griffin said. "Save for one thing. She had a chest where she kept her personal items and keepsakes, such as they were. A pair of baby shoes—perhaps her daughter's. The mourning card for your twin sister. A small lock of blond hair, knotted around a shark's tooth."

It felt odd to say, but... "I think the hair might have been mine? My hair was much lighter when I was a small child. What the shark's tooth means, I can't imagine."

Griffin's ankle pressed comfortingly against mine. "She had the Christmas cards you'd sent her as well."

"What so odd about all that?" Christine asked around a mouthful of fish sandwich. "The woman helped raise Whyborne—of course she'd keep mementos of him."

"It isn't odd at all," Griffin agreed. "What was strange were the words painted on the inside of the trunk's lid. Someone put a lot of time and care into the decoration—the script was fine and decorated with flowers and fish."

"Out with it," Christine prodded. "What did it say?"

"One for the land, and one for the sea."

I felt as if a cold hand had brushed the nape of my neck. "No. You're just-just joking at my expense."

"I'm afraid not, my dear. It seems Miss Emily knew of this prophecy, even if she wasn't a native of Widdershins. Whether she was the one to tell Guinevere, or what they believed it meant, I can't say."

"So it seems Miss Emily was more deeply involved in things than merely procuring a disguise for Guinevere." Christine gave me a sympathetic look.

I stared down at my half-eaten fish, all my appetite gone. The woman I'd thought of as a second mother had kept whatever she knew about Guinevere's death to herself, without telling anyone, even Mother. More, she'd kept some kind of secret for years, it seemed.

But what?

"Did Father know what it meant?" I asked.

"No. Nor did any of the other servants admit to knowing." Griffin turned his coffee cup around and around in his fingers. "I received the impression Miss Emily's closeness with your mother put something of a barrier between her and the other servants. No one admitted to ever even seeing her chest unlocked, let alone what she kept inside, and my instincts say they weren't lying."

Why did I eat so much? Acid clawed at the back of my throat, as if the fish tried to swim back up. I thought I'd known Miss Emily. Had I been deluded all along?

"Persephone," I said. "That was the other thing Guinevere said. "Persephone. One for the sea."

"Persephone," Christine mused. She scowled down at the crumbs on her plate. "Hmm. That seems to suggest the Lesters were involved."

Griffin frowned. "What do you mean?"

"They run a funeral business, don't they? Persephone is the queen of the underworld. Wife to the god of the dead."

"You're right," I agreed. How could I not have seen it earlier? "The Lesters must surely be guilty."

Griffin looked less than convinced. "Why wouldn't she simply name the Lesters, then? Guinevere was dying. Speaking the prophecy I can understand, but why give Whyborne an obscure clue to who had killed her, rather than just telling him? Could she have even come up with such a thing, in the condition she was in?"

"Oh." Christine frowned in disappointment. "I suppose you're right."

"Don't be so sure," I countered. "Perhaps it's a-a code name the Lesters used to cover their tracks."

"Perhaps," Griffin said skeptically. "But I've not uncovered any evidence they have financial ties to shipping, fishing, or anything else that might explain the ship disappearances. The Waites have been harmed by the loss of cargo and equipment for their cannery, so I don't imagine them to be involved."

"Thomas Abbott was at the party the other night." My heart beat faster. "Griffin, you overheard—Guinevere was trying to keep away from him. Thanks to her remark I thought he might be paying her unwanted attentions based on their old association, but perhaps there was more to it?"

"Perhaps."

"And Abbott's father was a member of the Brotherhood."

"According to your father, that would argue against him being a hybrid," Christine pointed out.

"Father is hardly omniscient. Perhaps he didn't know."

"Mr. Abbott seems the most likely candidate at the moment," Griffin agreed slowly. "But we need more proof of his involvement. I'll look into his finances further tomorrow. And I'll see if I can get samples of his handwriting to compare the note you found in Guinevere's room. With luck, I can do so legally instead of by tampering with the mail."

I poked at my fish. "What is the connection with Miss Emily? The myth of Persephone? This idiotic prophecy? The bracelet, the stone— we have a towering pile of clues, but none of them connect with each other. What the devil does any of it *mean?*"

Griffin rubbed his ankle against mine soothingly. "I don't know, my dear, but I intend to find out. Now finish your dinner and let's join your cousins at the docks."

As the steam launch the Endicotts had rented left the bay, the first tatters of fog rolled in.

Fiona steered the vessel. Christine, who wished to learn the operation of the small craft, sat in the seat directly behind her. Theo, Griffin, and I took the seats behind the boiler, which were sheltered by a canopy to keep off the worst of the soot. The moon had not yet risen, and the waves heaved beneath the craft. Thank heavens none of us were prone to seasickness.

Even so, I selected a seat as far away from the gunwales as possible. The waves surged all too close to the rail, in my opinion. Every bump and dip sent my heart to racing, some blind, animal part of me convinced we'd go over and drown.

The moon had yet to rise, and as the fog closed in, the only light came from the ship's lanterns. Bits of mist blew past, like the shrouds of dead men, thickening slowly as we drew further out to sea. The damp seemed to multiply the chill of the air, and I tugged my scarf closer to keep the wind off my neck. The scarf was one of those Miss Emily had knitted for me, though after learning of her involvement in Guinevere's death, I didn't know if I cherished the thing or hated it.

I half listened while Griffin told Theo of our discoveries. At least he had the tact not to bring up his horrid accusations about the Whyborne side of the family. I handed Theo the poem, which he read carefully.

"If you'll let me, I'll make a transcription and send it to England," he said. "Perhaps someone there will make heads of tails of it. Prophecies are always a nasty business, though—half the time they turn out to be the ranting of lunatics, and the other half their only purpose is to drive one insane worrying what *might* happen."

"You aren't concerned, then?" Griffin asked.

"Oh, I'm concerned, old chap." Theo met my gaze. "But I fear our Percival's friend was correct—the bloody things only make sense once they've come to fruition. Even so, we'll contribute whatever we can to deciphering the meaning."

"Thank you," I said gratefully. At least we had sorcerers with experience in the matter aiding us, rather than floundering about in the dark.

"We have news ourselves," Theo went on, leaning back in his seat and perilously close to the rail. He looked as at home on the boat as he did in the drawing room. "Uncle Ned sent us more information on the ketoi."

I tried not to look at the waves just behind him. "What did he have to say?"

"A good deal, and all of it ghastly." The fog flattened sound, made Theo's voice almost eerie even though he sat but inches away. "He believes they account for legends of selkies and sirens."

"I know sirens supposedly lure sailors to their doom," I said. "But I'm not familiar with selkies."

"Irish legend," Griffin supplied unexpectedly. When I glanced at him in surprise, he shrugged. "I may remember nothing of my mother tongue, let alone the Emerald Isle itself, but I've had occasion to pass myself off as a tried-and-true Irishman. I've spent more than a few nights listening to stories over a bottle of whiskey."

"It sounds as though you've had an interesting life, Mr. Flaherty," Theo said with a raised brow.

"Interesting enough," Griffin replied noncommittally. "At any rate, the selkies are seals who transform into men. Women who want a lover summon them onto land with seven tears."

"According to Uncle Ned, the ketoi are summoned by certain enchanted stones," Theo said. "Perhaps the 'tears' part isn't literal."

A little shiver went through me. "Enchanted stones? Do you think the one we found in Guinevere's possession could be such a thing?"

"I think it very likely."

Surely Guinevere had received the stone here in America, along with the bracelet. True, she had asked her husband's forgiveness before she died, but it could have been in reference to anything. And yes, she'd been married for many years before conceiving, but there was no reason to cast aspersions on her character. No reason to question the parentage of her son.

God, how could I even consider such a thing? The ketoi were monstrous. Guinevere would never allow such a creature in her sight, let alone touch her. Shame burned me, for the thought to have even crossed my mind for an instant.

Theo stared out into the ever-thickening fog, his mouth drawn in a pensive line. "The ketoi want to spread onto land, and rutting with the occasional human is one method to accomplish it. But sometimes, they make a more determined attempt. Apparently, in the thirteenth century, the ketoi all but overran a seaport in Suffolk called Dunwich. Our ancestors had to destroy a great deal of the town and drop some of it into the sea to stop them."

Griffin frowned. "What about the innocents living there?"

Theo's smile was thin. "I assure you, there were no innocents left in the town."

"You can't know that," Griffin challenged.

"Even if there were, we saved far more lives than we took." The wind ruffled Theo's hair, and the muted light bleached color from his skin. "These creatures drown sailors and drag ships down into the depths. Can you imagine the ruin their abominable offspring could wreak upon the land?"

Griffin looked troubled, but before he could answer, the boat slowed. A thick veil of fog surrounded us. In the distance, the Daboll trumpet began to sound, warning ships of the shallower water at our backs.

"Your show now, Theo," Fiona called.

"What do you intend?" Griffin asked.

"The area of disappearances is far too large for a single ship to hope to survey," Theo replied. "So we need a method of narrowing it down. Percival, did you bring the bracelet?"

I removed it from my pocket and displayed it silently. Theo took out a small bag he'd stowed earlier, along with a nautical chart, which had the sites of the ship disappearances marked on it. Taking the bracelet from me, he positioned it in the center of the cluster.

From his pocket he pulled an iron pendulum on a small chain. I leaned in closer, glad to have something to distract me from the rolling waves and heavy fog. Theo held the pendulum above the map and began to murmur softly. My skin prickled, and the scars on my arm tingled in response to the arcane forces gathering around him.

The pendulum swung, a deliberate movement unconnected with the motion of the launch. "Twelve degrees to starboard," he called above the chug of the engine.

The boat's direction altered in response. Theo continued to murmur his spell, occasionally pausing to call out adjustments to our heading. At last, the pendulum pointed straight down.

Into the depths.

"This must be it," he murmured. "Fiona! Hold steady! Mr. Flaherty, fetch the sounding line, and—"

There came an odd creak through the fog. Theo fell silent, and we all stared in the direction of the sound. Had it been some trick of the waves? An echo from our own hull?

The fog thinned directly ahead of us. No—it didn't thin. Something dark emerged from within it, bearing down on us.

"Fiona! Hard to port!" Theo shouted. I had just enough time to glimpse an iron prow cutting through the fog, before the sudden tilt of the launch flung me from my seat.

CHAPTER 15

SHARP CRIES FROM my companions pierced the fog, accompanied by a horrible grating sound as steel scraped against our hull. The larger ship's wake shoved against our little launch, tilting us further to port. Surely we would go over—

The boat righted abruptly, slid across the water, and rebounded from the hull of the other ship. Griffin's hand closed on mine, and I clutched at him. God, that was far too close. My heart pounded, and a cold sweat soaked my shirt.

"Nice spot of water magic there, Fiona!" Theo called. "Is everyone all right?"

"Y-yes." I swallowed and let Griffin haul me to my feet. His eyes were wide with concern, so I dredged up a small, shaky smile. "I'm quite all right."

"I'm glad." Griffin released me with some reluctance.

My legs remained shaky enough to make the short walk to the prow more of a challenge than it should have been. "Thank you, Fiona," I said, leaning heavily against her seat.

She nodded. "Any time, old chap. Of course, I shouldn't have had to, if the bloody fool steering the ship hadn't tried to run us down! No lights and in the fog? Sodding idiot."

I stared up at the black bulk above us. As Fiona had said, no light showed. Nor did I hear the groan of engines. The ship's name showed on the prow: *Oarfish*.

I cupped my hands around my mouth and shouted. "Ahoy!

Oarfish!"

Silence. No light, no movement. No answering voices. At the very least, the glancing blow they'd given our boat should have alerted someone to our presence. I might not be a sailor, but I'd grown up in a port town. There should be hands on deck already, calling down to us to make certain we didn't need assistance.

Griffin's lantern cut through the gloom as he came to join me. "Abandoned," he said, shining the light through the fog. "Look—the lifeboats are still in place, at least on this side."

"Just like the *Norfolk Siren,*" I said. God. The previous ship had been bad enough, in dock weeks after she'd been found adrift. But here, in the fog, so close to Widdershins... "Whatever happened must have occurred tonight."

Griffin shivered. "Yes."

"What are we to do?"

"Only one thing we can do, old boy," Theo said as he joined us at the front of the launch. "Go aboard."

Griffin's carpetbag contained a grapple, which we'd used on at least one occasion to scale a wall. Fiona maneuvered the tug to the leeward side of the ship. Once in position, I stood well back while Griffin swung the grapple, then sent it whistling through the fog at the rail of the *Oarfish* high above. The first throw tumbled free into the water, drawing a short curse from him. The next throw caught and held.

"I'll climb up," Griffin said. He began to strip off his coat. "There should be a pilot ladder aboard. I'll lower some lines to secure the launch and then let the ladder down."

I took the coat from him. My throat ached—what if horrors still lurked aboard? What if the ketoi were there, just waiting for anyone foolish enough to set foot on deck? I'd be down here, unable to protect him.

But the truth was, I had no hope of dragging myself up a rope. So I could only say, "Be careful."

He cast me a lopsided smile. "I'm always careful."

He caught the rope and hauled himself up, wrapping his legs about it for grip and pulling himself higher with his arms. The sight left me torn between admiration and fear. It was an appealing display of strength, but what if he fell? What if something above bit through the rope with sharp teeth? What if—

None of those things happened. A faint light appeared. "I'm aboard!" he called down. "Give me a moment and I'll throw down some lines."

A short time later, the launch was secured to the side of the ship. Griffin located the pilot ladder and dropped it over the side. I climbed up first, and Griffin helped me over the rail, clapping me on the arm as he did so.

"What now?" I asked, when the rest had boarded behind me.

Griffin picked up his salvaged lantern. "Look," he said.

A long smear of blood wended its way down the deck, as if some dying man had dragged himself along. The smear ended abruptly in a large puddle, but there was no trace of a body.

"Thrown into the depths," Theo said. "Food for the fish and sharks—if nothing worse. Poor bloke."

Christine muttered an oath. "I doubt we'll find any survivors. Still, a quick search may turn up some clue."

I stared at the bloody streak. The man who'd dragged himself along the deck, clinging to some vain hope of escape...who did he leave behind? Who did he think of in his last moments? A lover, a child, a parent?

What had Miss Emily thought while dying? Had she regretted her silence? Thought of her daughter? Of Mother? Of me?

"We must put an end to this," I said. My voice shook with emotion: rage or grief or horror, even I wasn't certain.

"We will." Griffin's hand rested lightly against the small of my back. "We should split up. It will make the search go faster. Mr. Endicott, Miss Endicott, would you take the upper deck and cabins? We'll see to below decks."

Wonderful. I hadn't the slightest desire to go down into dank holds infested with rats. Or ketoi. But we didn't have much choice.

Griffin was probably even less happy about it than I, having an aversion to dark, enclosed spaces. Although perhaps the motion of the sea would be enough to keep his phobia back. But if he was willing to go below decks, I could hardly complain about doing so.

Christine and I followed him to the hatch. Steep stairs led down into utter darkness, broken only by the shaft of light from his lantern. The rusty tang of blood mingled with the dank scent of the holds, and smears of red decorated the steel risers, as if bodies had been dragged up them. The steps rang beneath our shoes as we descended, and I winced at the sound. If anything lurked below, it would surely know we were coming.

At the foot of the stair, Griffin bent and picked something up. "Look," he said, holding it out for inspection. It was a simple knife, of the sort carried by sailors the world over. Blood coated the edge of its blade.

"Someone managed a good hit against the bastards," Christine said with satisfaction.

"To no avail." Griffin's lantern picked out a great deal of blood on the floor, as well as smears on the wall.

I shuddered. "Why do you think they remove the bodies? Do they...eat them?"

"God, I hope not." Griffin led the way down the narrow passage. "I wondered myself. The earlier ships vanished altogether, but first the *Norfolk Siren* and now this vessel have been left afloat with signs of catastrophe. It occurs to me perhaps whoever is directing the ketoi may have decided to spread fear, along with whatever else he's gaining from these attacks."

"Spreading fear—that sounds like something the Brotherhood would do," I said. "Abbott probably learned it from his father."

"We don't know he's the one behind this," Griffin reminded me. "Come. Let's take a look at the engine room."

We traversed the passage slowly. Pipes on the walls threw strange shadows, and open doors swung slowly to and fro along with the rocking of the ship. The air was close and damp, and reeked of fresh death.

A series of loud knocks sounded, echoing throughout the ship.

The fine hairs on the back of my neck prickled. "Something loose, swinging about with the motion of the ship?" Christine suggested.

"Then why did it stop?" I asked.

"Blast."

"I think it came from this direction," Griffin murmured, and started forward.

More knocking. The last in line, I glanced nervously back over my shoulder. Only blackness met my gaze.

The knocks came again, louder this time. Griffin cautiously pushed open a door. Beyond lay one of the coal storage rooms, immediately adjacent to the hull.

The knocks sounded once more, and there could be no mistake. They were coming from outside the ship.

"Griffin," I began, taking an uneasy step back.

Something struck me hard from behind, sending me into the wall.

"Ival!" Griffin leapt forward, the sailor's knife he yet carried flashing out. Something let out a hiss, like an angry cat, and the weight vanished from my back.

I pushed myself from the wall, just in time to see the light fall across the creature that had attacked me. Although I'd seen drawings and sculptures of the ketoi, and half glimpsed one in the cemetery, beholding one in the flesh was profoundly different.

Its slender, sexless form seemed honed to move through sleek water. Low fins rose from its calves and elbows, and its feet were long and webbed as a frog's. Although the skin of its face, throat, and belly was largely dead white, its back was dark gray, and spots and swirls of darker color decorated its face, arms, and legs.

Its hair, if it could be called such, was a nauseating mass of squirming tentacles like those of a sea anemone. The slits of its gills clamped tight to its neck, protecting them from the air. Jewelry of the strange gold alloy encircled its upper arms and forehead and formed a sparking loincloth across its hips.

But its eyes...its dark eyes were disturbingly, horribly, human.

The scent of the ocean flooded the passageway, as if a clean breeze had blown in with the creature. It hissed again, its mouth opening far wider than it should have, revealing row upon row of serrated teeth.

Griffin lunged at it, knife flashing. It snapped at him with its awful maw; at the same instant, I seized the back of Griffin's coat, pulling him away from its jaws. The scars on my arm tingled, and I fixed all my concentration on the steel decking beneath the ketoi's batrachian feet as I spoke the secret name of fire.

Had it been wearing shoes, the heat wouldn't have been enough to do it real harm. But the delicate webbing between its toes proved sensitive. A smell disturbingly similar to seared tuna filled the air. It let out a snarl of pain and sprang back from the suddenly hot metal. Then, with a final hiss, it turned and ran.

I gave chase.

Griffin and Christine both pounded after me—a good thing, since I had no lantern. I could just make out the figure fleeing in front of me. Even with wounded feet, it moved fast.

It made the stair leading back to the deck. As I raced up after it, I felt the currents of magic in the air and heard shouts and the chanting of Aklo from the deck above.

The twins were under attack.

I all but sprang from the hatch onto the deck. Fiona stood near the bow of the ship, hatless, her skirts blowing in a wild wind as she spread frost across the deck. The ketoi racing toward her slipped in it. She drove a cargo hook into the thrashing mass of tentacles on its head.

Theo wasn't far from her. He'd found a can of lamp oil somewhere, and splashed its contents on any ketoi who drew near, before setting them alight with a word. The Endicotts held their own, but another half-dozen ketoi climbed over the iron rail onto the deck.

I fixed all my concentration on the iron rail and called down lightning from the sky.

"Good show!" Theo shouted, as the aberrations dropped from the rail, dead or dying or burned. Then two more charged him, and he turned his concentration to them.

I fought beside the twins, dimly aware of Griffin and Christine at my back, holding off more ketoi with revolver, knife, and pistol. I pulled wind from the sky to fling monsters from the rigging, drew down lightning, and aimed fire. My blood roared in my ears, and those who would harm us fell away before me, before Theo and Fiona, before a great swirl of magic nothing could stand against.

My scars stung, a sweet burn, as I reached for wind and sky and felt them obey. The ship began to roll as the swells grew stronger, and the rigging sang in the sudden gale that shredded the fog into nothing.

In that moment, I felt only elation. All the doubts that plagued me the rest of my life fell away. There was no fear, no right or wrong, no constant questioning of every decision.

Just this. Just the power of my will, reshaping the world.

Some instinct caused me to turn. I beheld one of the ketoi, hanging from the lines, its eyes narrowed in rage and its shark teeth bared. Was it the one whose feet I had burned earlier?

No matter. I would deal with it.

The ship heaved suddenly, a wave raised by our spells striking it broadside. At the same instant, the ketoi launched at me.

Its sleek body slammed into mine, even as the deck tilted violently. My feet went out from under me, and I fell, until my back fetched sharply against the rail. Even then, I might have been spared, except for the weight of the ketoi coming down on me. For an instant, we hung poised. I thrust out a hand to keep back its snapping jaws, felt a sudden blaze of agony on my hand as its tentacle hair stung me like an enraged jellyfish.

Then the ship leaned just a degree further, and we toppled over backwards, plunging down, down toward the heaving ocean below.

Hitting the water felt like slamming into a wall. It drove all the air out of my lungs, and my entire body went rigid, pain and lack of breath overriding every other instinct. My thoughts scrambled, trying to understand what had happened.

The water closed over my head.

No! I flailed madly, as if I could claw my way to the surface. Which way was up? There was no light, no sensation except roiling water pressing in on me, my clothes dragging heavily at my limbs. What had happened to the ketoi who had knocked me overboard?

A hand closed around my ankle, claws biting into my flesh.

I found myself suddenly pulled down. My ears popped painfully, and my lungs burned. I tried to kick free, but the iron grip refused to let go. I was going to drown here in the black depths, my body torn apart by sharks or fish or the too-wide mouths of the ketoi.

An arm wrapped around my chest.

For an instant of panic, I thought a second ketoi had joined the first. But this arm sought to drag me toward the surface. My lungs ached, and I twisted wildly, kicking with all my strength at the grip on my ankle.

The hold on my chest let go. No—I didn't want to be left here, to be dragged to my death!

A hand grabbed my leg, but no claws sunk in. Something bumped against me—then the ketoi holding my ankle abruptly let go.

A moment later, I was headed for the surface, hands dragging me up. Even as my screaming lungs gave up the fight and I opened my mouth for an involuntary breath, my head broke the surface.

I gasped, sucking sweet air into my lungs. A second gasp sounded beside me, and the arm wrapped around my chest again. "Ival! Are you all right?"

We were still in the water, and terror told me to fight, to thrash, to cling. But I forced myself to go limp in Griffin's hold, to trust he wouldn't let me drown. "Y-Yes. I think so. My hand, though—the ketoi stung it." My heart had calmed a bit, and my skin itched and burned.

"Hold this." He pressed the knife he'd found on board into my uninjured hand. No doubt he'd used it against the ketoi clinging to my ankle. Once his hand was free, he struck out for the launch, dragging me after.

"Dear heavens, are you two well?" Christine called from the boat. She must have scrambled down the pilot ladder to reach us.

"Help us aboard," Griffin replied. "The ketoi stung Whyborne with its tentacles."

Fiona and Theo had reached the launch as well, and helped Christine haul me out of the water. "Where were you stung?"

I held out my hand. Angry red dots showed on the skin, but the pain had already begun to subside. "At least it doesn't seem swollen," Christine said.

"It's fine," I said, flexing my fingers. "It barely even hurts now."

"Thank heavens," Griffin said. "Come, sit down beneath the canopy."

"That was a bit more exciting than we'd planned, eh?" Theo asked, clapping me on the back as I passed.

"Fire up the boiler, brother," Fiona ordered as she went to her place in the pilot's chair. "Or else it will be even more exciting.

Remember, our craft isn't nearly so difficult to climb onto as a cargo ship."

Cʜᴀᴘᴛᴇʀ 16

Tʜᴀɴᴋꜰᴜʟʟʏ, ᴡᴇ ᴅᴇᴘᴀʀᴛᴇᴅ the area without any further attacks from the ketoi. Soaked to the bone, Griffin and I huddled together beneath the canopy, which at least kept out some of the wind.

"Go and get dry," Theo said sympathetically when we reached port. "Fiona and I will alert the harbormaster to the abandoned ship, before it can become a hazard to any other craft."

I wasn't about to argue. We departed with Christine, none of us speaking much, even when we parted ways in front of her boarding house. As for me, I was bone tired; the day had been long, and the drama aboard the *Oarfish*, combined with the shock of falling overboard, had taken whatever reserves I had left.

We were almost to our own walk when Griffin said, "You seem more comfortable with your...what do you call them, 'little spells?'"

Did he truly wish to have this conversation tonight? "I haven't called them such since Egypt," I replied.

We reached our gate. Griffin opened it and gestured me through. "I hadn't realized, but yes. You're right. Tonight it seemed to me you were more...adept? You haven't needed sigils for a while, but it seemed you've almost moved past words as well."

Curse the man. "So what if I have? Hasn't it come in handy?"

"If by 'handy,' you mean upsetting the ship to the point you fell overboard and nearly drowned."

"Enough!" I turned to him, fists clenched. "You do nothing but—"

"What's that?" he asked, brows drawing sharply together as he stared past me.

Startled from my vexation, I glanced at our door, where his gaze had fixed. A bit of white paper protruded from the crack between door and frame, just above the doorknob.

What the devil? I pulled the paper loose and unfolded it, revealing a note written in a familiar hand.

Percival,
Come immediately. These 'ketoi' have attacked your mother.
Yrs,
Niles Foster Whyborne

"Are you certain you're all right?" I asked Mother.

We sat in the downstairs drawing room. Griffin perched on the edge of his chair, as if ready to leap into action, although the time for it had already passed. Father paced angrily back and forth in front of the fire. As for Mother, she sat by me on the couch, wrapped in a warm dressing gown with a soothing cup of tea in her hands.

"I'm fine, Percival." She didn't look fine, though, her skin the color of fresh ivory. "I drove the creature off before it could gain access to the house."

"What exactly happened?" Griffin asked her.

Mother cradled her teacup, as if wishing to draw its warmth into her hands. "I haven't been sleeping well," she said carefully. I lowered my eyes; of course she hadn't, with Guinevere and Miss Emily murdered. "I awoke certain someone watched me. I thought perhaps one of the maids had come in, but the room was deserted. Then I saw *it* at the window."

I patted her arm. "They are horrible."

"Horrible," she repeated, then shook her head. "But...beautiful as well? Her skin—I'm almost certain it was a female—gleamed like mother-of-pearl in the darkness. She was sleek, like something born to the water. Not human, but now that I think back, there was something in her eyes...a look of grief, almost."

"Your mind is playing tricks on you," I assured her. "We just came from a ship where their kind slaughtered the entire crew."

Father and Mother both gasped at this. "The details will be in my report," Griffin told Father. "And some in the late edition of the newspaper, no doubt. Whyborne is right, however—the ketoi have neither remorse or mercy."

Mother nodded her head slowly. "I suppose you're correct. My mind no doubt conjured up a fancy after the fact because, at the moment, I only knew something inhuman tried to get into the house.

So I summoned the wind. The window burst outward, and she vanished."

"We found no trace of the creature," Father put in. "It must have used its claws to climb up the outside of the house."

I shivered. Too easy to imagine the thing scaling the stone, its batrachian feet finding purchase in cracks no human toes could have. If Mother hadn't waked, what would it have done?

The answer seemed obvious. "It meant to murder you," I said, my lips numb. Bad enough Guinevere had died thanks to someone striking an alliance with these monsters, let alone Miss Emily, but Mother?

The scars on my right arm pulled against my skin. We had to put an end to this quickly.

Permanently.

"Why attack Heliabel, though?" Griffin asked.

Father paused in his pacing. "No doubt they believed either Guinevere or Emily—or both—confided in her. Emily was her maid, after all."

Griffin looked troubled. "I suppose."

"Perhaps they mean to strike at the entire family." I sat up, my heart beating faster. "Do they assume we all know whatever secret Guinevere learned?"

"It will not happen." Anger flushed Father's skin. "The footmen will all be armed straight away, as will I. Bel, you'll move immediately to a small room, with fewer windows. Percival, you should return home as well."

"If by 'home' you mean here, don't be absurd." All this time, and the man still thought he could order me about.

His face darkened further. "Do not argue with me, Percival. We are all in danger, and I will not have your stubborn pride getting you killed."

"And I won't cower behind the footmen while monsters overrun the town!" I rose to my feet.

"You will not take such a tone with me."

The wind stirred, and a stack of sheet music slipped from the top of the piano. My scars ached. "Then don't take such a one with me. I'm not Stanford, to come whenever you call."

"God! Don't I know it!"

Griffin's voice cut into our argument, as surely as if he'd placed himself between us. "We shouldn't overtax Heliabel."

Curse it. He was right.

I took a deep breath, struggling for calm. "Someone needs to put a stop to all of this," I told Father. "And if you imagine I'd let Griffin and my cousins do so alone, you don't know me at all. Not to say you ever did."

I turned my back before he could make a reply. "Come on, Griffin. Let's leave Mother to her rest."

I threw the door open, intending to make a dramatic exit. Instead, I almost walked straight into Stanford. From the furious expression on his face, I suspected he'd heard what I said about him.

And why not? It was true, wasn't it? "Eavesdropping in the hall now?" I asked. "You should have just come in earlier."

The angry reddening of his face made him resemble Father even more than usual. "I wished to make certain Mother is all right," he snapped. "What are you doing here?"

"I sent for your brother," Father said in irritation. "And where have you been? If you've turned back to drinking and whor—other things," he corrected, recalling Mother's presence, "I won't be held responsible for the consequences."

"No need to worry." Stanford's eyes narrowed. From his tone, it seemed he and Father hadn't reconciled from the argument I'd overheard a few days ago. "I was attending to business."

Business, in the middle of the night? Even Father's doting gaze would see through such an excuse. Although Stanford didn't smell of either alcohol or cheap perfume, at least.

"There was some excitement down on the docks," he went on. "Another derelict has been found."

"Yes, your brother told us," Father said, waving a dismissive hand. "Well don't just stand there, come in if you wish to speak to your mother."

Stanford's face darkened. "You don't believe me. But you'll see."

"Don't be a fool," I said. "No one thinks you were 'doing business' at four in the morning."

He leveled a look of utter hatred on me, before pushing past, his shoulder striking mine. I didn't care. I just wanted to get out of the damned house.

Very little of the night remained by the time we finally arrived home, and as a consequence, I practically sleepwalked to the museum.

"Coffee, sir?" Miss Parkhurst asked sympathetically upon seeing me.

"Please."

"Right away. Dr. Putnam left word she'd like to see you as soon as possible about the Hallowe'en tours. I'm certain they'll be grand—I can't wait to see the gathering."

"You're coming?" I asked, surprised. A simple secretary surely wouldn't be invited to a donor event.

"I asked if I could help with the coat check. The galas are too grand for me, but I thought perhaps this would be an opportunity to see you—people," she corrected hastily. "People I work with. Away from the normal day-to-day."

For some reason her face had gone absolutely scarlet. Perhaps she thought I'd disapprove of her presence? "It sounds like a wonderful idea," I said. "And it will give me someone else to talk to besides Christine."

"Oh! I-I don't imagine I'll be allowed to mingle until after the donors have gone."

"Believe me, hiding in the coat check will be a welcome respite for me," I said ruefully.

"I—yes—I'll get your coffee," she said, and darted away. What an odd woman. An excellent secretary, though.

After obtaining coffee from Miss Parkhurst, I went straight to Christine's office. Ordinarily, it was far neater than my own, all of her books sorted and papers gathered. Various artifacts lay on shelves, awaiting analysis: canopic jars, a mummified cat, small figurines carved from hippopotamus ivory. Today, however, objects collected for the Hallowe'en tours crowded her desk and chairs. Huge spiders from South America—all of them long dead, thank heavens—necklaces made from human teeth, and every other ghastly thing she could find.

"If your object is to keep the director from ever asking you to do anything again, you've made a good start," I said, gingerly moving aside a foot, which seemed to have broken off a mummy sometime in antiquity.

"Let's hope," Christine agreed. Dark circles showed under her eyes, but she frowned at me. "You look terrible. Don't tell me your dip in the ocean last night resulted in you catching a chill?"

"Worse." I told her what happened at Whyborne House.

"The things are after your mother now? What the devil?" Christine frowned. "What if it is this Abbott fellow behind it all? Does he have a grudge against your family?"

"His father died thanks to me."

"And Griffin and I," she reminded me.

"True. Not to mention, he was in love with Guinevere at one time —I suspect she may have turned down a proposal from him." I frowned as a memory nagged at me. "And he and Stanford were arguing at the party the other night. Well, not arguing, but Stanford was clearly angry about something." Curse it—the man *must* be guilty. How it tied into the prophecy...well, as Amelie had suggested, maybe it would become clearer later.

"Let me know when you choose to beard the lion in his den," she said. "In the meantime, we still have this absurd showing of cursed artifacts. Dr. Norris finally deigned to answer us—apparently, the American History Department has some sort of sword. At any rate, the man is almost as much of a swine as Bradley, so you're coming with me."

"Why?"

"To keep me from strangling him with his own tie, of course." She rose to her feet. "Come along, Whyborne, and let's get this over with."

As befit a departmental head, Dr. Norris's office was large and airy, with windows looking out over the garden and fountain nestled between two of the wings. His desk would have taken up most of my office, let alone the sideboard well stocked with decanters of brandy and whiskey, or the large cabinet displaying a collection of Thomas Jefferson's dishes. A gigantic portrait of George Washington loomed on the wall behind the desk. I hoped it was well secured; should it ever fall, it would probably crush Dr. Norris like a bug beneath a flyswatter. A sword with no scabbard lay on his desk, looking wildly out of place.

Dr. Norris sat in his leather-backed chair, trimming a cigar. "There you are," he said, as if he'd been waiting on us, rather than had his secretary keep us cooling our heels outside for twenty minutes. "Pitman, Windleby."

Christine's eyes blazed, and she drew in a deep breath. Hoping to cut off any vitriol that would only prolong the interview, I hastily said, "You had something for the private tours, Dr. Norris?"

"Yes, yes." He lit his cigar. The odor of burning socks filled the air. My upbringing insisted I chide him for smoking in front of a woman without first asking her permission, but I had the feeling Christine wouldn't appreciate the sentiment, so I kept silent. "Brilliant idea the director had, wasn't it? I was just telling some of the board members what a genius Dr. Hart is last night, while we were at the club."

Now Christine wasn't the only one grinding her teeth. "Yes," I forced out. "Brilliant."

"Of course, it took us a while to come up with anything in *our* department," he went on, apparently taking great pride in the fact. "None of that superstitious twaddle here—we Americans confront curses head on, don't we?"

My smile felt as if someone had pasted it onto my face, and not done a very good job at it. "You aren't from Widdershins, are you?"

"Not at all, Wembly. I was born in Philadelphia—our fine nation's original capital, if you recall."

"Yes," Christine grated out. "I'm also from Philadelphia."

"Are you, Miss Pembroke?" he asked, sounding as if he rather doubted it.

Christine reached for the sword on his desk. I managed to seize her arm before she could touch it. "Is this the item for the private showings?" I asked hurriedly.

"Yes, yes. It belonged to a Brother Matthew, who claimed to be a Knight Templar or some such nonsense. We've only a fragment of diary left, and it's badly burned, but apparently he believed the sword allowed him to kill witches by giving him immunity to their spells. He came to Widdershins a decade or two after its founding, apparently intent on wholesale slaughter." Norris shook his head. "Fellow was completely delusional by then, I suppose. At any rate, no one knows what happened to his body, but the sword and diary survived. The blade itself is of Spanish make, fourteenth century."

"And the curse?" Christine prompted.

Norris blinked. "Curse? Well, I suppose if you were a witch it would be a curse, wouldn't it?"

"We'll take it," I said, and snatched it up.

My hand went numb, and pain sliced the scars on my arm, as if someone had taken a penknife to them. I cried out, snatching my hand back. The bare blade gouged a strip of varnish out of Norris's desk as it fell with a clang.

"Careful, there, Worthington!" Norris exclaimed.

"Are you all right?" Christine asked, reaching for my hand.

I cradled it to my chest. "Just nicked myself on the blade," I lied.

She picked up the sword, muttered thanks in Norris's direction, and hurried me out the door. As soon as we were safely in the hall outside the secretary's office, she asked, "What actually happened?"

"It might not be cursed, but the sword is definitely enchanted," I said. I flexed my hand—at least the feeling had begun to return. "And since it affected me and not you, I'm going to suggest the story is true, and it really does act against those of us who use arcane power."

"How odd." She inspected the symbols etched into the blade. "How does it know?"

"I couldn't say without taking a closer look." But I recalled the pain in my scars. "Hold onto it a moment—I want to try an experiment."

I'd naturally reached for the hilt with my right hand before. This time, I carefully pressed a fingertip of the left to the blade.

Nothing.

I lay the length of my left hand against the cool metal. A little sizzle of pain flashed through my right shoulder, where the scars began.

"How strange." I spread my hands out in front of me: the left unmarred, the right laced with a pattern of scars like frost on a window. "I wonder..."

"Wonder later." Christine started down the hall, forcing me to jog to catch back up to her. "We've finally found something safe enough to display in the foyer."

"Safe? It's a sword with a four-foot blade!"

"True. But at least it won't turn the guests into werewolves, like the Celtic ring, or drive anyone violently insane, like the locket." She grinned a bit ferociously. "And if we're lucky, Dr. Norris will drink too much champagne and skewer himself on it. Now that would be a lovely birthday present, wouldn't it?"

CHAPTER 17

AN HOUR OR so later, I knocked on the door of the rented house on Wyrm Lane. When I'd arrived back at my office, it was to find Theo had sent a note, asking me to stop by during my lunch break.

Theo answered my knock almost instantly. "Percival! I'm very glad you could join us." He ushered me inside. "We have exciting news for you."

"I have news as well," I said. "Although not good."

Theo's face fell. "Oh dear. We'd best go straight to Fiona, so she can hear as well. Come—she's in her lab."

When we reached the room at the top of the house, it was to find Fiona hunched over her worktable. Before her lay what appeared to be a short staff, made from some dark wood and polished until it shone. Carving knives, gold wire, and a few crystalline gemstones lay scattered about. At the moment, Fiona affixed a slender crystal, some four inches long, to one end of the staff.

"Is that a wand?" I asked in surprise.

"It is," Fiona said. "Not of the same magical tradition as the one you used in Egypt, but it can still be used to channel arcane energies." She put it down and smiled eagerly at us. "Did you tell him, Theo?"

"Not yet. Percival has some news of his own to share."

I told them of the attack on Whyborne House and Mother. As I spoke, their faces grew more and more grave.

"Bloody ketoi," Fiona said fiercely, when I was done. "We'll send them all to hell for this."

"And whoever is the 'one from the land,'" Theo added. "We must put an end to this, and soon."

"Perhaps the wand will be of some use," Fiona said. "Theo?"

"We asked you to come because we wanted to show you something." Theo took out the map of Widdershins we'd used to mark the locations of the arcane lines, and spread it out on the table.

"You finished it!" I exclaimed.

"Yes—we spent yesterday marking more lines, while we were waiting to go out on the launch. Last night, we began to draw the lines connecting the places we'd marked on the map, and well, see for yourself!"

Scores of arcane lines ran into the town, curving like the currents of a whirlpool. They ran from the land and curled in from the sea, all meeting in a single eye of power where the Cranch River entered the ocean, atop the Front Street bridge.

"You were right—it is a whirlpool," I said.

Theo shook his head. "It's not a whirlpool—it's a sodding maelstrom. None of the whirls of arcane energy we've ever seen come close to this."

"Do you think Blackbyrne knew, when he founded the town?"

"Look at the direction of rotation," Fiona said. "The current moves anticlockwise."

"Widdershins," I breathed.

"Indeed."

I stared at the map. "Why did he perform his works so far out from the eye, then? He used this island in the Cranch, not the very mouth of the bay."

Theo leaned his hip against the table. "I suppose he didn't want to lose control over his workings. The magical energy at the center must be phenomenal. You said Blackbyrne was summoning things from the Outside, correct? Any pinprick in the veil between the worlds near the heart of the maelstrom would be blasted open by its power to form a tear in reality itself. As for other spells, tapping into a source of such power directly would be suicidally dangerous. Much safer to work a bit farther out, where you have access to power but can maintain control of it and not burn yourself up like a scrap of paper in a fire."

"A tool such as the wand would help—the energy would be funneled through it rather than the sorcerer," Fiona added. "But it would still be a huge risk. Believe me, if we use this wand anytime soon, it won't be on the bridge."

I lightly traced the lines of converging power. So much magic, lying under our feet, unseen and unguessed at save by a few. "The bridge is the oldest in Widdershins. I wonder if Blackbyrne put it there just in case. Or was it just to form part of the Brotherhood's symbol?"

"We'll never know, and it doesn't really matter." Theo smiled at me. "It's just a good thing we came here."

"Yes. I can't express how grateful I am for your assistance. And friendship."

"Of course. You can call on us at any time. For any reason." Theo put his hand to my shoulder, his blue eyes sincere behind the shields of his spectacle lenses.

The touch on my shoulder reminded me. "Something odd happened at the museum today." I told them about the sword and the effect it had on me—or, specifically, on the parts of my body marked by the scars.

"Strange," Theo murmured. "They were left by a lightning strike, you say?"

"Yes. I called lightning down using the Egyptian wand, directly above a line of arcane power I found in the desert. The strike destroyed the wand altogether."

"Can we see the scars?" Fiona asked.

"Er..." My ears grew hot. "They go rather high on my shoulder, you see..."

"Just roll up your sleeve, then," Theo said. "Here, I'll take your coat."

Striving to control a blush, I slipped off my suit coat and handed it to him. Were Griffin here, he'd no doubt laugh at my reticence. I undid my cuff and started to push up the sleeve.

"Here," Theo said. Having hung my coat over a chair, he took over the matter of rolling my sleeve neatly up, well past my elbow.

"Oooh," Fiona said. "It must have hurt."

The scars were yet new enough to be red, although I supposed over time they'd fade to white. They ran from the backs of my fingers up my arm, forming a pattern like frost on a windowpane.

Theo's hands lingered on my rolled-up shirt. Instead of dropping them, he slowly ran his fingers down my arm, tracing the pattern over the bicep, then down into the hollow of elbow. His touch was warm, and yet my skin pebbled beneath his fingers. Somehow the gesture felt shockingly intimate, and I looked away quickly, striving to control my body's blind reaction.

"It's beautiful," Theo murmured.

Surprise caused me to look back at him. They were scars, a disfigurement. How could they be beautiful?

Theo met my gaze, a little smile on his lips meant only for me. "Lines of power, inscribed on your skin by arcane fire, summoned by your will. I've never seen anything quite like it. But then, I've never met anyone quite like you, either."

"I-I should get back to the museum," I stammered, pulling away and tugging down my sleeve.

"Will we see you tonight?" Theo asked.

"I don't know. Griffin meant to look into Abbott's finances today. I should go home. Talk to him," I babbled. "I'll send word as soon as I know."

"Until we meet again, then." Theo leaned against the table and watched me pull my coat back on. "We'll await word from you most eagerly."

That evening, I entered our house and hung up my coat and hat. The rattle of cookware led me back to the kitchen, where Griffin stood at the sink. The savory smell of a roast filled the air; he'd already placed it on a platter, beside a bowl of mashed potatoes. He'd stacked pans in the sink, but seemed to have lost his train of thought, staring out the window blankly.

"Griffin?" I asked uncertainly.

He turned, offering me a welcoming smile. "Forgive me, my dear. I heard you come in, but the case has me rather distracted."

I should have been with him, instead of wasting my time at the museum on the absurd Hallowe'en fundraiser. Curse the director.

"Of course." I crossed to him and pressed my lips to his. He tasted of the sage he'd used to garnish the roast, and I slid my arms around his trim waist, pulling him closer. "I could distract you from your, er, distraction."

Griffin grinned. "The roast will get cold. Help me set the table, and we'll discuss things first. You can distract me all you like after dinner."

I released him and went to the silverware drawer. Soon enough, we sat on either side of the table, the roast sliced and wine poured, and Saul begging shamelessly for scraps.

"You've already been fed, you beast," I scolded.

Griffin raised a brow. "He might take your admonishment to heart, if you weren't slipping him a scrap of beef as you gave it."

Saul and I both pretended not to hear him. "So what has your thoughts so occupied?" I asked, cutting my slice of roast into neat chunks. I preferred fish over the flesh of terrestrial animals, but Griffin's years in Chicago and the west had instilled a love of beef in him. We compromised, as with all else.

Griffin frowned at his plate. "I haven't been able to find any link between Abbott and the disappearing ships—the *Oarfish* is the only one I haven't been able to yet look into. However, I obtained a sample of his handwriting on some legal documents. It matches the note you found in Guinevere's room."

My stomach contracted around the bites of roast. "It's him, then. Thomas Abbot murdered Guinevere and Miss Emily."

I'd stood only feet from him, the night of the party. If I'd known, I should have struck him down, should have saved everyone from his evil.

But I hadn't known then. I did now. And he would pay.

Griffin frowned, his gaze focused on the empty air. "I don't know."

"What do you mean? His guilt is certain!"

"Is it?" Griffin countered. "The note is disturbing, yes. But I heard Guinevere's voice when she spoke of him the night of the party. It seemed obvious to me she considered him an annoyance, nothing more. Her tone was quite different when she pleaded with you to meet her at the saloon. If he had something to do with the prophecy, surely she would have sounded more concerned."

What the devil was wrong with the man? "Guinevere only interacted with three families before the night of the party. You've ruled out the Waites and the Lesters, and now shown Abbott threatened my sister!"

"And yet it doesn't change the face Guinevere spoke of him as a separate matter from that of the *Norfolk Siren*," Griffin countered, irritation showing in his voice. "Think, Whyborne!"

"I am thinking!" I put down my fork, my appetite utterly gone. "Abbott threatened Guinevere and argued with Stanford. What more proof do you need?"

"Some link to the disappearing ships would be nice."

"Clearly he has a grudge against our family! Guinevere spurned him, I was indirectly responsible for his father's death, and God only knows what Stanford did. Why not try to destroy our finances at the same time?"

"I spoke to your father," Griffin reminded me sharply. "The ship disappearances haven't harmed the Whybornes—quite the opposite, in fact."

Why would he not see what seemed so obvious? "Then the ships are part of some grander scheme. The man has a vendetta against us!"

"You don't know that."

"So what are we to do? Just wait for some—some proof of his guilt good enough to satisfy you? My sister is dead, and my mother has been attacked!" I crumpled up my napkin in my lap. "Will my corpse be the one to convince you?"

"Damn it, Whyborne, don't you think I'm worried?" Griffin hurled his fork onto the table; it bounced off and hit the floor beside Saul.

"Your Father has turned Whyborne House into a veritable fortress, arming all the footmen and carrying his Remington from the war on his person. But accusing the wrong man won't help anything."

"I mean to do more than accuse him."

"I know, which is why I'm asking you to give me more time." His green eyes grew dark with memory. "Don't you think I've seen men in the Pinkertons, or the police, so certain of their convictions, so blasted overconfident they condemned suspects without sufficient evidence? Do you know what it feels like to see a man's widow crying over the corpse we gunned down, only to find out a week later he wasn't the guilty party after all?"

"That isn't the case here."

"You don't know. You can't."

A knock sounded at the front door. We both fell instantly silent and exchanged glances. "I'll answer it," Griffin said, in a tone that left no doubt our argument wasn't over. I followed him into the hall and leaned against the kitchen door, arms folded over my chest.

As Griffin's hand reached for the doorknob, the door burst inward.

A heavyset man charged into the hall, a wicked-bladed knife in his hand.

Griffin leapt back, and the knife passed through the air in front of him, just inches from his skin. Even as a cry of alarm escaped me, Griffin snatched my coat off its hook and hurled it onto his attacker.

The man dodged the coat, but it gave Griffin enough space to retreat toward the parlor, where his revolver lay within a desk drawer. The thug rushed after him, and I sprang forward, ready to leap on the man's back if I had to in order to keep him from Griffin.

A second shape slipped in through the front open door, all squirming tentacles and shark teeth. The ketoi's unsettlingly human eyes met mine, and it hissed like some eldritch cat.

I bolted for the stairs. The sound of its claws on the wooden floor tracked its progress at my back. Was this the same horror that had sought to kill Mother, or some other?

The narrow risers foiled the abnormally long feet of the ketoi, slowing its ascent. I practically flew up the stairs and into the study. A throw lay on the couch; I snatched it up and turned back to the landing.

The ketoi bared its rows of shark teeth from the top of the stair. I hurled the heavy throw over it, covering its head and shoulders in the thick folds. It scrabbled at the cloth, swaying dangerously unbalanced.

I struck it as hard as I could in the chest. The thing went over backwards, snarling and flailing in the folds of the throw, flesh thumping on the hard edges of the risers. It came to a halt at the foot of the stairs.

I rushed down after it, not giving it time to gather itself. Springing from the sixth stair up, I landed on it with both feet. Something gave way beneath me with a wet snap, and I pitched forward. My palms burned against the hall rug.

There came the crack of a revolver. I couldn't breathe—who had fired the shot? Had Griffin reached his weapon in time?

The thuggish man who had broken down the door stepped into the hall.

Time slowed to a crawl, each second like an ant trapped in treacle. They'd killed Guinevere and Miss Emily, and threatened Mother, and, oh God, not Griffin, not him, anyone but him.

No rational thought existed, only terror and rage, and the rivers of power crawling beneath Widdershins. My throat ached, and belatedly I realized I'd screamed Griffin's name, but everything felt very far away.

Wind shrieked through the house, ripping pictures off the wall, sending my hat flying from its hook out the open door, battering down the man in the hall. I would kill him.

I'd kill them all.

I'd slay every hybrid abomination in this town, then take a boat to the ketoi city and dive deep, rip their hearts out from their ribs—

A heavy weight struck my back, knocking me to the floor. The revolver roared a second time, and the weight on me jerked away.

Then I was blinking in confusion, as the ketoi and hybrid fled out the door, both trailing blood. Griffin stood in the doorway to the parlor, his face grim and his smoking revolver in his hand.

I lurched to my feet with a cry. Griffin ran to the door, peered outside for a moment, then slammed it shut and jammed the umbrella stand beneath the knob. "Are you all right, Ival?" he asked.

My head felt light, my chest full of air. I grabbed him, his arms solid beneath my fingers, and pushed him back against the wall. His eyes widened in surprise.

"I thought they'd killed you," I said raggedly. Then I kissed him, desperate to erase the terrible moment when I'd feared the worst.

He kissed me back, hard. Perhaps he had the same fears, or perhaps it was simply the violation of our home, the one place we'd felt safe. Should I have obeyed Father, gone to Whyborne House and kept these monsters away from Griffin?

"It's all right," he murmured when our lips parted, although it seemed he said it as much to reassure himself as me. "I'm uninjured. Are you hurt?"

"No. I avoided those damned tentacles this time," I said with a shaky smile.

"Good. I'll make certain the house is secure. You find Saul."

Wrapping my hand around the back of his neck, I pulled him closer and kissed his forehead. Then I let him go and went to locate our cat.

Saul hid beneath the couch in the study, tail still half-bushed and ears canted back. I retrieved a can of sardines from the pantry and lured him out. By the time Griffin joined us, Saul had reverted to his usual purring self.

"No sign of them," Griffin said. "I secured the gate, and downstairs is locked up as well as it can be. Still, I'm not certain how much sleep I'll get tonight."

"Do you think they'll return?" If they did, I'd be ready. They wouldn't escape so lightly a second time.

"I don't think so. It's just...unsettling." He sat on the floor beside Saul and me. "Of all the times I've been attacked in my life, none have ever been in my own home. Or the string of apartments I thought of as home while in Chicago."

"I know. We're supposed to be safe here." My voice trembled with anger. Outside of these walls, so much of the world was turned against us. But here...here we were free to be ourselves. To sleep in each other's arms without fear.

Damn Abbott for doing this to us. The attack on our home must surely prove his motive a vendetta against my family. It had taken two years, but he'd finally found a way to turn whatever arcane knowledge his father left behind against us.

I didn't bother to say it aloud to Griffin. He didn't understand.

But the twins would.

The night we'd roamed the streets of Widdershins...had I ever truly even considered living so without fear before? Casting off all the shackles of convention and self-doubt and finally being free?

Of course not. Freedom had been something reserved for Stanford, who did as he pleased the entire time we grew up.

No more. Abbott wouldn't threaten my home with Griffin. I'd destroy him first.

And once he was gone, I'd tell Griffin everything. Show him we didn't have to live just within these walls. With my protection and that of the Endicotts, we'd do whatever we pleased, and no one would dare threaten us ever again.

CHAPTER 18

THE NEXT NIGHT, I stood on the street corner not far from the museum. The wind blew in from the ocean, cold fingers rifling through my hair and chilling my ears. I bounced in place, unable to stay still, but not from nervousness.

From anticipation.

"Cousin," Fiona greeted me with a fierce grin.

I turned to greet them with a grin of my own. Fiona wore a tweed skirt and coat—she might have been going out with a shooting party on the moors of her homeland. Theo's attire was a bit more elegant, the colors darker.

"Percival," he said, and clasped my gloved hand in one of his. "Time to put paid to Mr. Abbott and bring and end to this madness."

I'd sent a note to them that morning, telling them of the attack and my decision. Later in the day, I'd informed Griffin I needed to stay after hours to work on the Hallowe'en tours with Christine. No reason for him to worry, should this take longer than expected.

But there were three of us, and only one of Abbott. How long could it possibly take?

Perhaps we'd go out to a saloon again, afterward. Or maybe I'd just go home and drag Griffin into bed, make love to him until we were both exhausted, our throats raw from screaming each other's names.

"The Abbott mansion is on High Street," I said.

Fiona bowed with a little flourish. "Lead the way."

The three of us strode abreast down the sidewalk. We didn't precisely force anyone out of our path and into the street—rather, they took one look at us and melted aside. The electric lights competed with the moon, and shouts and song poured from within restaurants and theaters. The cold, crisp October air flooded my lungs, invigorating and wild. I wanted to laugh with the joy of being alive and untrammeled.

Fiona snatched a bottle of beer from a man talking with his friends, took a swig from it, and handed it back. They all gaped at us in shock, seeming not to know how to react to such outrageous behavior from someone dressed as she was. Two young women with their beaus left off their conversation to watch us pass by, and Theo smiled and tipped his hat to them. It was as if they could sense we were different, set apart, as if we radiated some strange magnetism which both attracted and repelled.

As if they knew we were strong, and we were free, and nothing could possibly stand against us.

"There it is," I said, as the Abbott mansion came into view. "See how there are only a few lights? Abbott lost a fortune after his father died. Threw it away on bad investments and racehorses."

"Not much of a sorcerer if he couldn't hex the other beasts," Fiona said with all the disgust of a professional for the dilettante.

"He barely has any staff left. Can't afford to pay them all." Staring up the mansion's darkened windows, something seemed to reach inside my chest and twist my heart. I couldn't save Guinevere or Miss Emily, but I'd be damned if I let the evil within this house take Mother or Griffin.

I could put an end to it tonight. *Would* put an end to it, alongside Theo and Fiona. As sorcerers—as Endicotts—it was our responsibility to act. While others might hesitate a fatally long moment, we would step into the gap and do whatever needed to be done.

"What do you think would be the best way to enter?" I asked. I couldn't pick locks, the way Griffin did, but perhaps we could still sneak in through an unsecured door.

Theo draped his arm lazily over my shoulder and leaned against me. "Why, through the front door, old chap. What other way is there to make an entrance?"

Of course. I was still trammeled in my thinking. "None at all," I murmured.

"Oh, let me," Fiona said, clasping her hands with excitement.

Theo laughed. "By all means, sister. Go ahead."

She strode toward the house, Theo on her heels, and I *felt* the world around them still, as if waiting for their will to guide it.

God. This was what I'd always wanted, without even knowing it. This control, this purpose, this certainty. Thanks to Father—thanks to society—I'd spent my life second-guessing every move, every thought. Even Griffin, who loved me, cast a dark eye on my arcane studies and strove to hold me back.

But now I didn't have to wonder, or worry, or fear. I would save Griffin, and Mother, and everyone else I loved. The twins and I would put an end to this. The guilty would be punished, the monsters slain, and we'd all be safe. Free.

Fiona held out her hand as she walked, sketching sigils in the air and shouting in Aklo. A gust of wind smashed open the door, all but ripping it from its hinges. The huge vase sitting on a table just inside crashed to the marble tiles, bursting into pieces of blue ceramic, which crushed into powder beneath our shoes.

A man in butler's attire ran into the hall, and was promptly hurled into a wall. He struck it hard and collapsed to the floor, dazed.

Theo seized him by the chin, jerking his head back. "Where is your master?"

The butler blinked. "I...I..."

"Where!"

"The library! Second floor!"

Theo released the man. Stepping back, he wiped his hand on his trousers, as if he'd touched some contamination. "Second floor it is."

The twins headed for the grand staircase winding up from the entry hall. I paused by the butler, whose dazed look was slowly giving way to one of fear. "Stay out of our way," I warned. If he was at all like Fenton, he was deep into his master's most filthy secrets, nearly as guilty as Abbott.

Whatever other servants Abbott kept, they had less loyalty to their master or more terror of us. A maid screamed and dropped a pile of linens, fleeing for some perceived shelter. The rest we glimpsed only as shadows: the edge of a skirt, the sound of steps. The same presentiment of power that had cleared the sidewalk for us yet held force, sending the servants scurrying for their lives.

The second floor landing opened onto a long corridor leading from one end of the great house to the other. We walked along it, power swirling around us in a haze. The mirrors lining the walls shattered as we passed. We ignored most of the doors by common consensus, until we reached a pair of heavy oak, which could only lead to a room of importance.

This time, I summoned the wind, funneling it down the corridor and slamming into the doors. Fiona clutched at her hat and laughed in delight as they burst open.

We entered as one; Fiona watching our left, Theo our right, and myself straight ahead, as if we'd practiced this a thousand times before. The library proved to be a large room, books lining three walls, the fourth hosting enormous windows to let in light during the day. Tonight, only the moon and a single lamp illuminated the room.

Thomas Abbott sprawled in one of the overstuffed chairs, coatless and holding a glass of liquor in his hand. Books lay open around him in a rough circle, as if he'd been in the act of consulting them before giving it up as a bad job. Even a glimpse showed arcane sigils and gutter Latin, Aklo and Cabalistic designs.

We came to a halt before him. This man had killed my sister, murdered Miss Emily, and threatened both my mother and my lover. And how many others had died at his behest, aboard the ships at the hands of the ketoi? How many widows and mothers and siblings now wept because of him?

He deserved to die for his crimes.

"Thomas Abbott," I said, and my words burned with barely leashed power.

Strangely, he didn't seem surprised to see us. Instead, he saluted me with the glass and drained it. "Percival Endicott Whyborne. Funny. I'd never thought you'd be the one Stanford sent for me."

The man must be drunk. "Stanford didn't send me."

Abbott peered at me blearily, as if he'd mistaken my identity. Then he shook his head. "Of course he did. Why bother to deny it? I got desperate and stupid." He waved his empty glass vaguely in our direction. "I thought, it's not like you Whybornes don't have plenty of money, right? And I know just what Stanford's been up to. And then Guinevere comes back, and I've got her too. The way she used to dance on my cock..."

The glass exploded in his hand, and he let out a startled cry. The wind began to rise, ruffling my hair, just waiting for my word. My mouth tasted of smoke, fire longing to be unleashed. "You murdered her, you filthy bastard!"

Terror seemed to cut through his alcoholic haze. "Murdered Guin? What the devil? She's—she's dead?"

"Don't lie to me!" The pages of the books ruffled in the gale blowing through the room. One of the windows came unlatched, banging open. "We know what you've done. You summoned the ketoi. Sunk the ships or killed the crew and left them adrift—"

"Destroyed ships?" He stared at me as though I had gone utterly mad. "The goddamned *Oarfish* just washed up the night before last. I invested every last penny I had in her. I'm ruined."

"*Liar!*" I screamed. "We found the threatening letter you sent to

Guinevere! You said you'd kill her, said none of us could save her!"

"No!" Abbott shied back in his chair, eyes wide with horror. "I admit I was blackmailing her, all right? Told her I'd find a reporter eager to make his name through scandal and reveal everything that used to go on in Newport. Something to make the Vanderbilt divorce seem like schoolyard gossip in comparison. The papers here might be afraid to print anything your father doesn't like, but the ones in Boston or New York would be more than happy to drag her name through the mud. I wanted to convince her the Whyborne name couldn't save her if she didn't cooperate, but I didn't kill her, I swear!"

"What a pathetic attempt to save your worthless skin," Fiona said. "We know about the prophecy."

"I don't know what you're talking about! Believe me, please!" he begged.

"Even if we did believe you, it wouldn't be enough." Theo pointed at the books lying open around Abbott's chair. "It's clear you've been learning sorcery. You're a danger to everyone, Mr. Abbott, whether you killed Guinevere and are working with the ketoi or not."

"I don't know what the ketoi are! Please!" Abbott shrank in on himself, all drunken bravado gone now. "The books—my damned father—this was his legacy. I wasted a year trying to learn it, trying to get even the smallest result from it. But there was nothing."

"No," I said, because it couldn't be true. I'd mastered the fire spell in a single evening, and even if these books were poorer teachers than the *Arcanorum,* Abbott should have learned their secrets in a year of study.

He shook his head wildly. "I thought it was just nonsense. I was giving up. But you...it isn't, is it? God, please, I'm sorry! I should never have turned to blackmail, not of one of the old families, anyway. Please don't kill me!"

Theo's eyes narrowed behind his spectacles. "You're a liar and a sorcerer. There is no reprieve."

"Stop!" Griffin cried.

Griffin and Christine stood in the doorway behind us, both of them out of breath as if they'd run here. Griffin clutched his revolver, but held it pointed at the floor.

"What are you doing here?" I demanded. Blast, he wasn't supposed to find out about any of this until I was ready to tell him.

"I came to the museum, to tell you the loss of the *Oarfish* will leave Mr. Abbott ruined." Griffin's mouth was nothing but a hard line. "Only to discover you lied about working late."

"And didn't tell me!" Christine put in. "I must say, I'm hurt. I thought we were friends."

"We *are* friends. And, Griffin, I didn't tell you because I knew you'd never approve!"

"Of you killing an innocent man? You're certainly right about that."

"Innocent?" Fiona asked with a laugh. She strolled around the back of Abbott's chair. He shrank down, as if he thought he could vanish into the seat cushion. "Mr. Abbott here isn't innocent. He's already confessed to blackmail and to attempting to learn the arcane arts." She reached down and trailed her fingers through his hair. He whimpered. "So run along home like a good boy, and let us do what needs to be done."

Griffin raised his revolver and pointed it at her. "Step away from him."

"Griffin! What the devil are you doing?" All the blood seemed to rush from my extremities. "He killed Guinevere!"

"Guinevere wasn't afraid of him," Griffin countered harshly. "Damn it, Whyborne, she knew he meant to blackmail her the night of the party, and she didn't care! Either she thought she could pay him off, or it paled to insignificance beside the real threat. Whatever the case, blackmailers go to jail, not the gallows."

"Look at these books," Theo all but snarled. "He means to learn sorcery!"

"It doesn't matter." Griffin kept his gaze trained on Fiona. "I won't stand here and let you kill a man because you think he *might* do something terrible eventually."

"I really would suggest you put the gun away right now," Theo said, and the threat in his voice was clear.

God—they could set fire to the powder, blow the damned thing up. Leave Griffin mutilated or even killed.

I put myself between the gun and Fiona. "Griffin, stop."

His eyes widened, and he lowered it instantly. "Whyborne, you have to see how wrong this is!"

"Do I? Blackmail, sorcery—Abbott may not have killed anyone, but surely it's only a matter of time." I gestured in Theo's direction, although I kept my gaze locked on Griffin's. "We're going to make this town a safe place to live, Griffin. Cut out the darkness from its heart."

"Like your ancestors did with Dunwich?" he asked.

Damn it. He had no intention of listening to reason and backing down.

"Have it your way," I grated through clenched teeth. "Mr. Abbott gets to live another day. If he's wise, he'll use it to leave Widdershins behind and never come back."

"Percival," Fiona objected.

"Hush, Fi," Theo said. I could feel his gaze on me. "So long as Mr. Abbott leaves his books with us and agrees to stay far away from sorcery in the future, the solution is workable."

"Y-Yes!" Abbott moaned. "Yes, I swear! Please, just don't kill me. I'll do anything you want."

Fiona sighed. "Sod it. Starting running, worm."

Abbott didn't need to be told twice. He bolted out of his chair and past us. The thud of his feet on the floor vanished toward the other end of the house and the stairs leading outside.

I locked gazes with Griffin again. "Happy?" I asked coldly.

"Not at all." He turned his back on me, shoulders stiff, and started in the direction Abbott had gone.

Curse the man—I'd done what he asked. What more did he want? Hurrying after him, I grabbed his shoulder and spun him around before he reached the stairs. "What's wrong with you?"

"I could ask the same thing!" Green fire snapped in his eyes. "You nearly killed a man tonight for a crime he didn't commit! You lied to me about your whereabouts—"

"Perhaps I wouldn't have to lie to you if you'd ever, for one *moment*, supported me." Both hands clenched his shoulders now; I had to resist the temptation to shake some sense into him. "Time and time again I've saved us with magic, and you've never done *anything* but hold me back."

The color drained from his face. "I've begged you to exercise caution—"

"You've tried to keep me trammeled, keep me bound by fear!" My voice rose louder and louder, but I no longer cared who might overhear our argument. "Now, for the first time in my life, I'm truly free."

Griffin wrenched from my grasp. "Is that what you call this? *Freedom?* Because I call it being utterly out of control."

"You don't understand the arcane, so you've let fear rule you—fear of my cousins, of me—"

"I've always been afraid *for* you, damn it!" Griffin gripped his sword cane in his hand, as if throttling it. "But given the way you've acted tonight, perhaps I should be afraid *of* you instead."

"Devil take you." My heart beat so loud I could barely hear my own voice. "Tonight was for you. It's all been for you. You and Christine almost died in Egypt, and I vowed I'd do whatever it took, learn whatever it took, to protect *you*."

Griffin stepped back toward the stairs. "Then perhaps we shouldn't be together."

I hadn't heard him aright. "What?"

"If *this*"—he gestured in the direction of the library—"was to protect me, then I don't want your protection."

"But..." He couldn't mean it. He'd misunderstood, somehow, or I had. "But I love you."

His eyes shone bright in the gaslight of the hall. "And I love you. But apparently it isn't enough."

He turned and descended the stairs rapidly. I started after him, but Christine caught me by the elbow. Good heavens, had she heard our entire argument?

"Let him go," she said. "He needs time away from you to think." Her lips pressed into a narrow line. "We both do."

"Christine," I began.

"Don't. Not now." Turning her back on me, she started down the stairs, leaving me alone in the hall.

CHAPTER 19

I SAT ON the edge of a bed in one of the guest rooms in the Endicotts' rented house. The light of a single candle struggled to banish the gloom, and a slightly dusty scent hung in the air. The smell reminded me forcibly of my old room in Whyborne House, of Griffin making love to me there in hopes of replacing bad memories with good.

Griffin.

I replayed his words again and again. Had he truly walked away from me, from our relationship? Left me alone once again?

I'd only been trying to do what was right. Protect him. Protect my family, and my town, and everyone else.

But Abbott hadn't been guilty, at least not of murder. Griffin's instincts had been right and mine wrong.

On the other hand, Abbott had been trying to learn sorcery. He'd done a terrible job of it, but what if he'd made some breakthrough? He'd already proved himself willing to blackmail my siblings for their scandalous acts. What might he have done with real power?

I tried to recapture the feeling of certainty, of invincibility I'd possessed earlier, but grief and worry crowded it out. What if Griffin's decision was permanent? What if he left me?

I leaned forward and buried my face in my hands. My belly clenched; at least I hadn't eaten dinner. Had he? Was he in bed even now? Or sitting alone in the study? Did he miss me, or was he too angry?

I should have insisted on following him home. Perhaps it was for the best, though. A few hours would give him the chance to think rationally. To calm down. Tomorrow I'd find him, and we'd talk. Griffin loved me, of that there was no question. I'd convince him, somehow. I'd say whatever I needed to make him take me back.

A soft knock sounded on the door. I composed myself hastily. "Come in."

Theo entered, carrying one of his spare nightshirts and a shaving kit. "I fear the nightshirt will be short on you," he said, "but it should do."

I summoned a grateful smile from somewhere, even though I'd seldom felt less like smiling in my life. "Thank you. Truly."

Theo laid the nightshirt over the back of a chair and came to sit beside me on the bed. "Mr. Flaherty doesn't deserve you."

"He worries for me."

"If he worried so, he wouldn't have kept us from doing what needed to be done." Theo shook his head in disgust. "Listen to me, Percival. Whatever qualities Mr. Flaherty may have, he's not one of us. He doesn't truly appreciate the dangers these other sorcerers pose, and so can't understand that sometimes one must act in haste, or else it's too late. England would have been overrun generations ago by ketoi hybrids and God knows what else, if our ancestors held back in our dealings with them. We are the ones with power, which makes it our responsibility to stand fast against the darkness. Whatever the cost."

I didn't know what to think anymore. I remembered again the feeling of euphoria, when I called and the world answered. The sensation of rightness, as though I was finally doing what I'd always been meant to do.

Theo put his hand over mine, tracing the scars with his thumb. "Flaherty wants you tamed. Safe. Common. Bound by society's niceties. He fears you'll grow beyond him, and so tries to keep you down on his level." Theo leaned closer. The heat of his body warmed mine, even though an inch of air still separated everything but our hands. "I don't. I want for us to reach new heights. Together."

He kissed me, mouth soft and tasting of wine. And I longed to kiss him back, because I desperately wanted everything he represented. Craved the life he and Fiona led, filled with energy and excitement, devoid of fear. Outside all the rules of society, because their constant defense of humanity had earned them that sort of freedom.

I threaded my fingers through his hair...and pushed him gently but firmly away.

"I'm sorry," I whispered. "I can't."

For a moment, I thought he might kiss me again anyway. Then he sat back with a crooked smile. "Well, I won't pretend not to be disappointed."

"I'm sorry," I repeated. "But I love Griffin, and I can't do this."

"I'm not asking you to give up on him," Theo said. "He walked away from you, though. Why spend the night in a cold bed if you don't have to?"

It was a sentiment Griffin would probably have agreed with, back in his wilder days in Chicago. "Because it isn't my way," I said with a rueful smile. "It isn't that you're unattractive." I remembered the feel of his fingers on my arm, tracing my scars. "If things were different..."

"But they aren't." Theo rose from the bed. "I'll leave you to your rest." He went to the door, then paused and glanced back at me. "If you change your mind, my room is the second door on the right."

The door closed softly behind him, and I was once again left alone.

I didn't sleep well. The absence of Griffin's arms was a constant ache, and his final words seemed to echo in my skull. I finally fell asleep sometime shortly before dawn, only to wake later than I'd intended. I had just enough time to use the borrowed shaving kit, before rushing to the museum.

A note from Griffin arrived with the morning mail. Feeling a bit of trepidation, I opened it. The sight of his familiar handwriting drew a twinge from my heart.

> *Ival,*
> *We need to talk. You're frightening me with your behavior. Come home tonight and just listen.*
> *Yours always,*
> *Griffin*

I sighed and rubbed at my aching eyes. I'd done nothing *but* listen to him. He was the one refusing to listen to me. I loved the man, but at the same time, I wanted to throttle him.

But at least he hadn't shut me out completely. There was still some hope for us.

A knock sounded on my door. "Come in—oh."

I'd almost forgotten Griffin wasn't the only one angry with me. Christine glowered from the doorway, her arms folded tightly across her chest. "Care to explain your behavior of yesterday?"

"I don't have anything to explain."

She crossed to stand in front of my desk, but didn't sit down. "You could have told me you were going to confront Abbott. I would have come with you. Instead you lied, to Griffin and me."

"I had Theo and Fiona with me," I snapped. "We didn't need your help."

"Clearly you did, since you almost killed the wrong man!"

"Damn it!" I rose to my feet, towering over her. She only glared up at me, completely uncowed. "You and Griffin both refuse to understand what's at stake here. At the moment, yes, it seems Abbott is only a blackmailer, which is bad enough. But what if he decides to find other members of the Brotherhood, or joins forces with some cult? What if a year from now, or five, or ten, he comes back with a lot worse than blackmail on his mind?"

"You can't go about killing people based on what ifs." Her nostrils flared in anger. "And you're right, I don't understand. I don't understand what's become of you lately."

"I'm finally being true to myself." My hands clenched, scars tugging. "I've spent my life conforming to society's expectations, and I've had enough. I'm done cowering, done hiding my magic, done sitting around waiting for something horrible to crawl out of the woodwork and threaten everyone I care about."

"I'm all for giving the boot to society's expectations, but not like this."

"Of course not like this." Anger and frustration coiled into something malignant inside me. "You want me properly cowed, don't you? To be someone you can just order about without any fear of contradiction. Just as Griffin wants some meek scholar overawed by his accomplishments with the Pinkertons."

"How dare you!" Christine's face went white, save for two spots of color high on her cheeks. "Are you mad, or merely stupid? I will not stand here and listen to this absurd nonsense! If you wish to apologize, you know where my office is."

She swept out of the room, nearly colliding with Dr. Gerritson as she did so. "I wouldn't advise speaking to Dr. Whyborne," she said loudly. "He's utterly irrational at the moment."

Dr. Gerritson watched her leave. He wore a brown sack suit today, although chances were excellent what lay beneath it would be unconventional. I hoped so—here was a man who didn't allow society to press him into a preconceived mold.

"Pay Christine no mind," I told him.

"Oh, I shan't." Gerritson gave me a sympathetic smile. "People often call me irrational. I've learned not to apply the label to others."

"Please, have a seat." I took my own, willing my pulse to calm.

Gerritson settled across from me. "I came to tell you I received a reply from my friend in Boston."

I'd entirely forgotten about his enquiry. Once I knew the jewelry's true provenance, I should have told him not to bother. "Ah. Thank you."

"Sadly, I doubt it contains more than you already knew."

His words caught me off guard. "What do you mean?"

"The necklace in Boston is another of yours," he said cryptically. "Here's the copy my friend made of the provenance."

Now completely baffled, I took the folded paper from him. The record was neatly typed on letterhead, and read:

Purchased at auction in Widdershins, MA, 1892. Previous owner: Mrs. Niles Whyborne, sold by her in 1887 as part of a collection. Inherited from her father, Mr. Isaiah Endicott. Isaiah Endicott received from his father, Michael Endicott, who inherited from his father, Gabriel Endicott. Received from his mother, Mrs. Zachariah Endicott, who brought it to the marriage as a dowry in 1780.

Prior origins unknown.

Less than an hour later, I stood on the doorstep of Whyborne House.

Clearly, Gerritson's colleague had made a mistake. Mother had indeed sold her jewelry to fund my studies at Miskatonic University, but the auction house must have gotten its records jumbled.

Just a mistake. A strange coincidence, but strange coincidences happened every day, didn't they?

Still, I would confirm the error, just to keep it from preying on my mind. Mother would laugh at the very idea. We'd have a cup of tea, and I'd return to the museum, shaking my head at my own foolishness.

A footman opened the door. I hadn't any idea of his name, but made out the bulge of a pistol beneath his coat. "Dr. Whyborne!" The footman hastily drew back, bowing to me. "Your father and brother are both out."

"I'm here to see Mother," I said. "Is she still in her old rooms, or did Father convince her to change them?"

"The former, sir." He bowed a second time, more deeply.

I went directly up to Mother's room. The windows stood open to the cold October air. Mother stood before one, her hair unbound and blowing in the breeze. Half-finished letters lay scattered everywhere in a drift of paper, and a stream of smoke rising from the wick of a candle showed it had just been blown out.

"Mother!" Concern cut through every other emotion, and I hurried to shut the windows. "You'll catch your death."

"I've been practicing summoning the wind. In case the creature, or more like it, should return."

I took her hands; they were icy cold. "The chill isn't good for you."

"My daughter is dead. My friend is dead. What does a chill matter?" She looked up at me solemnly. "Are you not proud of me?"

"Of course I am." Griffin had never been proud of my arcane accomplishments. I wouldn't make the same mistake. "You're amazing." I kissed her forehead. "Shall I call for tea?"

"No." She pulled her dressing gown closer. I ushered her to the divan and wrapped a thick blanket around her carefully. "I'm glad to see you, but shouldn't you be at your work now?"

"I needed to ask you something." I settled into a chair beside her and took the bracelet from my pocket. "We found this among Guinevere's belongings. I know it might sound strange, but have you ever seen jewelry of this sort before?"

She would say no, of course. It was the only possible answer.

"Ugly, isn't it?" she asked, making a face. "I can't imagine why Guinevere would have brought it with her from England. I can barely believe she took it with her in the first place."

"I..." Was that a yes? "It's familiar to you?"

"Of course." Mother plucked the bracelet from my palm, turning it over in her hands. "It belonged to my great-great-grandmother. I had more pieces like it, an entire set, but the style...well, there was no question of ever actually wearing it. But since it had come down to me, I felt it only right to pass at least one piece on to Guinevere." Her eyes grew misty for a moment, then she shook herself. "The rest I sold for your university fund. And an excellent trade it was—can you imagine anyone wearing this to a party?"

I stared at the bracelet. The pearls glowed richly in the light, as if mocking me. There was some explanation, some ordinary explanation. There had to be. "Where...where did she get it? Pirate loot, perhaps?"

She laughed. "Pirate loot? Percival, really. Have you been sneaking looks at the adventure fiction Griffin reads?"

"But it must have come from somewhere."

"I'm sure it did." Mother shrugged. "I assume she inherited it herself, or else her husband gave it to her. In all honesty, I don't know much about her—not her name, or even where she came from."

"Can you tell me anything?" God, she had to. "Any details at all?"

A concerned frown creased her face. "Very little. She brought her own servants to the marriage. Emily was descended from them actually. Her mother was responsible for saving my mother, when

Father..."

"Went mad." I'd heard the tales before. Isaiah Endicott, my grandfather, had gone mad shortly before his wife gave birth to their first child. Mother. He'd attacked my grandmother, screaming he'd cut "it" out of her, then committed suicide shortly thereafter.

God. Zachariah Endicott had murdered his brother and fled England. And done astonishingly well for himself, for someone who arrived on foreign shores with nothing but the clothes on his back.

He'd probably known about the ketoi, about their deals with humans, whispered through the legends of selkies who sought to spread their seed to the land. Their copious golden jewelry, which they wore like barbarian kings. Had he traded his bloodline for the wealth to start over in the sort of comfort he'd known all his life in England?

No. The Endicotts hunted monsters. They didn't marry them. Didn't lie down with some shark-toothed creature. It was impossible.

Wasn't it?

An unknown wife. Mysterious servants, bound to the family for generations. If Isaiah hadn't known what his great-grandfather had done, if he'd only learned the truth shortly before his own child was to be born, had he tried to put an end to it?

An end to a line of monsters?

Griffin and Christine had been right. Daphne, or Nitocris, or whoever she'd been at the time, had been right.

There were indeed hybrid monsters amidst the elite of Widdershins. And I was one of them.

CHAPTER 20

"**I HAVE TO** go." The words spilled from numb lips, and I only distantly recognized them as my own.

"Percival?" Mother reached for me. "Are you all right? What's wrong?"

"Nothing." It was a lie, perhaps the biggest I'd ever told. "I'll see you later."

The house swayed and reeled around me as I descended the steps. It all made sense now. Somehow, Guinevere had discovered our true heritage, before she'd ever returned to these shores. Otherwise, she wouldn't have brought the jewelry with her.

Once back in America, she'd recruited Miss Emily, who had must have known the truth all along. She—they—knew the ketoi were behind the ship disappearances, and meant to warn someone who might believe them.

Me.

I wasn't human. Whatever I had believed about myself, it was all a lie, wasn't it?

What would Christine think, if I told her? Or Theo and Fiona? How proud I'd been when the twins praised my arcane ability. No wonder I seemed to have an uncanny knack for the spells. A line of sorcerers, crossed with a line of abominations...of course Abbott had to study for a year what had taken me a night. He had at least been human.

Theo and Fiona had encouraged me...but they thought they

prompted a human man. Not some blasphemous horror crawled out of the deeps. I was the very thing our family was supposed to hunt and kill, an abomination that talked and walked like a man, but wasn't. The twins would turn away in utter disgust at the very sight of me, and with every reason.

And Griffin...

I clutched at the bannister to keep from falling. If he found out...if he learned the *thing* he'd had in his bed wasn't even human, realized he'd let a monster perform such intimate acts with him...

He'd hate me. Hate himself.

Nausea roiled in my belly, but I choked it down. I had to get out of this house. I had to think.

Once on the street, I paused and took a deep breath. The fishy scent of Widdershins flowed over me, reminding me forcefully of what Griffin had always said. I smelled of the ocean. Of good things, he'd claimed. But he'd been so very wrong.

My very blood tainted me. No wonder my life had turned into a dime novel—surely a monster must attract other monsters.

I was dangerous to everyone around me, wasn't I? Christine...I'd have to give up my position at the museum. And Griffin...

If only I could make everything all right. Fling myself at his feet and beg forgiveness. But no amount of groveling would change what I was. All the words the Endicotts had spoken about my true nature echoed inside my skull, mocking me.

My true nature was the sea and blackness, stinging coils and shark teeth. No wonder the dweller in the deeps had chosen me to call upon. Dear heavens, when it had communicated with me, it had spoken of "humans" as if they were something apart from us both. At the time, I'd never realized how literally its words were meant.

I stumbled through the streets, as if movement could distance me from my own thoughts. I bumped into a man's shoulder—he turned to shout at me, but his face went ashen. I must look truly deranged, and yet I couldn't bring myself to care.

I found myself standing at the gate to the house I'd shared with Griffin. The only place I'd ever truly felt at home. The one place I could never go again.

Thank providence, he wasn't there when I entered. Saul ran to me, rubbing against my legs and mewing loudly, as if he wished to comfort me. I picked him up and cradled him, smelling the woodsy scent of his marmalade fur for the last time.

"I'll miss you, old tom," I whispered.

I grabbed my valise and flung random items into it; when it was full, I couldn't even remember what I'd packed. Not that it mattered.

Father would see to it I had whatever I needed.

In the parlor, I scribbled a note, explaining after our argument, I'd decided to return home to Whyborne House. As an afterthought, I added Griffin's services were no longer needed by any of us. We still didn't know who had murdered Guinevere, but it would be utterly wrong to involve Griffin in our tainted doings a moment longer.

I picked up the note and pressed my lips to it. "I love you," I said helplessly. "Oh God, I'm so sorry."

I wanted to stay. Wanted to curl up on the couch and cry until Griffin returned. Wanted him to hold me and tell me everything would be all right.

But it wouldn't. I'd have to confess the truth. See the horror and revulsion on his face, as he realized I'd contaminated him.

So I laid the note carefully on the desk and walked out, locking the door gently behind me.

I stood on the sidewalk outside of Whyborne House. Rain had moved in, and thunder rumbled, far off but drawing closer. I'd left my umbrella at home—no, it wasn't home anymore. I couldn't think of it as such. At Griffin's house. Cold water dripped down the back of my neck and beneath my collar, and my coat smelled of wet wool.

My grip tightened on my valise. I'd sworn I'd never return here. Never spend another night in the somber prison of my third-floor room.

I could turn away. Find an apartment for rent. But ordinary people would be exposed to me then. Far better to keep all the monsters locked up in one place, where the only people they could savage were each other.

I'd thought I was finally free. God, what an idiot I had been.

The footman seemed surprised when I came in through the door. "Sir—you're soaked. Let me get your coat."

I shed it and handed the valise to him. "Take these things to my old room and have it aired out. Has Father returned?"

"Yes, sir. Just a little while ago. He's in the study."

Of course. Best to get this over with. To hold on for a little while longer, before I could lock the door to my room behind me and unravel completely.

The walk to the study had a dreamlike quality. Or perhaps a nightmarish one. How often had I traversed the hall leading to this room, knowing Father would shout and berate me? How often had I silently told myself to be strong, to not give in?

I should have given in. It would have saved us all time, and maybe been less painful in the end. At least then I wouldn't have had a glimpse of some other life.

Father sat behind the desk, frowning at some papers in front of him. "Percival?" He set the papers aside and frowned at me. "Have you news?"

"I've come back." Perhaps if I said the words quickly enough, they wouldn't hurt so bad. "I belong here. I see that now."

His brows climbed toward his hairline, and his mouth opened slightly. Then his features relaxed into a smile, and he nodded. "I always knew you'd return. It's why I kept your room for you."

"Yes." I just wanted to get this over with.

"I'm pleased you've given up on your nonsense," he went on. "Will Mr. Flaherty be a problem?"

What? "No!" I said, perhaps a bit too hastily.

Father's brows lowered. "I won't ask what caused you to come to your senses. But if it resulted from a quarrel, there's always the risk Mr. Flaherty might wish some compensation in exchange for his silence. He should know I won't tolerate a threat to this family. It's my duty to protect us, even if it means doing unpleasant things from time to time."

Oh God. God, he sounded like me, like I had last night, threatening Abbott.

Bile stung the back of my throat as I stared at my father. I'd always told myself I was nothing like him. Taken a perverse sort of pride in our differences. Believed if I held his position, with money and power, with people who relied on me, I'd do better.

Instead, the moment I got a little bit of power...I turned into him.

"I'm a monster on both sides," I said aloud. A hysterical laugh tried to escape, and I barely bit it back.

Father's scowl deepened. "Have you been drinking?"

"If only I had. It's not enough to have gotten the blood of abominations through Mother, but now I find I'm turning into you. At least it takes a spell to become a full ketoi, but apparently the Whyborne side doesn't even need that!"

"What the devil are you going on about?" he demanded. "Did Mr. Flaherty repeat his nonsense to you? Bad enough he had the gall to suggest I might know something about these creatures. I won't hear such things from you as well."

"Did you?"

"Did I what?"

"Did you know?" The papers on his desk rustled, the wind rising around me. I didn't care enough to stop it. "Did you know we're not human? Not Mother, not Stanford, not Guinevere. And not me."

"I won't put up with this nonsense. Go to your room and don't return until you're sober."

He didn't know. "Christine asked if I was a changeling." The wind grew more violent, scattering papers. "But no, we're a bunch of cuckoo's eggs, slipped into your nest where you thought to find human children."

"Enough!" Father surged to his feet, face darkening with anger. "Cease this at once, Percival! How dare you say such things about our family?"

"Because it's true! Zachariah Endicott married a ketoi woman, and we're tainted with her blood. Even your precious Stanford."

"Get out," he ordered, pointing a shaking hand at the door. "I won't—I won't hear such things."

"You'll listen to me! For once in your damned life, you'll hear what I have to say!" Papers flew about us in a whirlwind, and a picture wrenched free of the wall with a crash. "I might be a monster, but you're worse! I *hate* you, and I hate this house. How could you imagine, even for a second, I'd return here of my own will? I finally thought I was free. And instead, here I am, back in the same place I started, the same cage!"

The crystal decanters of whiskey and brandy along the sideboard exploded in a shower of glass and alcohol. The wind howled along with me, and the lights flickered madly. Father shouted something, but I could no longer hear him, hear anything beyond the roar of blood in my head.

Hands grappled me from behind. "Ival!" Griffin yelled in my ear. No.

Everything stopped, the only movement that of papers slowly fluttering to earth like dying birds. Griffin's hold on me relaxed.

I wrenched free and stumbled away. He wasn't supposed to be here. He wasn't supposed to see me, to find out, to know...

"Ival," he said again, more gently this time. His hair was in disarray from the whirlwind, and he reached out to me, a pleading expression on his face. "What's happening to you? Talk to me, please."

I ran.

The cold rain had turned into a storm. Lightning crashed, and stinging hail pelted me, but I didn't care. The deserted streets transformed into rivers, utterly soaking my feet the moment I stepped into them.

It didn't matter. I staggered blindly, lost. So lost.

I felt hollow inside, all my rage gone. Nothing remained but grief. I'd never thought I could return to Whyborne House without going mad, but the process had taken a great deal less time than I'd ever imagined.

I didn't belong anywhere. Not with Griffin, not in my childhood home. Certainly not among decent people.

My wet feet carried me without a conscious destination. Eventually, I looked up, and found myself near the docks.

Had the sea been calling me home? My ancestress had slithered out of the ocean and birthed our line of hybrids. Maybe I belonged in the deep. Maybe I should just crawl back beneath the waves.

By the time I stepped onto one of the long piers, the rain had soaked me to my skin. I shivered violently, the cold air leeching the last bit of heat from me. I raised my head to look at the heaving ocean and discovered I wasn't alone.

A ketoi stood on the pier. Although its body was nearly sexless, something about the bones of its face suggested a female to me. The pattern of light and dark skin matched the creature I'd chased in the cemetery, the night we'd laid Guinevere to rest. Golden jewelry formed her only clothing, and the tentacles on her head lay very still, swaying just a little in the rain. She watched me solemnly with eyes I recognized from the mirror every day.

"Percival," she said. Her voice was rough but not unpleasant.

I swayed a bit. Was this some hallucination? Had I lost my senses at last? Was this thing actually talking to me? How did it know my name?

"Who are you?"

"My land name is Persephone."

So Griffin had been right, and Guinevere's last words had nothing to do with the Lesters after all. "Guinevere knew you."

"Our sister," Persephone said sadly. "Yes."

The rain clung to my lashes, and I blinked rapidly. "I don't understand. *Our* sister?"

She nodded and stepped forward. "Yes. Once we were together, in the sea of the womb, you and I. I am your twin."

"No." I ached to run, to fling myself into the water. Or wake up in bed with Griffin and discover the last week had been nothing but a hideous dream. "My twin sister died when we were born. When Mother lost her health."

Facts slid into place in my mind. When had the Endicotts done their ritual to kill the ketoi? About thirty years ago on Hallowe'en, Theo had said. Had it more precisely been twenty-nine?

It killed the young and the old, and pregnant females. As far away as Widdershins was from Cornwall, had some thread of blood connected us to the ketoi sacrificed in their ritual? Had it been our own hellish kin?

No wonder the doctors had failed to help Mother. The origins of her malaise lay not in disease, but ancient sorcery, wielded by those who would keep humanity safe from...us.

"I did not die." The ketoi—Persephone—cocked her head to one side, peering up at me. "But I might have, had I stayed. We were dying. The servant, Emily, feared both would be lost. So she chose to give one to the sea."

"One for the land, and one for the sea." But no, that was absurd. Whatever the meaning of the prophecy, it had nothing to do with me. "Why did she never say? All these years...why hide the truth?"

Persephone shrugged, a startlingly human gesture. "Our grandfather went mad and tried to kill our mother before she was even born. You chased me from the cemetery. Our mother tried to kill me, when I climbed to her window."

"If we'd known..."

"Perhaps it would have been different. I don't know. Perhaps it simply seemed too great a risk. Matriarchs rule beneath the waves, so Emily chose me to take. She summoned the ketoi and gave me to them. The transformation spell saved my life."

I closed my eyes, then opened them again. Nothing I'd ever believed was true. Not about me, or my sister, or anyone. "And the dead girl in the post mortem photograph? The one buried in the casket meant to be yours?"

"We survived that night. Others did not."

And Mother never knew. Father didn't. All these years, their daughter had swum beneath the waves, alive but monstrous.

Despite her inhuman form, I hadn't felt any fear of her at all the entire time we'd stood on this pier. Perhaps some deep part of me recognized the twin who had curled beside me in the womb.

"Why now?" I asked. "Why—"

The sound of running feet drummed on the boards behind me. Griffin raced toward us, his face white with fear and his sword cane in his hand. "Ival! Get back!"

"No!" I flung out my arms to either side. "Griffin, wait."

There came a soft splash. I spun about to find the pier behind me empty. No fins broke the heaving, wind-tossing waves.

Griffin halted beside me. "Why did you stop me?"

I stared bleakly at the empty waves. "Because the ketoi is my sister."

CHAPTER 21

GRIFFIN SHEATHED HIS sword cane. The rain plastered his curls to his face, and I longed to brush them away from his eyes. But I couldn't bring myself to touch him.

"What do you mean?" he asked cautiously.

"What I said. You were right...Daphne was right...we're hybrids." The entire story spilled out of me, from Theo and Fiona's comments on my magical proficiency, to the provenance of the jewelry, to my realization the horrors plaguing the town, killing sailors, and murdering everyone who might stand against them, were my own people.

My own blood.

When I'd finished, Griffin stared at me numbly. "Oh." He took a deep breath, then let it out slowly. "I wondered...but I dismissed it, as you did. How could my love be one of the very monsters we've fought against?"

Each word laid me open, like a razor against skin. "I'm so sorry." My throat tried to close against the words, but I had to get them out now, while I still could. "Just...try to forget you ever met me."

His brows drew together. "I didn't mean—" he began, reaching for me.

"Don't touch me!" I jerked away. "Don't you understand? Aren't you *listening?* I'm descended from the ketoi. A part of me isn't even human. I'm...I'm tainted."

He grasped my arms, fingers tightening when I tried to pull away.

"You are not tainted. Or corrupted, or anything else. I don't give a damn who—what—your ancestress was. I only care about you."

My eyes burned. "You just said I'm a monster."

"No!" He stepped closer, until his thighs pressed against mine. "Listen to me, please. If you're one of the monsters we've fought against, then—then they can't *be* monsters. No more so than humans, at any rate. Some terrible and some good, but not inherently evil."

"What if you're wrong?" I swallowed hard. "You've already seen what I'm capable of. With Abbott. And that came from the non-aberration side of my family. What if...what if there is some darkness in me? Something terrible inside?"

"Then we'll face it together." Griffin touched my face with one hand, fingers tender. Finding the hotter wetness of tears amidst the cold rain. "You are the love of my life."

"But it isn't enough," I echoed the words back at him.

"I should never have left last night. I should have waited and talked. I knew I'd done the wrong thing as soon as I got home. Because I realized no matter how frustrated and angry and scared you make me, I won't give up on you." He shook me gently. "Do you understand, Ival? I love you, and I will *never* give up on you."

I tried to speak, but a sob tore its way out of me instead. Crumpling into his arms, I buried my face in his hair and wept while he held me tight.

"I'm sorry," I said yet again. I sat shivering on the hearthrug in the study, my sopping clothes removed and a blanket bundled around me instead. Despite the crackle of the fire only a few feet away, I couldn't seem to get warm, as if the cold day had crawled in through my skin.

Griffin carefully set a tea tray on the table beside me. He'd exchanged his wet clothes for dry, but forgone shirt and vest alike, only wrapping himself in a dressing gown while he went down to make tea.

"What are you apologizing for?" He poured a cup, then gave it to me. The heat scalded my fingers, but I cradled it gratefully in my hands.

"There's rather a lot of choose from, isn't there?" I asked ruefully. "My behavior has been abominable, I know. It just seemed so right at the time. So easy."

"The magic?" he guessed. Pouring a cup of tea for himself as well, he settled cross-legged in front of me.

"Yes." I sighed. "I should have listened to you. I wanted to protect us, you and Christine and everyone else. My arcane studies saved our lives, and I only wanted to see their usefulness, not any dangers. When Theo talked about our true natures, about how we don't bow to society, but make society bow to us..." I shook my head miserably.

"It's a seductive thought," he agreed with a wry twist of his lips. "Those men I spoke of before, the Pinkertons or the police, began wanting to help people. Believed they *were* helping people. 'One can't make an omelet without breaking eggs' and all the other platitudes which let them sleep at night. When you're certain your cause is just, it becomes easy to excuse almost anything to further it."

"You were right all along, though. About the sorcery. I rushed ahead and didn't think, didn't consider the consequences. I lied to you and ended up lying to myself." I bowed my head. It wouldn't be easy, but it had to be done. "I'll give it up. All of it. Stay out of your investigations. Never cast another spell. Go back to being boring old Why-were-you-born."

"The one thing you've never been is boring, my dear." He set his tea aside and rested his hands on my ankle. "But before you make any drastic decisions, will you hear my apology?"

"You have nothing to apologize for."

"You're wrong." Sadness darkened his eyes. "If I hadn't been so against your sorcerous studies, you wouldn't have felt the need to hide them from me again and again. I thought magic was just something you did. But now I realize I was wrong. It's something you *are*. Whether by your ketoi blood or your Endicott, or some strange combination of the two, I don't know, and it doesn't matter."

His words felt true in my gut. "Still, I don't have to practice it."

"I won't ask you to clip your wings." He took my teacup from my hands and set it aside, then twined his fingers with mine. "I've seen how you've bloomed, my dear. Discovered yourself, your confidence. And although I'd like to think our relationship might have something to do with it, I'm not quite so arrogant as to claim full credit. We could have spent the last two years talking about your sorcery, about the good your spells have done for all of us, including you. And discussing, as well, the dangers of taking it too far. Instead, I made you feel as though I wanted to hold you back."

I winced. "Griffin—"

"Ival." He squeezed my hands. "I'm sorry. I don't want you to feel like you have to hide anything. If you wish to learn some new spell, do so here, and don't fear I'll chastise you. Just promise to discuss it with me, and listen if I raise a concern."

"Are you sure?"

He nodded. "I'm sure. Magic is a part of you, the way it isn't other people."

I looked away. "You mean humans."

"I mean other people." He let go of one hand so he could catch my chin with his fingers and turn my gaze back to him. "I love you—all of you. I love that you want to protect Christine, and your family, and me. And despite your zeal to see justice done at any cost when it came to Abbott, you didn't hurt your father today. You got angry and wrecked a bunch of his possessions, but you didn't hurt him."

"I'd already done enough harm." I found the courage to meet Griffin's gaze. "Thank you. For not turning your back on me. I thought once you found out the truth about my heritage, you'd be disgusted."

"And why would I be?" he asked, arching a brow.

"Because...well...all the things we've done together. Er, intimately. To know you've..."

"Been buggered by a fish-man?" he suggested.

"No!" My cheeks heated. "Well, yes, but I wouldn't have put it like that!"

Griffin laughed. "I'm sorry. Should have said seduced by a shark-man?"

"You're not taking this nearly as seriously as you ought," I grumbled, but in truth, I was desperately glad he could make such a joke.

Griffin shifted closer, until our knees pressed together. "Whatever you are," he said, "you were the same thing yesterday. And last week, and last month. Nothing has changed."

"Easy for you to say. You're not the one who just discovered he has a fish-woman for a sister."

"True. Do you think the prophecy might refer to the two of you?"

"No."

"You seem awfully certain."

I shrugged. "*The time will come for one to rise, To ride the foam and touch the skies*—does that *sound* like me?"

Griffin leaned in to kiss me, slipping one hand beneath the blanket as he did so. "Parts of it," he murmured against my lips.

I snorted. "I don't think that's the kind of 'rise' it means."

"Then I like my version better." He tugged the blanket from around me and spread it on the floor. "Lie down," he murmured. "Let me show you just how I feel about you."

I did as he asked. He trailed his gaze appreciatively over my naked form, without even a flicker of revulsion. It was more than I could ever have asked for, and my eyes burned again with emotion.

Griffin stripped off his clothes, the firelight painting his skin with gold. The sight of him stole my breath: firm muscles and broad chest, the dusting of freckles across his shoulders and the darker line of hair curling from navel to groin. My member roused in response, and he smiled. "Do you like what you see?"

"Very much," I whispered. "Do you?"

He bent over me, lips feathering across my temple, my cheek. "Yes," he whispered into my ear, before drawing back and kissing me hungrily on the mouth. He tasted of the tea we'd drunk, and I was reminded sharply of Theo's kiss last night.

"Last night," I said.

He stilled. "Yes?"

"Theo kissed me."

"I see." For a long minute he stared off into nothing. Then he met my gaze. "You know I'll forgive you, if it was more than a kiss."

"What? No!" I ran my hand over his face, tracing the lines of cheekbone and jaw. "I know you would, but there's nothing to forgive. I refused him immediately. I just...I didn't want to start anew by lying again, even by omission."

He looked at me searchingly...then his lips curved up into a smile. "I won't pretend I'm not relieved to hear it. An educated man... another sorcerer...that British accent..."

"Hmph. Perhaps I ought to be the one who's jealous."

He laughed softly and kissed me again, more leisurely, driving any thoughts of Theo out of my head. "Tell me what you want," I said. I reached for his length, but he caught my hand.

"I want to touch you for a while." His fingers skated over my collarbone, down to my nipple, pausing to tease. I gasped softly at the pleasure and arched my back in silent invitation. But he only grinned and took my right hand in his.

He traced the lacework of scars the lightning had left behind: down my fingers and hand, up my wrist and over my forearm, lingering on my elbow. "Do they trouble you?"

"Not really. Occasionally. When I use magic, mainly, as if they're sensitized to it."

He traced them all the way up to my shoulder, then said, "Roll over."

I obeyed. The lightning scars came to an end on my right shoulder blade. On my left showed another knot of scars, these caused by the vicious bite of Nitocris, queen of the ghūls. Although the infected bite had nearly cost my life, not even an ache remained now.

I lay on my belly, hard cock tucked down to point between my slightly parted legs. Griffin kissed first one shoulder, then the other, and the brush of his skin on mine made me shiver with desire. His cock slid against my crease, and he kissed the back of my neck. He breathed deep and nuzzled my hair. "You smell so good."

I closed my eyes at the reminder. "Like the ocean?"

"Like companionship." He kissed my neck again. "Like love."

He worked his way slowly down my spine, planting a little kiss on every vertebra, his hands tracing the curve of rib and flesh. An involuntary yelp escaped me when he bit me on one buttock. He laughed and repeated the same action on the other.

He gripped my buttocks in his hands, spreading me open. My breath grew short with anticipation, and after a moment, I was rewarded with the touch of his tongue on my fundament.

I bit my lip against a needy whimper, felt the soft breath of his chuckle on my exposed flesh. He licked and kissed until I squirmed beneath him. Then he dragged his tongue lower, over my balls and onto my cock, hard against the blanket.

"Griffin, please," I whispered.

"Turn over."

The request startled me; I'd assumed he meant to take me. But I did as he asked, rolling over onto my back. He nuzzled my thighs, then moved to my length and took me into his mouth.

After a heavenly few minutes, he drew back. His eyes were dark with lust, his lips full and red from sucking on me. "You taste so good." He moved to straddle my hips, so his prick lay against mine. "Smell so good. I love it. I love everything about you."

I slid my hands up his thighs to his buttocks, firm beneath my questing fingers. "You feel good, too."

"I'm glad." He leaned over me, bracing his hands to either side of my shoulders. "Hold us together and let me make it feel even better."

I wrapped one hand loosely around our cocks. The other I slid around the back of his neck, fingers tangling in his hair. His hips flexed, sliding us together, the slow, slick pleasure of his hard length against mine. I caressed the tip, gathered the liquid seeping from us both, spread it mingled together over our members.

"Look at me," he whispered. "I want you to know just how badly I need this, need you."

Only thin green rings showed around his dilated pupils. His lips were parted, damp from our kisses, from sucking on me. The expression on his face was one of desire, as raw as the friction of his cock against mine, the gasp of his breath. All the hollow spaces inside were filled with his presence, and I whispered his name over and over again.

He responded, rocking against me with greater urgency. "Yes, this, Ival," he said and a shudder of pleasure went through him. "This. Us, together."

It was too much. I dragged him down with my hand around the

back of his neck, kissing him hard, my tongue sliding in and out of his mouth like a cock. He sucked on it, and suddenly I couldn't stand it any longer. I moaned into his mouth, lights dancing behind my eyes, shattering and breaking in a wave of pleasure that dragged me down like an undertow.

His back arched, mouth pulling free from mine. The cords stood out against his neck, and his arms shook as he spilled onto my belly.

With a soft sigh, he lowered himself down onto me, kissing me softly. "Have I convinced you no part of you repulses me?" he asked.

"Yes." I returned his kiss. "Most effectively."

"Good." He took my hand and led me to the bedroom, where we slipped together between the icy sheets. I lay my head on his chest, listening to his heartbeat, while he stroked my hair tenderly in silence.

We would have to talk further about my sorcery. About what I had done, or almost done, to Abbott. But, impossible as it would have seemed just a few hours ago, I felt more hopeful than I had in a long time. We were finally together in full, all the pieces of our lives joined into one thing, and it didn't matter if they didn't all fit perfectly just yet.

I opened my eyes in the pre-dawn light to discover a ketoi clinging to the window and staring back at me.

I yelled and jerked upright. Then my muddled mind recognized the dark eyes blinking curiously at us. "Persephone," I gasped. "What the devil are you doing?"

"Let me inside," she called.

Griffin froze beside me, every muscle stiff. Not knowing what else to do, I wrapped the top layer of blanket around me, trying for some semblance of modesty while I went to the window. "What are you doing?" I repeated.

"We need to talk. Let me in."

Uncertain what else to do, I unlocked the window and slid it up. She eeled through, the claws on the tips of her fingers digging into the wood. No doubt it was how she'd scaled the house. And come to Mother's window, now to think of it.

God. Mother. She didn't know we were descended from sea-born aberrations, or that her youngest daughter still lived, or any of it.

"Couldn't you knock on the door?" I asked Persephone, clutching the blanket closer.

"But you were here," she pointed out. She peered at Griffin. "Why is this one hiding?"

"Because it isn't proper for you to just—just crawl into a man's bedroom when he's not dressed," I exclaimed. Although as she wore nothing but a flimsy loincloth of gold netting and a few gems, no doubt she had rather different ideas of modesty.

"I've seen land men before," she said with supreme indifference. Cocking her head to one side, she sniffed the air. "This one is your husband?"

"What?" Her questions kept catching me off guard. "That is, no, of course not. Only a man and a woman can wed."

"Truly? Land people are stupid, then." She held out a clawed hand to Griffin. "This is your custom, yes? My land name is Persephone, and my sea name is Sings Above the Waves."

For once, Griffin looked even more flummoxed than I felt. He extended his hand cautiously. "I'm, uh, Griffin Flaherty. Pleased to make your acquaintance."

"You don't sound pleased."

Dear God, did the ketoi have no manners, or was she blunt even for them? "You crawled in the window of our bedroom!"

Her tentacle-hair writhed, almost thoughtfully. "Ah. This is not polite. I have erred. Forgive me."

"Just—just wait downstairs," I told her. "Please."

"Yes." She turned and departed. Her long, webbed toes made her gait awkward, and I heard her shuffling gingerly down the stairs a few moments later.

"Well." Griffin slid out from under the covers, shivering as he reached for his clothes. "I already like her better than Stanford."

CHAPTER 22

IT WAS, WITHOUT a doubt, the strangest breakfast I'd ever eaten.

Persephone sat at our table, her appearance even more shocking against the backdrop of our ordinary kitchen. When we came down, we found Saul in her lap, purring so loudly the neighbors could probably hear him.

"Would you care for breakfast?" Griffin asked politely. "Coffee? Birthday waffles?"

Dear lord, it was Hallowe'en. Our birthday.

"You cook your fish. Disgusting," Persephone declared. She cocked her head to the side. "I don't know these 'waffles.'"

"Then this will be an adventure for us all."

I sat across from her, unaccountably nervous. It seemed impossible the twin sister I'd always believed to have died at birth was alive and a creature from the depths of the sea. "So...Emily was the one who gave you to the sea?"

"Yes." She scratched delicately behind Saul's ears with the tips of her claws. "The matriarchs told me the story, when I was old enough to understand. I had been born on land, hurt by sorcerers who sought to destroy our kind. My brother lived there still, and my mother and father. I wondered about you often."

"I see." Emily had known. She'd held the secret of our true nature —and presumably her own—all these years and never spoken it aloud. She'd had a daughter with no known father—did he live beneath the waves?

If she'd only told me...but what then? What would I have done with the knowledge? Would I have ever dared let Griffin touch me, or would the weight of my secret have driven us apart before we even had a chance to begin?

There was no way to know. Perhaps I ought to feel grateful rather than betrayed. "Are you a sorceress?" I asked. "Theo and Fiona—our cousins—said twins are often magically adept in our family."

In reply, Persephone held out her hand toward Saul's water bowl. The water swirled, lifted from the bowl in a streaming wave, like a fountain in slow motion.

Then it splashed down again, spreading water across the floor. I winced and shot Griffin an apologetic look.

God, I'd just met my sister, and here I already felt I had to apologize for her. We really were related.

"The ketoi have no sorcerers of their own," she said. "This is all I can do. But I think I could learn more." Her voice held a wistful note in it.

"It's amazing you've learned this much," I assured her. "Have you been happy, living beneath the sea?" Were abominations from under the ocean happy? I'd never wondered before.

She nodded. "Yes. For the most part. Until recently, when the Eyes of Nodens betrayed us."

I stiffened. "The Eyes? You mean when they tried to enslave the dweller in the deeps?"

"Yes. You saved the dweller." She smiled, revealing a mouth full of shark's teeth. "The god has returned to the abyss, but we still hear its dreams on certain nights."

Thank heavens I'd shielded my mind against such tampering. "Er, glad to be of service."

"When the Eyes of Nodens betrayed us, our influence on land was diminished." Persephone's face became serious again, which was far less disturbing than her serrated smile. "We could not trust the humans, the ones who do not share our blood. Some argue we should find those willing to take wives and husbands of the sea, so in time we might again have many eyes and ears upon the land." Her eyes darkened. "But others do not believe this. They call for war against the land. To kill or enslave those who do not have our blood, and to force the change to ketoi form upon those who do."

My fingers went cold. I wrapped them around the coffee cup Griffin set in front of me.

"And which side is winning?" Griffin asked. The smell of cooking waffles filled the air, but I knew he paid close attention to our conversation.

She made a sound of frustration. "I don't know how things are done on the land, but we have many cities. Families live within them, most related, but not all. The matriarchs appoint the city's chieftess, yes? The one who listens to the counsel of the matriarchs, but makes the final decision herself."

"That's...not how it is here." I wished Christine could hear this.

"Not all chieftesses agree what is to be done. Nor those of us within a city. The chieftess who met our sister Guinevere wished for a peaceful solution."

"Guinevere?" But of course she'd known, somehow.

"She went from this place," Persephone flapped her hand at our environs, "to another, near to a different city of ours."

"The one off Cornwall," Griffin said. "It must be."

"I do not know how she learned of their presence. There are many old legends among land people, it is said, of how to find a lover from the sea."

"Selkies," Griffin said, at the same moment I asked, "Lover?"

"Her land husband could not give her a child." Persephone shrugged her thin shoulders. "So she took a husband from the sea."

"God." I sat back in my chair, badly needing its support. The horrible thought I'd had on first hearing the legend had been right after all. No wonder she'd begged the earl's forgiveness in her last moments. The child he raised as his heir didn't belong to him. Or to any human father. "Oh, Guinevere, you fool."

"She summoned her lover, and he knew her for one of our blood," Persephone went on. Whatever ketoi mating customs might be, she clearly didn't find Guinevere's behavior particularly scandalous. "She learned of her heritage and our city here. So she wrote of it to our brother, Stanford."

"Wait, Stanford?" My head reeled. *Stanford* knew? "Why on earth would she tell him and not the rest of us?"

"I do not know. We were told only he needed our help." Persephone spread her hands, claws glistening faintly in the electric light. "His place in the land world was threatened, but we could save him. Our chieftess, who rules the city here, wishes war. Stanford told her which ships needed to vanish, and we took their sailors down into the depths to drown."

Was it true? Could Stanford be so selfish? "But surely such a war wouldn't benefit him," I said. "Even if the disappearing ships aided our family's investments, the rest of it...Guinevere's death, and Miss Emily's..."

Persephone leaned across the table and put her hand on top of mine. Her skin was slick and cool, like touching a dolphin. "I do not wish war. I spoke out, drew down the anger of our chieftess, Dives Deep. She sent me into exile."

The droop of her tentacles suggested she hadn't found exile an easy burden. "I'm sorry," I said.

"As am I. Dives Deep believes she is fulfilling a prophecy, and many agree."

"One for the land, and one for the sea," I said.

"Yes. She rules beneath the waves, and soon Stanford will command the town."

Damn it. What had Stanford said to Father the day I'd heard them arguing? About taking Whyborne Railroad and Industries to heights Father had only dreamed of? *The town will rise to his hand.* Did Stanford actually believe he was destined to take over Widdershins, even more than our family already had? And then what—make war on the rest of the land?

"Stanford certainly strikes me as the sort who would like to imagine himself the subject of a prophecy," Griffin said. He placed waffles and maple syrup on the table in front of us. Persephone frowned and sniffed skeptically.

"Yes." She poked at the waffle with a claw.

I winced. "Like this," I said, demonstrating use of fork and knife. She looked at me as if I were mad. Perhaps she was right; teaching table manners to a ketoi wasn't quite how I'd envisioned spending my birthday.

"Emily brought the stone Guinevere had summoned her sea husband with and used it to call me," Persephone continued her tale. "One of our land kin had a place where we might meet in safety. I would find you and Guinevere there, and we would speak together of how to stop the coming war."

What had her note to the bartender said? To expect one wet and one dry? One ketoi and one land-dweller, it must have meant.

"The bartender was a hybrid?" At least we knew the connection with the saloon now. Another thought occurred to me, and I lowered my fork and knife to the plate. "Amelie. Her mother taught her the poem. She must be a hybrid as well." No wonder her connection with the dweller in the deeps had been so strong. "I wonder if she knows?"

Persephone managed to slice off a piece of waffle, stab it with her fork like a savage, and maneuver it to her mouth. For a moment, she looked confused...then her face brightened. "Good!" she exclaimed, displaying a smile full of terrifying teeth and waffle fragments.

"I'm glad you like it," Griffin said, charming even under these circumstances. Actually, his smile rather gave me the impression he liked her despite her monstrous form.

If Miss Emily had chosen differently, I would have been the one on the other side of this table, with a razor-lined mouth and tentacles in place of hair. I ran my hand automatically through my unruly locks —I'd never complain about them again.

"Someone else knew Guinevere was going to meet us," I said. "And they killed her to keep it from happening. But who?"

Persephone licked syrup off her thin lips. "I do not know."

"If Stanford found out..." Griffin mused.

"Surely not!" I could believe a great many terrible things about my brother, but not this.

"He's behind the ship disappearances," Griffin said gently. "Guinevere knew—about the war against the land, about the prophecy, about the *Norfolk Siren*. Who else could it have been?"

"I don't know—but—but you don't have any evidence." I seized on the hope. "If I was wrong about Abbott, you might be wrong about Stanford."

"True," he said, but he didn't sound as if he believed it.

Our family might be many things, most of them terrible. Greedy and ambitious, willing to sweep aside any who got in our way, to use any method foul or fair, so long as it promised the most reward...and that was those of us who *weren't* aquatic monsters. But guilty of fratricide?

Zachariah fled England over the murder of his twin brother. And Isaiah had tried to kill his unborn child.

Fine. But Stanford and I weren't our ancestors. Whatever they had done, we weren't cursed to repeat their mistakes.

"We need to confront Stanford, either way," I said. "If he believes this wretched prophecy means he's destined to take command of the town somehow, we must stop him."

"Will your father help?" Griffin asked.

I started to ask Griffin if he'd lost his mind, but caught myself. "I don't know. We'll need to be very convincing indeed—this is Stanford we're talking about. And after my behavior yesterday, Father might not even let me set foot in the house. But we can try."

"Something is planned for tonight," Persephone said. She'd finished off her waffle while we spoke and stared sadly at her empty plate.

"Tonight?" I pushed my half-eaten portion across the table to her. "What?"

"I do not know." She helped herself to more syrup and tucked in. "But I met in secret with my friend, Stone Biter. He says it will happen at the place of bones."

"The cemetery?" I asked.

"I do not know."

"It would have to be," Griffin said. "What else could it mean?"

I rubbed tiredly at my eyes. "An even better question is: what does Stanford have planned in the accursed cemetery?"

"Necromancy?" Griffin speculated.

"He's no sorcerer," I pointed out.

"Neither was your father. That didn't stop the Brotherhood from finding sorcerers within their ranks, or outside of it when needed."

Blast. He was right. Weren't monsters from the sea bad enough? "We need to stop this," I said. "Theo and Fiona will help us, once I explain things to them. But what of the ketoi? If your chieftess is determined to start a war with the land...can we prevent her from doing so?"

Persephone's tentacles stirred thoughtfully. Crumbs of waffle decorated her upper lip. "Perhaps. There is an old law, seldom invoked in these days when the seas rattle with the noise of engines and few humans remember how to summon a lover from the waves. But it must be done face to face." She met my gaze. "I will need your help, brother."

This was the strangest morning of my life. "Y-yes. Yes, of course."

"We'll do whatever is needed," Griffin told her.

"Thank you, brother's husband." She glanced at the window. "Dawn is coming. I should not risk being seen. Meet me tonight, before the taste of the river turns to metal and blood."

"I don't have the slightest idea what you mean," I confessed.

"Upstream from the cannery?" Griffin guessed.

Persephone huffed. "Near to where I went into the river, when you chased me from the cemetery. There is a bridge."

I nodded. "Oh! Yes. We'll be there."

She rose. "Thank you for the food. And..." she hesitated, her manner suddenly diffident, almost shy. "It was a good thing, to meet you."

"And you." I could hardly believe I was saying it, but it was the truth. On impulse, I reached out and took her hands. They folded carefully over mine, the claws just resting against the backs of my fingers. "I'm glad to know you're alive."

She gave me her shark's smile. We opened the back door for her, and she slipped out into the rapidly lightening morning.

"Well, my dear," Griffin said as I shut the door. "After all of this, I feel better than ever about searching for my own brothers. Whatever faults they may have, I'm quite certain they will at least be human."

Shortly after dawn, Griffin and I stood on the walk in front of

Christine's boarding house. When she came out on the wide porch and saw us, her step hesitated, and for a moment, I thought she might go back inside and slam the door in our faces. Instead, she squared her shoulders and marched down the walk determinedly.

"Well?" she demanded, stopping a few feet away from me. "Have you come to apologize?"

"Yes."

"Oh." It took the wind out of her sails, but only for a moment. "Get on with it, then."

I glanced around nervously. The landlady peered out from behind the curtains of the downstairs parlor, a sour look on her pinched face. "Can we step away, please? Or find somewhere a bit more private?"

Christine huffed and led the way out onto the street. "We're away."

I accepted it was the best I was going to get. At least the neighborhood was a quiet one, with only a few people hurrying to work at such an early hour. "I'm sorry. My behavior was inexcusable. I had no right to say such things cruel things to you. You're my best friend, and I hope you will forgive my foolishness."

She eyed me a moment then thrust out her hand. "Very well. I forgive you."

We shook on it, but my nervousness only increased. The apology had been the easy part. "There's something else I have to tell you."

She frowned at my tone and glanced at Griffin. But he only looked at me. "Go ahead, my dear. I'm right here."

"Dear heavens, what is it?" Christine asked in alarm. "Don't tell me you have some incurable disease."

"What? No!" I stared at her in shock. "Why would you think such a thing?"

"You certainly looked upset enough. What is it then?"

"I'm trying to tell you! I'm...well. It seems I'm a ketoi hybrid."

"Oh." She blinked. "Are you certain?"

"I'm afraid so." I explained everything to her, including our early morning meeting with Persephone. When I finished, she looked away, as if something in the street suddenly fascinated her.

"Christine?" I asked tentatively.

"Of all the things for Nitocris to have been right about," she said.

"I know." When she still didn't look at me, I said, "Are you all right?"

"Yes. It's just a bit of a shock."

I bit my lip. "Do you want me to leave?"

"What?" She finally looked at me. "Don't be daft just because I need a moment to think."

"I'm sorry. Take all the time you need."

"Oh, do stop looking at me like that." She thumped me lightly on the shoulder. "I don't give a fig who—or what—your ancestors were. Although I would have liked to have met Persephone. She sounds like a sensible fish-woman."

"Christine..." I said, torn between relief and exasperation.

"I can't believe you're some sort of hybrid fish-man, though," she went on, ignoring me. "What sort of abomination from the sea is afraid of water? You're really terrible at the whole monstrous creature thing."

I glowered at her. "It isn't funny, Christine."

"That's your opinion." Her grin faded. "Truthfully, Whyborne, I'm a bit surprised, but you're my dear friend. That hasn't changed. You are still the same person you were yesterday. I really don't see the problem."

Had we not been on the street, I would have hugged her. Instead, I only said, "Thank you. I was afraid...well. I've given you rather a lot to look past when it comes to our friendship. Sorcery. My inclinations. I feared inhuman blood might push you to your breaking point."

Christine sighed. "Was he like this with you?" she asked Griffin.

"Yes."

"Then you have my sympathies."

"Christine," I said, vexed. "This hasn't been easy for me to accept. How can I ask anyone else to?"

Her expression softened. "You're right, of course. And I don't mean to make light. But Griffin and I love you—not in the same fashion, obviously, but we're not going to let a little thing like being a shambling horror on your mother's side change our opinions. I mean, we've both met your father and not abandoned you, after all."

I couldn't help but laugh. "You do make a valid point." My mirth died away. "Speaking of Father...Griffin and I discussed things once Persephone left. If we can confront Stanford this morning and expose him, we can disrupt whatever he has planned for tonight. Father won't tolerate such goings-on. If we can just convince him, he'll call Stanford to heel."

"Or join him," Christine said darkly.

"I don't think so. If Guinevere hadn't died...well." I shook my head. "Even if her death came through some accident or mistake, Stanford's schemes were still responsible. Father won't overlook that."

Christine nodded slowly. "I see. Very well, then. Let's see what we can do."

CHAPTER 23

I HESITATED ON the walk outside Whyborne House. "Father may not even let me in the door after yesterday."

"You told him how you felt. Forcefully," Griffin allowed, "but you didn't hurt him. Despite all the chaos, it was clear to me even then you didn't mean to actually harm the man."

It seemed a low bar for good behavior. But this was my family we spoke of. My great-great-great-grandfather had murdered his brother. The Endicotts of thirty years ago had almost killed three of us, if unwittingly so. And if Griffin's worst suspicions were correct, and Stanford had indeed murdered Guinevere...

I'd been upset about being related to inhuman monsters from under the ocean? How absurdly naïve of me.

I took a deep breath and stepped up to knock on the door. Fenton answered this time. His face was pale, and he looked as if he hadn't slept much. Did he fear attacks by monsters?

At least I could tell Father there was no need to guard the house. Which also meant explaining the ketoi that had frightened Mother was in fact his own daughter.

My head ached at the thought. "We're here to see Stanford," I said.

Fenton shuffled slightly. "He's not in, Master Percival."

I glanced incredulously at the sun, which still hung low on the horizon. "This early, and he's already gone out?"

"I don't think he came home last night, sir."

Oh. That didn't sound good. But perhaps I was being paranoid. Perhaps Stanford was drunk in a gutter somewhere, or had fallen asleep in some dockside brothel.

What had our family come to, when total dissolution was the best scenario I could imagine?

"And...Father?" Hot shame rushed over me at the thought of confronting him again. He would be angry, and any truth my words of yesterday might have contained would be brushed aside.

"He left yesterday." Fenton paused, uncharacteristically uncertain. "He took some of things with him."

"What do you mean?"

"I believe he and your mother had strong words. Your father stated his intention to find other lodgings."

I gaped at him. Father had *left?* Walked out of Whyborne House, his pride and joy?

I'd told him that his wife and children were monsters. Had he been unable to accept such a thing? "What did they quarrel about?"

"It isn't for me to say. Would you like to see her?"

I took the hint. "A moment, if you will." I turned to Christine. "There's no reason for us both to miss work. I'll send word as soon as we find Stanford, but until then, it might be best if you go in to finish up whatever remains to be done for the tours tonight."

"All that remains is for the curators," she said. "But I'll go in and make some excuse for you." She hesitated. "What about tonight?"

"With any luck, we can head things off in time for us both to get to the museum before the tours start."

"Hmm, yes. What is the likelihood?" She waved me off. "Never mind. I'll tell the director you're ill. Ghastly symptoms. Should things go awry, perhaps he'll believe I caught it as well, and we won't both end up unemployed tomorrow."

She strode briskly away. Griffin and I followed Fenton inside. "This might be best done in private," I told Griffin apologetically. "Not to suggest Mother doesn't consider you one of the family, but..."

"But it will be best from you alone," Griffin finished. "I understand."

"Fenton, please show Mr. Flaherty to the private parlor."

"Very good, sir."

I climbed the familiar path to Mother's room. She called for me to enter when I knocked. I stepped inside, and found her still at her breakfast. A half-eaten piece of toast lay before her, smeared with raspberry jam, beside an almost untouched cup of coffee. She still wore her dressing gown, and at the sight of me rose to her feet. "Percival? Is something wrong?"

"Yes," I said. "I'm afraid quite a few things, actually."

"Your Father said you'd returned yesterday. That you claimed we're hybrids."

Curse it. "It's true."

She sank to the divan. "I...I see. He yelled at me. Accused me of lying to him, of concealing my true nature. I called him mad."

Damn him for shouting at her. "I'm sorry. He had no right."

She looked up at me, mouth a thin line. "Sit down and tell me everything."

I began with the true nature of Zachariah's mysterious wife, and ended with Persephone's visit. When I finished, Mother sat in silence, her face white as the pages of the book forgotten at her side.

"I'm sorry," I said. If it felt unreal to me, how must it seem to her? I'd gained a sister, but she a daughter. As for what she thought of Stanford's actions, I couldn't guess.

"I see." She closed her eyes.

"Mother?" Had the shock been too much? I reached to touch her, but she stood up abruptly and walked to the window.

"Damn you, Emily," she whispered, staring out the glass. "Damn you to the lowest reaches of Tartarus."

I rose to my feet, but didn't approach. "Mother?" I repeated like a fool, but I didn't know what else to say.

"She knew." Her voice trembled with suppressed rage. "I thought her my friend. I thought we shared confidences. When she wanted to keep the child in her belly, I fought Niles not to turn her out. But she hid everything from me. Everything."

I couldn't imagine how Mother must feel. "She must have known your father's reaction to finding out the truth," I said. "She meant to protect you."

"I don't need protecting!" Mother spun, her eyes flashing fire. "In the name of protection, she denied me my birthright. Worse—she denied me freedom! If she'd told me the truth, when I lay weak and in agony from giving birth, I would have begged her to take all three of us to the sea. You, me, my daughter, all of us. We could have been happy together, and strong! Instead, I've wasted all the years of my life in this *cage*."

The look on her face was utterly savage, and at that moment, I understood her as I never had before. I'd wondered before whether her true nature was the socialite Father had fallen in love with, or the scholar I'd always known.

But the truth was neither: she'd simply picked the only path open to her. And if I'd doubted whether she ever loved him, I doubted it no longer.

She hadn't. As with everything else, he'd been the most acceptable of the only choices human society offered.

"I'm sorry." I felt stupid for repeating the words yet again, but I'd never felt so helpless. Nothing I could say would change anything; it had all been set in motion before I was old enough to speak a single word of protest.

She took a deep breath and reached for me. I took her hands. "You have been my only joy," she said fiercely. "The best thing I've ever done. But I regret your wasted years as much as my own. Among the ketoi, away from your father and brother, away from the society that condemns you, you might have found happiness so much sooner."

I sighed and tugged her closer. "At least Emily might have trusted you to make your own choice. Even if your choice had been to run insane like Grandfather."

"Or you." She shook her head. "Really, Percival."

"It was a shock!" I protested. "On top of an unpleasant fight, which I haven't mentioned because it's of a personal nature."

"I see." She gave me a skeptical look. Then, after a moment, dropped her gaze to our hands. "Do you think I might meet her? Persephone?" She swallowed. "Did Emily name her that? Persephone, the daughter given to the underworld. I want to know what her life turned out to be. Who she is. I feel terrible I drove her away the other night."

"You had no way of knowing her identity. And yes, I'm sure she'd love to meet you." I drew her hands to my mouth and pressed a kiss to her knuckles. "Will you be all right? I should return to Griffin, but if you need me to stay, I shall."

"I'll be fine." Her expression turned wistful. "Angry, perhaps. Sad. Worried about Stanford."

"I'll do whatever I can for him," I promised.

"No you won't. You'll do whatever you have to, even if it means standing against him." She let go of my hands. "I named you truly, Percival. My knight. Of all the things in this world, you are the only one I never doubted."

With no idea where to look for Stanford or what lodgings Father might have found, Griffin and I went next to Wyrm Lane and the Endicotts' rented house.

"After the other night, I'm not entirely comfortable with them or their decisions," Griffin told me as we walked. "I understand we need their assistance for this, but I can't agree with their methods otherwise."

"I know." I stuffed my hands in my pockets. "It's hard to explain. The feeling that everything you do is right because you're the one doing it. The way they live, without fear, above society..."

"They're able to do so because they have the power—and willingness—to destroy anyone who might try to censure them." Griffin gave me a keen look. "You do realize that, don't you?"

"It isn't that," I protested. But what had they said, about having earned the right to do as they pleased? About how the world owed them for saving it, time and again?

"It's precisely that." Griffin sighed. "There's a difference between being free and feeling no responsibility to anyone else. You express disapproval over the men who have a wife and children at home, but frequent the bathhouses at every opportunity. But one could argue they're simply living without the artificial constraints of society, couldn't one?"

"I suppose. But the Endicotts have saved lives, time and again. They take their responsibility seriously."

"It doesn't give them the right to pass judgment on whomever they please."

On Abbott, he meant. But also Dunwich. How easily Theo had dismissed Griffin's concerns the night on the boat. "I know."

He touched my elbow lightly. "I'm sorry, my dear. And I swear I'll try to get along with them, for as long as this takes."

"Thank you. And I'll try to convince them not to move to Widdershins after all."

He stopped dead. "Move to Widdershins?"

"Oh. Er, yes." I felt my face heat. "I spent more time with them than you knew. I didn't want to lie," I added in a rush. "I just felt they accepted me. All of me."

Griffin's eyes darkened, and he glanced down at his shoes, then back at me. "I'm sorry I made you feel thus. I never intended...but the result was the same, whether I intended it or not."

"We've worked this out between us, haven't we?" I asked quietly.

"Yes. We have."

"Then stop fretting and come along."

When we arrived at the rented house, we paused on the sidewalk outside. "Perhaps you should remain out here," I said. "Otherwise, I fear we'll be distracted by arguments about methods."

"Agreed." He leaned against a lamppost. "Fetch me once you've smoothed the way, as it were."

Theo answered my knock on the door, a bright smile on his face. "Percival! Come in; come in. We were growing concerned, since we hadn't heard from you."

"No need," I said. "Or, well, perhaps there is need. I'll explain everything to you both."

"Come up to Fiona's laboratory, then. She's putting the finishing touches on the wand."

"Good. It might prove useful." If we failed to stop Stanford from taking over the town and making war against the land alongside the ketoi, the ability to draw upon the arcane power of the maelstrom might become necessary.

Fiona greeted me effusively from her workbench. "Look!" She held the wand out to me.

I took it. A deep buzz trembled in its length, in my bones, as if it vibrated to some force that touched nothing else in the room. I could feel its power, feel the maelstrom beneath my feet, nearly hear its roar as the lines of power curved and met only a few streets away.

A little breeze sprang up and touched my hair. I handed the wand back to her hastily, before I accidentally unleashed a gale in the small room. "Impressive."

"Thank you."

"Percival has something to tell us," Theo said. He found a chair and sat in it, gesturing for me to do the same.

My belly clenched with nerves once again...but my fear was foolish. Griffin and Christine had accepted my confession easily enough. Theo and Fiona would be no different. "I have bad news. It seems Stanford is the one collaborating with the ketoi."

"No!" Fiona's eyes widened. "One of our own? How could he do such a thing?"

"And he killed Guinevere?" Theo asked.

"I don't know. I hope not. Perhaps he sent someone, some other hybrid working for him, and when she fought back he panicked."

"One moment." Theo frowned. "What do you mean, 'other' hybrid?"

I took a deep breath. "We're—the American branch of the Endicotts—ketoi hybrids. When Zachariah fled England, it seems he took up with one of the ketoi from an underwater city off the coast of Massachusetts. My twin sister, the one I thought died...it turns out she was taken to the sea and transformed. I think the Endicott spell is even what almost killed us, believe it or not. But I've spoken to her, and she's the one who told me of Stanford and the rest."

Shocked silence followed my pronouncement. Fiona and Theo shared a look. "It's not possible," Theo said. He sounded numb. "Are you...are you certain?"

I swallowed past the knot in my throat. "I'm afraid so. I was as surprised as anyone, but it's true."

Theo recoiled in his chair, his lips parting. Fiona's eyes widened in alarm. "A ketoi-sorcerer hybrid," she whispered, and the horror in her voice was impossible to mistake.

"No!" I exclaimed, rising to my feet and holding out my hands. "Well, I mean, yes, but nothing has changed! I'm still the person I was when we parted the other night. It's just the situation is more complicated—not all the ketoi are our enemies."

"God, that alone proves he's already been corrupted!" Theo said. "Quickly, Fiona!"

Fiona snatched up the wand and pointed it directly at me. I didn't even have time to protest before a wall of wind punched into my chest.

CHAPTER 24

I FELL BACKWARD, through the open door and onto the steps. For a moment, all was confusion as I tumbled down them, risers striking my head and body, a wrenching pain in my left arm, the taste of blood in my mouth. I fetched up against the landing and lay still for a moment, stunned.

The uppermost stairs creaked.

Theo stalked toward me, his expression one of mingled rage and disgust. "You tricked us," he snarled. "Tricked me. Thank God I never fucked you—I'd have to kill myself from the shame."

I scrambled to my feet, hands shaking. "Theo—no—we're friends —cousins—"

"You're no cousin of ours, abomination," Fiona spat. She held the wand in her hand, her eyes wild with fury. "Traitor!"

"No!" I shouted, and summoned the wind.

It howled up the stairs, shoving them both back, interrupting whatever spells they might have been casting.

Then I ran.

My feet pounded down the steps, and I almost fell again. Footsteps sounded behind me, drawing nearer. As soon as I reached the first floor, I stretched my legs to their full length, gaining the front door even as they emerged into the room behind me.

Frost slicked the wood beneath my feet, and I fell heavily against the door. The knob burned my flesh when I touched it, but I ignored the pain, ripping open the door and scrambling out to the street.

Griffin looked up in alarm. "Run!" I shouted.

He reached for me, grabbing my elbow as I passed. Then we both fled down the street, away from the house. I didn't think even the twins would murder us in broad daylight, but I had no desire to make certain of it.

We slowed our pace a few blocks away. "They didn't follow," Griffin said, looking back over his shoulder. "Are you all right? Your chin is bleeding."

My scalded palm ached, and bruises made themselves known from various parts of my anatomy. I slumped back against the side of a building, feeling the roughness of the brick through my hair as I tipped back my head. Now that we'd escaped, reaction began to set in. My knees trembled, and my stomach rolled. The memory of Theo's anger and betrayal burned worse than my palm. He'd been so disgusted, as if his attraction to me had been some sort of filthy snare into which I'd lured him.

"What happened?" Griffin asked.

I closed eyes, but only saw Theo's face again. "They didn't take it well," I said. "My lineage. I suppose I should have guessed how they'd react, given the things they said earlier, but I thought because it was me..."

"They would see things differently." Griffin put a hand to my shoulder. Although I couldn't feel his warmth through my coat, the firm grip comforted me, reminded me I wasn't alone. "I'm sorry, my dear."

"After you and Christine, I thought my fears had been nonsense." I sighed and shook my head. "I'm a fool."

"I should have insisted on joining you. But I believed my presence would be a distraction." Griffin squeezed my shoulder, then let go. "Very well, it looks like we can't count on the Endicotts to aid us tonight. We'd best redouble our efforts to locate Stanford well ahead of time. Any ideas?"

I straightened from the wall. My hurt and disappointment meant nothing beside the dangers Stanford posed. "Perhaps he's fallen back into bad habits, and spent the night at a saloon or brothel?"

"Perhaps." Griffin didn't look convinced. But then, neither was I. "It's somewhere to start, at least. Let's go."

"Damn your brother," Christine said, shortly after sundown. "He's going to cost us both our jobs."

Griffin and I spent the day hunting for Stanford, with no luck whatsoever. We could hardly search every rented house or room in the town, but we did our best, canvassing his old haunts. No one admitted to seeing him, and eventually we were forced to admit defeat. An afternoon check at Whyborne House revealed neither he nor Father had returned or even sent word.

God, I hoped I hadn't gotten everything wrong, and Father really was in cahoots with Stanford. With any luck, he was safely out of the way at the museum by now. Where Christine and I should have been.

Instead, we waited in the cold with Griffin, so we could confront my idiot of a brother and prevent him from taking over the town. We stood on the bank of the river, not far from the cemetery, where I'd first seen Persephone. Storm wrack filled the eastern sky, and no moon lit the sky. The wind held a breath of frost as it rustled the vast bulk of the Draakenwood behind us.

God, I hoped Stanford wasn't stupid enough to go in there at night. Any night, really, but tonight seemed even more ill-omened, given the rites Blackbyrne had once practiced within the confines of the forest.

Sunset ushered in the official start of Hallowe'en according to the ancient Celts. All across Widdershins, people celebrated: either with cards and silly games, or darker rites handed down from their ancestors. The private museum tours would begin any moment, wealthy donors crowding inside to exclaim over the cursed items, before retiring to the buffet and champagne.

"Perhaps Dr. Hart will believe your story about the fever?" I suggested hopefully.

"Perhaps, if we hadn't spent the entire time complaining about the blasted tours." Christine sighed. "Ah well. We'll simply have to become highwaymen to feed ourselves."

"Gold miners in the Yukon."

"You could find a job waiting tables at Le Calmar. Or would you worry the fish stew might consist of near relatives?"

"Christine!"

"Hush, the both of you," Griffin ordered. "I heard something."

We fell instantly silent. I strained my ears, but the only sounds stirring nearby were the sigh of the breeze, the hiss of our breathing, and the rustle of leaves. More distantly, dogs barked, and a faint strain of odd music blew in on the wind, before vanishing again just as quickly.

There. A splash. Ripples spread across the surface of the river, and a fin breached the surface. I started forward, but Griffin grabbed my arm and yanked me back. "We don't know it's her."

Dear lord—the cemetery behind us lay silent, so far as I could tell. Had the ketoi not come on land yet? Were we about to be greeted by a...school? pod?...of them?

It was almost impossible to make anything out in the starlight, but the faintest outline of a form rose from the water. Alone.

"It's her," I said, with more certainty than the situation probably warranted. But there was no question in my mind, as if some part of me recognized some other part of her.

Griffin unshuttered his lantern. Persephone's jewelry flashed back at us in the light, and she squinted. Her tentacle-hair thrashed around her shoulders violently, and I caught a quick flare of gills to either side of her neck, before the slits closed tight. In her hand, she held something resembling a crude sword: a length of bone, set with razor-sharp bits of obsidian.

"What is that?" I asked, approaching her.

She hefted it. "This is for Dives Deep. I will use it to cut off her head."

"Oh, I like her," Christine said.

I'd let my manners lapse. "Dr. Christine Putnam, this is my, er, sister, Persephone. Persephone, Christine is my dear friend."

"A pleasure to meet you," Christine said staunchly, and thrust out her hand. Persephone eyed the rifle slung over Christine's shoulder warily, but shook hands.

"Where is our brother?" Persephone asked. "Where is Dives Deep?"

"We haven't seen them yet," Griffin said. "Perhaps we can find a place of concealment among the crypts and lie in wait?"

Persephone frowned, an expression I found far less disturbing than her smile. "The warriors left before me. I watched from a distance, waited until they were well past, then came after. They are not here?"

The cemetery behind us lay dark and silent. "Perhaps they sneaked in, before we arrived," I suggested. "Or...there was a reason Stanford chose this place. Maybe a crypt opens into some underground cavern via a secret entrance in a tomb."

"Good gad, man, what utter nonsense!" Christine gave me a disgusted look.

"It's as likely as anything else," I shot back.

"And more so in Widdershins than anywhere else, I'd say." Griffin touched my arm lightly. "Come. I'm going to lower the beam, and we'll enter the cemetery. Surely we'll spot them, or at least evidence of their activity, soon enough."

We crept cautiously to the low wall and scrambled over. A fat rabbit broke cover and fled before us, and handfuls of golden and scarlet leaves from the Draakenwood drifted on the breeze, but otherwise nothing moved. There was no trace of water dripping from ketoi fresh from the river, no sound of low chanting, no light of torches or lanterns. No flicker of magic at all, except for the slow tug of the arcane maelstrom beneath us.

When we reached the edge of the forest, it became clear we were the only living creatures in the cemetery tonight. "I don't understand," I said, turning around and around, in the vain hope of spotting some glimmer of light or motion. "Persephone, you're certain of what your friend said? They were going to the 'place of bones?'"

"Yes." Frustration roughened her voice, and she struck the ground with her weapon. "Stone Biter is no fool. And he would *not* have lied to me."

"Then he must have been wrong," Christine said. She perched on a convenient headstone and glared at the nearest crypt, as if its inhabitants might be persuaded to emerge and give us answers. "What a devil of a night. No Stanford, no ketoi army, no Theodore and Fiona, and no jobs because we skipped the damned tours in favor of in this accursed cemetery. The only thing which could possibly salvage it is if the blasted hadrosaur collapses on top of Bradley."

"What is a hadrosaur?" Persephone asked.

"A giant creature, which lived a long time ago, so long even its bones have turned to stone," I explained.

"Its bones." Griffin met my gaze, and my heart began to beat faster. "The hadrosaur in the grand foyer. And the other exhibits behind it, of ancient beasts."

"The place of bones." Horrified realization swept over me. "Not the cemetery at all. Whatever Stanford has planned, it's taking place at the museum."

We ran down the road leading to the Ladysmith. On the streets around us, revelers in masks and costumes traveled to parties. Bonfire smoke perfumed the air, and candles gleamed within jack-o-lanterns set out on porches and in windows.

A young woman let out a mock-scream at seeing a man dressed as a bear. Then she spotted us and let out a genuine shriek at the sight of Persephone, dressed like a barbarian queen in nothing but jewels and a golden loincloth, clearly inhuman even in the dimmest of light. The fellow in the bear costume howled in fright as well, before lumbering off. Other screams followed—curse it, how many people could there be on this street? I could only imagine the headlines tomorrow: WHYBORNE SON TERRORIZES TOWN IN COMPANY OF FISH WOMAN.

On the other hand, if that was the worst thing the papers had to say about one of us in the morning, perhaps I should count us lucky.

By the time we reached the museum, my side felt on fire, my

lungs gasped for air, and my legs ached. With a final burst of strength, I plunged up the stairs to the great doors of the Ladysmith. I grabbed the handle and swore when it proved to be locked.

"Stanford's already here," I said. God, what could he possibly intend? Had he gone utterly mad?

"We can slip around the side, check the staff entrance," Griffin suggested.

"No. We don't have enough time." I met his gaze. "I'll summon the wind and break down the doors."

I expected him to hesitate, as he always had, whenever I spoke of using sorcery. But he only nodded. "Do it."

"Step aside, then." He did so, drawing Christine with him. Persephone withdrew as well, but watched me curiously. The same magic that moved in my blood filled hers also, even if she'd never been trained to its use.

I turned all of my concentration on the doors. The wind began to rise, ruffling my hair. I could feel all the forces of nature, gathering to respond to my command.

"Now," I said.

The wind roared down the street, hurling Hallowe'en decorations into the air and knocking over the sign announcing the private tours. It tore at my clothes, whipped through my hair, pressed against my back like a hand urging me forward.

The doors exploded inwards with a tremendous crash.

Griffin was through them instantly, revolver drawn. Christine charged in behind him, and Persephone and I followed.

The elite of Widdershins filled the grand foyer: some in ordinary eveningwear, others dressed in elaborate costumes glittering with diamonds, pearls, and rubies. Most of the women clung to the sides of their escorts, husbands, or fathers. Orange and black streamers covered the floor where they had fallen, and a smear of blood showed on one of the special exhibits of cursed objects. A long buffet lay to our left, and the abandoned instruments of a string quartet sat scattered on the floor of a discreet alcove on the right. Three guards lay dead, either stabbed with crude spears or mauled and stung. The hadrosaur loomed above all, empty sockets staring mockingly out.

Ketoi lined the perimeter of the room, far greater in number than I'd hoped to face. Stanford stood before the crowd of staff and donors, at his side a ketoi woman holding a spear. Father crouched on hands and knees at his feet.

Father?

Griffin and Christine had both halted, bodies tense and weapons pointed toward the floor. Did we dare attack with so many vulnerable to reprisal by the ketoi?

"Dr. Whyborne, Dr. Putnam!" exclaimed the director. He huddled with Mr. Mathison, the museum president, and a number of the staff, including Bradley and Dr. Gerritson. Poor Miss Parkhurst clung to Dr. Gerritson's arm, her eyes bright with tears.

"Sorry we're late," Christine called. "But I apologize for my earlier doubts, Dr. Hart. You were indeed correct about needing our expertise for this event."

Stanford's eyes narrowed at the sight of us. Of me. "Percival," he spat.

The ketoi woman beside him looked equally contemptuous. "What are you doing here, exile?" she asked, baring her teeth at Persephone.

"Just—just stop, everyone." I held up my hands, showing myself to be unarmed. Conventionally, anyway. "Stanford, whatever it is you think you're doing, it isn't too late to stop."

Stanford's face flushed red with anger. "Stop? You coward. To think Father actually began to favor you." He aimed a vicious kick at the figure crouched at his feet.

Father's body rocked from the impact, but he didn't fall or cry out. One eye was blackened, and blood crusted his lips, but he still held firm.

It made no sense. Father had always adored Stanford as the perfect son, the one I could never compare to. Why was Stanford treating him so? "What are you doing?"

"What I'm doing, or was, before your rude interruption," Stanford said, "is addressing the elite of Widdershins." He indicated the huddled men and women. "You might have fought off those I sent to teach you your place, but you can't win this."

Stanford had sent the ketoi and hybrid to our house, to attack me? To attack Griffin, and in our own home? "You're wrong. I fought your lackeys, and I can fight you," I said with more bravado than I actually felt.

"I have a destiny which will not be denied," Stanford said.

"You mean the blasted prophecy."

Stanford's eyes narrowed. "Scoff if you want. This town will rise to my command, one way or another. *Widdershins always knows its own.*"

"That could mean anything."

"What it means is that I'm destined to control this town, and soon every other." Stanford grinned, and the expression sent a chill through my blood. He indicated the ketoi beside him. "My counterpart Dives Deep, the queen beneath the flood, already rules the seas. Everyone here knows of the missing ships, the derelicts. All meant to prove a simple point: nothing can pass in or out of this port, unless we allow it."

Horrified murmurs spread through the crowd. Stanford preened, and with a sick twist, I realized he was *enjoying* this. Spreading fear, having everyone under his control.

"So much for the sea," he went on. "As of this afternoon, I was able to *convince* Father to cede me complete control of Whyborne Railroad and Industries. Now nothing can pass in or out of Widdershins by land or sea, without our permission. So I came here tonight, where you so conveniently gathered all of the old families, to make certain they understand who their new master is."

I wanted to argue the damned tours weren't my idea, but it seemed rather beside the point. "And what comes next? Your friend here wants to wage war against the land."

"Only those who do not bow to us," Dives Deep said.

"With the railroad in my control, I hold the lifeline to many a town on the prairie." Stanford indicated the ketoi warriors. "When it comes to larger cities, or those served by other lines, a few rail cars packed with my friends here will surely be enough to convince them to surrender to me."

Dr. Hart stepped forward. "You can't do this!"

"Can't I?' Stanford laughed and turned to the crowd. "Consider the fate of Thomas Abbott. Ruined, thanks to his investments in the *Oarfish*, which I ordered destroyed. As for where he is now, well, I'll find him soon enough. Anyone who threatens me will suffer and then die."

"And what about Guinevere?" I asked. "Did she threaten you, too? Is that why you had her killed?"

Stanford's grin faded away. "Guinevere was an accident," he said. "I only meant to talk to her, to stop her! But she tried to fight, and—and I didn't have a choice. She made me kill her."

Chapter 25

Oh God. Stanford had killed Guinevere with his own hands. Even I hadn't expected it would be this bad.

Father went utterly white, and he swayed, just a little. "You k-killed your sister?"

"It was an accident," Stanford repeated. He licked his lips; a sheen of sweat sprang out on his forehead. "She was a woman—didn't have the strength to do what needed to be done. She meant to betray me to Percival."

"And Miss Emily?" I asked.

"She knew too much. She would have betrayed me eventually—she had to die."

All the blood seemed to drain into my feet, leaving me light headed. I'd suspected, but to hear the truth from his own mouth was worse than I'd ever thought it would be.

Father staggered to his feet. His face had gone white as chalk, and his voice cracked on the words, but anger gave him strength. "How could you, Stanford? How dare you—"

Stanford struck Father a hard blow across the face. "How dare I?" he shrieked. "How dare you? I did everything to please you, *everything*, but it was never enough. I spent my entire childhood following your every order."

Had I been jealous of Stanford's freedom? Resented how he'd passed through life with such ease?

I'd been wrong. We were both trapped, in our own ways. Twisted out of whatever shapes we might have taken otherwise. Only Stanford hadn't been strong enough to walk away.

"You dragged me back from New York the moment you thought I'd escape the leash," Stanford went on, "then had the gall to parade this fairy I have to call brother in front of me, as if he were the lord of the manor. We'll I'm done. I'm done begging and scraping for your approval. I will build an empire of land and sea, far greater than anything you could have imagined. Your time is *over*, Father."

He turned on me. "Guinevere forced me to kill her. I didn't want to do it. But you? I'm going to cut your heart out and laugh while I do it." His eyes flicked to the ketoi. "Kill them—"

"Dives Deep!" Persephone shouted. "I challenge you for the chieftainship!"

Oh. So this was what she meant when she'd spoken of some old law.

A ripple ran through the ketoi. Several hissed in anger, and I took it they didn't particularly approve of her gambit.

Dives Deep bared all of her teeth, and there certainly were a lot of them. She held her spear easily, like someone used to killing with it. What did she usually hunt? Dolphins? Sharks? Whales? Certainly she looked more than capable of spitting Persephone.

"Sings Above the Waves." Her voice practically purred with contempt. The tentacles on her head squirmed in a lazy cloud around her face. The pattern of markings on her skin left her arms and legs almost purely white, and only two tiny dots of black decorated her face. Multiple necklaces hung around her neck, and her limbs were banded with gold. Something like a spiky crown with a huge black pearl in the center adorned her forehead.

I could sense Persephone trembling beside me, but when she spoke, her voice remained calm. "Yes."

"She's trying to distract you!" Stanford exclaimed. "Kill them all now and be done with it!"

"You can't!" one of the other ketoi shouted. "Sings Above the Waves has issued the challenge according to ancient law."

"Be silent, Stone Biter!" Dives Deep snarled, turning on him. He flinched back, but his eyes remained locked on Persephone. I felt the tremors in her limbs ease, as if she drew strength from him.

"Stone Biter is right," another ketoi called.

"Sings Above the Waves is an exile!" cried another.

"The law doesn't say exiles can't issue challenge," Stone Biter replied with a trace of satisfaction. Had Persephone's friends planned this with her? "If the prophecy is true, if Dives Deep is meant to rule, then what has she to fear?"

Dives Deep growled. "I do not fear. You would challenge me, little halfbreed exile? I am many times your elder. I have hunted the fish of the vast abyss, and stood before the dweller in the deeps."

I probably should have kept my mouth shut, but I couldn't resist. "Stood there?" I asked with an arch of the brow. "*I* actually did something besides stand there. I saved the god."

If the chieftess could have killed by sight alone, I'm certain I would have dropped dead on the spot. "Is that so?" Her lip curled to reveal rows of serrated teeth. "Do you offer challenge to this other one, then?"

"What?' I asked, shocked.

She grinned at me, and I shuddered at the sight. "He claims dominion over this town. Will you fight him for it?"

"No!" exclaimed Stanford. "This isn't how we do things. Nor should you! Have your men kill her—it's what they're for, isn't it?"

"Most of them are women, you idiot," I said. It was just like Stanford to make an alliance and not bother to learn anything about his allies.

"I'm not fighting this—this—"

"Are you a coward, then?" I demanded. Stanford's face flushed, and I knew then if he hadn't intended to kill me before, he surely did now.

"By our laws, the challenge must be carried out immediately, or else forfeited," Dives Deep said. "To death or surrender."

"Oh, there will be a death, all right," Stanford growled.

"Is this your wish?" Dives Deep asked me. "Do you challenge your brother?"

I could feel everyone's eyes on me. Dr. Hart, Miss Parkhurst, Mr. Mathison, all the museum staff and the guests. All of them depending on me to prevent the grand foyer from becoming an abattoir.

Stanford had spoken of sending ketoi warriors by rail to take over other towns. A great many other people were going to die if we couldn't stop him tonight.

I looked over my shoulder and met Griffin's eyes. His pupils were tight with fear, and his lips parted, as if he would say something. Then he swallowed and gave me a tiny nod.

I turned back. "Yes," I said.

"Fuck you," Stanford snarled. Then he pulled a gun from his pocket and shot Griffin.

Griffin's body jerked, and his revolver fell from his hand. He clutched at the hole in his coat, even as dark blood welled around it.

No.

Everything stopped: time, my heart, the world, the universe. A drop of red fell to the floor, like a discarded gem, no longer needed. Griffin's body followed it, knees striking the marble. Christine cried out, gripping his arm to keep him upright.

I ran to him and tore aside his coat. The shot had struck his left side, and blood darkened his vest. Shock and pain drained all the color from his skin, even as Christine tried to staunch the wound with her coat.

All around us, people screamed. Persephone snarled in rage as she closed with Dives Deep. And behind me, my brother laughed.

Laughed.

I rose to my feet and turned to face him.

"Are you going to cry?" he taunted, grinning. "Cry over your—"

Wind howled through the open doors, tearing apart the streamers and crape ghosts, ripping hats from heads. The force of it slammed into Stanford, sending him into one of the special exhibits. His gun flew away, spinning off across the floor.

More screams, and some part of my mind recognized I'd just performed sorcery in front of donors and co-workers. But any worry was distant, small and crushed beneath the raw fury igniting my blood.

I stalked across the floor toward Stanford. My throat hurt; the sound coming out of it didn't even seem human at all.

Stanford's lips drew back from his teeth, and he spat on the floor. "You think you're something because you know a few magic tricks. But what would you be without them?"

He shoved the exhibit beside him, sending the glass case crashing to the floor. Even as I gathered the wind again, he snatched up a sword from amidst the glass shards.

"Cease this at once!" Dr. Hart bellowed from amidst the others held captive by the ketoi. "That is a priceless artifact, sir!"

I flung out my right hand, the scars on my arms pulsing with pain, from shoulder to fingertips. A gale built, and I didn't care what it destroyed, so long as Stanford hurt, so long as he paid—

He swung the sword, and I *felt* the magic come apart on its edge. The wind died.

Stanford gave me a hideous grin. "Well, well, what do you know? The 'curse' on this one is real."

The witch hunter's sword. And I'd been the one to convince Christine to put the blasted thing in the exhibit.

"Now the fight is even," Stanford said. "Except I'm going to gut you like a fish."

He charged at me, swinging the sword like a scythe. I leapt back—

not fast enough, the edge of the blade slicing though my coat, vest, and shirt. Numbness spread from where it had touched, and an instant later a thin line of blood appeared against my exposed skin.

"Run, Whyborne!" Christine shouted at me.

Christine. Griffin. Oh God, Griffin...

I risked a glance, even with Stanford chasing me. Three ketoi surrounded Christine, their spears pointed at her. No doubt she'd tried to interfere. Griffin rested against her, pale but still alive.

Stanford's heavy steps sounded just behind me. Where had his gun gone? Could I find it and use it against him?

"Coward!" Stanford roared. "But running won't save your sniveling life!"

I raced for the exhibits in the back of the enormous hall. More bones lurked here: saber-toothed tigers, an Irish elk with horns wider than a man was tall, the heavy carapace of a giant armadillo. Beyond these lay the glass cases displaying wax statues of ancient hunters clad in furs and beads, replicas of their spears in their hands.

"Stanford, no!" Father shouted. It was the only warning I received.

I flung myself full-length to the ground, the sword whistling past where my head would have been and crashing into the brown bones of the Irish elk. Fragments of bone went everywhere, and Dr. Hart howled in outrage.

I rolled and kicked blindly in Stanford's direction. I missed, but an instant later, a pair of snarling figures hurtled into him. Persephone and Dives Deep had both lost their weapons, and now tore madly at one another with claws and teeth. Both bled profusely, but the chieftess was clearly winning.

Dives Deep pinned Persephone beneath her. Her tentacle hair thrashed wildly, and blood coated her teeth. "You should have stayed in exile," she hissed.

I snatched up a fragment of fallen bone and smashed the front of the hunter's display. The wax hand came off when I tore the spear free.

If Dr. Hart hadn't already fired me, he certainly would now.

I stabbed Dives Deep with the spear, the point biting into her shoulder. She jerked back, and Persephone heaved her off.

"Here!" I exclaimed, holding out the spear.

She took it and pursued Dives Deep, who rapidly retreated toward their dropped weapons.

Unfortunately, I had no time to search for the gun. Stanford had made it back to his feet, the sword still in his hand. And I'd just given away the weapon I'd hoped to use against him.

I ran again, hoping I might by luck come across the gun. Stanford came after me, panting and cursing. One of the shrunken heads lay on the floor; I scooped it up and flung it at Stanford, forcing him to duck aside.

Crape streamers tangled my feet. I fell heavily, almost cracking my head against one of the display cases. I rolled onto my back, saw Stanford above me, the sword raised high to chop off my head.

"Stanford, no!" I cried.

No trace of regret showed in his eyes. Only hatred. His lips drew back from his teeth, the expression bordering on maniacal.

"Die, you disgusting sodomite," he snarled, and brought the sword down.

"No!" Father shouted, locking his arms around Stanford's shoulders and heaving him off-balance.

I scrambled to my feet as they struggled. Fixing my eyes on the pommel of the sword, I whispered the secret name of fire.

Nothing. Damn it, the sword itself resisted any magic worked against it.

"Stop this, Stanford," Father ordered. "Percival is your brother! You can't—"

"You don't get to tell me what I can do, old man!" Stanford roared. His shove sent Father sprawling across the marble floor. "I'm not your lackey any more."

I started forward, but Stanford spun to face me, sword lashing out. I leapt back, and collided with the enormous hind leg of the hadrosaur fossil.

Stanford's grin turned bloodthirsty. I was backed into a corner, with no magic to protect me and nowhere left to run. So I did the only thing I could.

He swung the sword with all his strength, meaning to take off my head. At the same moment, I let my legs go limp. The blade passed so close I felt it touch my hair, just before it smashed into the unyielding stone of the fossil.

The blade shattered, and I felt something *give*, whatever enchantment it bore unraveling with the metal fragments raining down around me.

I called down the fire.

Stanford let out an angry bellow as the hilt flared suddenly hot in his hand, the guard scorching against his fingers. It hit the ground, and he clutched his wounded hand to his chest.

I scooped up a length of elk bone and struck him as hard as I could on the head.

Stanford collapsed in a heap at my feet. I stood above him, panting for breath. I should hit him again. I should keep hitting him, over and over, the way he'd stabbed Guinevere. I should make him pay for hurting Griffin. I should bring down bloody vengeance for every wrong he'd ever done me, from the time we were boys until this very moment.

Instead, I flung aside the bone.

There came a loud, wet *crack*. I spun, just in time to see Persephone hold up the head of the dead chieftess, now completely severed from its body.

Utter silence fell over the room. Some of the humans had fainted, but even those who hadn't only stared in mute horror. The ketoi remained silent as well, watching Persephone with a sort of awe. Stone Biter grinned fiercely, and a few more of the donors fainted at the sight.

"Dives Deep is dead at my hand," Persephone declared, her voice ringing in the grand space. "And the other lies defeated at the feet of my brother Percival."

Father started badly. He didn't know. Stanford had never bothered to tell him about his other daughter.

"Their power is broken," she went on. "*A new queen shall rule beneath the flood.*" She glanced at me. "One for the land."

"And one for the sea," I whispered. Had Griffin been right, when he asked if the prophecy referred to us?

Persephone lowered the grisly head. "Come. Return home. This war is at an end."

The ketoi obeyed her, a soft shuffle of claws on marble. Three of them lifted Dives Deep's headless body and carried it out with them. Persephone watched them go. As the crowd behind us began to whisper, then cry out in relief and anger, I ran to Griffin's side.

He leaned heavily against Christine, his face white and his hands red with blood. He wore only his shirt above the waist, and Christine had used the arm of his suit coat to create a makeshift bandage. Spotting me, Griffin smiled weakly and held out one hand.

"Well done," he said. His voice was hoarse but strong.

"You need medical attention." I went to my knees, afraid to touch him.

One of the donors hurried up. "I'm a doctor," he said.

"The wound isn't serious," Christine said. "The bullet scraped along the rib, I think, but fortunately Stanford's aim was terrible."

Stanford. I glanced back over my shoulder. Several of the men had rolled Stanford onto his stomach and bound him. Another doctor tended to Father, whose face was almost as pale as the marble floor.

No doubt he'd received the greatest series of shocks in his life tonight.

The cold air streaming through the open doors brought with it the sound of a motor car's engine. A moment later, footsteps pounded up the steps to the entrance. Fenton appeared, his eyes wild with fright. They went even wider when he beheld the destruction within.

"Fenton?" What on earth was the man doing here?

He blinked again at seeing me. I must look a state—my hat long gone, my coat torn, my shirt bloody. The sight of Persephone caused his mouth to gape...but after a moment, he seemed to collect himself. "M-Master Percival? Thank God!" He swayed where he stood, one hand to his chest, as if his heart troubled him. "It's your mother."

"Mother?" Cold fear washed through me.

"Y-yes. Your cousins—the Endicotts—they came to the house. Forced their way in using unnatural powers. They said—they said to tell you they mean to wipe this entire cursed town off the map, and if you do anything to stop them, your mother will pay with her life."

CHAPTER 26

I STARED AT him for a long moment in disbelief. The Endicotts had been shocked at my revelation, disgusted even, but for this to be their solution...

Then again, perhaps I should have expected it. Our ancestors had dropped half of a medieval town into the sea. What had Theo called Widdershins, the day we mapped the arcane lines? A bloody nightmare?

They'd meant to stay and help me cleanse it of whatever magic they deemed unacceptable. Any besides than their own, in other words. The truth of my lineage must have convinced them there was no saving Widdershins. The corruption ran too deep.

It was their solemn duty to put an end to us. And what better night than Hallowe'en, when the arcane energies would be at their height?

God. Did they mean to use the maelstrom? They had the wand to help them tap into its power, after all.

I rose shakily to my feet and looked around. Griffin was hurt, and even though the injury wasn't critical, he was in no shape to fight. Christine, however, met my gaze calmly.

"I'm with you, of course," she said.

I shook my head. "No. You can't."

Her black brows snapped together. "Damn it, Whyborne—"

"No!" She fell silent at my shout. "They're sorcerers, Christine. If you bring your rifle, they'll set fire to the powder and blow it up in your hands."

"A sword, then or an ax—"

"You don't know how to fight with one," I cut her off. "And the Endicotts have been doing this their entire lives. They know far more magic than I. They think destroying the town is the right thing to do, and they won't hold back, not for anyone. I can't fight them and keep you safe."

Rising to my feet, I looked out over the foyer, the broken exhibits and damaged fossils, the destroyed decorations and fainting donors. Dr. Hart and Mr. Mathison had both begun to approach, but stopped when they'd heard Fenton's words. Now they looked at me in confusion.

"I'm sorry," I said. "I'll turn in my resignation tomorrow morning. If I survive, I mean."

Miss Parkhurst ran up to me, giving Persephone a wide berth. "I don't know what's happening, but good luck, Dr. Whyborne," she said, and kissed me quickly on the cheek.

I blinked in surprise and touched the spot, even as she fled, her face burning. Turning back, I saw Griffin struggling to his feet, most of his weight on Christine's arm. "Look after Father," I said to them. "I... I'll see you later."

"Ival," Griffin reached for me. I stepped closer, and he gripped my arm. "The Endicotts have been doing this their whole lives, as you said. And maybe they know more magic." He met my gaze, and I read there all the love he had for me. "But you *are* magic."

I wanted to reply, but my throat was too tight with emotion. So I only nodded. He squeezed once, then let go.

Ignoring the burning in my eyes, I turned to my sister. "Persephone? Will you help me fight them?"

Her tentacle hair rose in an angry halo around her head. "Yes."

"Sir?" Fenton asked, and a note of fear quivered in his voice. "Shall I drive you?"

"Yes," I said. "Thank you."

Not daring to look back at Griffin and Christine, I hurried out the doors, Persephone and Fenton behind me.

I clung to the motor car's seat as Fenton drove us through the winding streets with reckless speed. The storm clouds I'd noticed at the cemetery had rolled in while we were inside the museum, and now fat drops of rain began to pelt from the sky, stinging painfully against our exposed skin.

"Can you summon the other ketoi back?" I shouted over the rush of wind and rain.

Persephone perched in my lap, her arms loosely around my neck and her tentacle hair crushed against my face. Fortunately, the stingers appeared to be under some sort of conscious control. The tentacles themselves felt odd but not unpleasant, if I ignored their occasional wriggle.

"No—not without a stone." Her mouth tightened in a frown. "I should not have dismissed them—but I thought it would make things easier for the land people, allow me to show the danger is passed."

"It was a good idea. You didn't know the Endicotts would do this. Threaten the town. Kidnap Mother."

If the twins hurt Mother, I didn't know what I'd do. Did they have her out even now in the soaking rain? Was she afraid? Hurt?

"We're almost there," Fenton shouted over the rumble of thunder. At least he hadn't questioned I knew where to go. If the twins truly meant to wipe Widdershins from the face of the earth, they'd need immense power to do it. Despite the dangers, they'd go to the heart of the maelstrom. The ancient bridge over the Cranch, where it entered the bay.

The streets grew darker as we neared the bay, and the downpour strengthened, until we were all soaked. I could *feel* the arcane rivers beneath us, swirling fast and tight toward the center, in a way I'd never been able to before. Because of the date, the ancient Witches Sabbath? Or because, having touched its power several times now, I'd become in some way attuned to the flow?

Or because Widdershins knew me, as the poem-prophecy said?

We turned onto Front Street, and Fenton brought the motor car to a halt. The electric lights of the bridge shone in the darkness, although we were still far enough away to make out only indistinct shapes on the span. Two appeared to be wearing robes, which flapped and snapped in the breeze.

Persephone and I climbed out of the motor car. A stiff wind blew from the ocean, ruffling my hair and bringing with it the sound of chanting. "Go back to the museum," I told Fenton. "Take Father, Griffin, and Christine as far from here as you can."

Fenton nodded. "Yes, sir. Where should we go?"

"Given the family history, as far away from the ocean as possible."

I walked down the street, every nerve alive and thrumming, Persephone at my side. Thunder rumbled again, and lightning cracked out to sea.

We reached the bridge. Fiona's wand stood upright in its center, somehow jammed into the solid stone. Chalked sigils marked the road all around it. As we approached, Theo took up position at Fiona's side, near the low stone railing.

Persephone and I froze, side-by-side, mirrors of the Endicott twins. One pair human, the other monstrous, and at the moment, I wasn't even sure which was truly which.

Fiona held Mother in front of her, one arm tight around her waist. The other pressed the tip of a vicious blade to her chest.

"Stay back," Fiona warned. "Unless you want to see her die before your eyes."

Mother was pale, and a dark bruise showed on one cheek. They hadn't taken her easily. She gripped Fiona's wrist with both hands, as if holding the dagger back from her flesh. But years of illness had sapped her strength, and if Fiona chose to stab her, there was nothing she could do to prevent it.

Mother's eyes widened at the sight of us. "Persephone?"

Persephone nodded. "Yes."

"How touching," Theo said, his lip curling. "The mother of monsters and her litter, together at last."

"Let her go." My voice trembled, and I swallowed hard against my fear. "There's no need to threaten her."

"No need?" Theo let out a bitter laugh. "This town is a blight on the face of the earth! Your woods are haunted, your most powerful families poisoned by dark magic. The very streets were designed by a necromancer. Even the public museum is filled with cursed objects and tomes that ought to be shut away or burned. There is every need!"

"But it's all right," Fiona said. "The sea will wipe everything away and make it clean again."

No. She couldn't truly mean it. "You're raising a tidal wave? But—but that's madness! You'll die, too!"

Fiona's eyes gleamed in the light. "Yes. If such is the price we must pay for protecting humanity from monsters like you, then so be it. We've lived life to the fullest, and now we can die without regret, so long as we take you with us."

She truly believed her words. She—and Theo—looked at me and beheld a horror. No different from the ghūls, or the yayhos, or the abominable Guardians. She and Theo were saving the world, and nothing I could say would convince her otherwise.

And in the meantime, she held my mother tight against her, a tiny dot of blood forming on her bodice where the knife pressed a little too hard.

"But we're not without mercy," Theo said. "Surrender, don't fight us, and we'll let Heliabel go. She might even escape what's already in motion."

Already in motion. The spell was cast. The wave on its way.

"No!" Mother shouted. Her eyes narrowed, and she gave Theo

such a look of scorn he took a step back. "You will not use me to hurt my children."

She met my gaze then, and the anger slid away, replaced by love and something very like grief. "Send them both to hell, my knight," she said.

Then she jerked Fiona's knife to her instead of pushing it away.

The blade slid into her chest, all the way to the hilt. Blood instantly darkened her bodice, and she let out a choked sound of anguish. Fiona shouted in surprise and instinctively pulled the knife free, springing back from the sudden gush of blood that followed it.

"No!" The sound tore its way out of my throat. Persephone and I ran onto the bridge, but we were already too late.

Mother stumbled back, her life flowing out of the terrible wound. Her legs struck the stone railing—and she flung herself over, back, and into the river.

She was gone.

The world stopped. Or maybe just my world.

Nothing remained but a pool of blood, already washing away in the rain. A roaring sound filled my ears, and the bones of my arms and legs didn't seem to work correctly anymore.

I'd expected to lose her, ever since I was old enough to understand the meaning of death, to know there was no other possible end to Mother's long illness. But not like this.

Send them both to hell, my knight.

I screamed, and the world screamed with me.

Wind howled across the bridge, funneled by nothing save my desire to see Theo and Fiona pay, to see them hurt and broken and shrieking. Rain pelted them, accompanied by a sudden onslaught of stinging hail. The gale caught their robes, tangling the fabric about their bodies. Fiona stumbled, the hood temporarily blinding her.

Theo dropped to the ground, hands pressed against the bridge. I started toward him, my pulse slamming in my ears, my only thought to rip out his heart.

The stones of the bridge turned soft beneath my feet, my shoes sinking into them like mud. Taken off guard, I glanced down, only to see the stone resolidify, trapping my shoes. I jerked against its grip, but it held fast.

"You're too late, cousin!" Theo shouted. The wind died along with my concentration, and he scrambled to his feet. "Look—the river level is already dropping as the sea retreats. What's coming over the horizon will cleanse this hellhole of ketoi and dark sorcery alike."

I tried to shatter the stone holding me fast, but command of earth had never come as easily to me as the other elements.

But I wasn't alone in this fight. Persephone let out a growl of fury, and the scars on my own arm tingled as she grasped the river beneath us with her will. A wall of water heaved up from beneath the bridge, curling as it prepared to smash down on the Endicotts and flatten them against the stones.

Fiona spun and faced the side of the bridge, both hands flung up before her. The wall of water stopped, churning, as her will held Persephone's back.

Before I could call a warning, Theo struck. A blast of wind hit Persephone, sending her into the wand still rooted in the center of the bridge. The wand snapped under her weight, and both hit the railing. She tried to scramble to her feet, but he struck her again, hurling her over the rail at the same point Mother had fallen. The river collapsed back into its banks, Persephone's spell shattered.

I finally succeeded in wrenching free of my trapped shoes. The stones of the bridge felt cold beneath my socks.

Frost raced over my skin, biting and stinging, and the rainwater under my feet turned to a sheen of ice. I tried to draw on fire to melt it, but before I could, Theo hit me with another gust of wind. My feet went out from under me, and I struck the bridge hard enough to knock the breath from my lungs.

"Give up," Theo said. He stalked toward me, his expression one of fury and hate. "Why waste your last moments fighting us both, when you can't possibly win?"

My last moments.

I felt the maelstrom beneath me, arcane energy swirling in from both land and ocean, fast and wild as a riptide. The tidal wave rolled in, still out to sea but closing quickly. The sea wall wouldn't be enough to blunt its fury, and a good part of Widdershins would be swept away. These wouldn't just be my last moments, but Griffin's as well. Unless Fenton had performed a miracle of driving, they'd surely be caught up: Griffin and Christine, Father. Miss Parkhurst, Dr. Hart, Bradley, everyone I'd known. Hundreds of souls packed into the tenement houses, the sailors along the wharf. Thieves and whores and beggars; husbands and wives and children. All were going to die, and most of them would never even know why.

Beneath my hands lay the flood of magic that had drawn Blackbyrne to Widdershins two centuries ago: too dangerous and raw for anyone to touch directly. Even knowing he would die tonight, Theo had diverted it carefully into the spell, funneled through the wand.

If only the wand hadn't broken, perhaps I might have made use of it. But as it was, I had nothing except myself.

"Then the town will rise to his hand," I whispered. "One for the sea, and one for the land."

I opened all my senses to the maelstrom. The scent of the sea intensified: cold water and ancient things, deep as time. The stones of the bridge pressed against me, and I could almost taste the quarry they'd been taken from centuries before. Wind stripped the heat from my skin, but at the same time, I could hear the hiss and crackle of fire.

I threw aside every mental barrier and called on the maelstrom. And Widdershins answered.

Energy flooded into me, a feeling of power like nothing I'd ever experienced, even with the dweller. The dweller had been a separate thing—but this magic wasn't. This magic *was* me, or I was it. Or maybe there had never been a me at all.

Lightning danced across the sky, the electric lamps going out all at once. But it didn't matter, because the entire world was filled with light. The arcane rivers burned in my sight with blue fire, pouring in from the land and the sea, meeting in a swirl of current, which became a gigantic whirlpool, slowly rotating counterclockwise. The eye of the magical storm lay in the center of the bridge, but the energy didn't simply disappear, draining off to some deep place in the earth. Instead, a huge spire of blue-white light shot up from the center, vanishing into the clouds above.

"What is he doing?" Fiona shouted, sounding panicked. "Dear God, look at his eyes!"

I rose to my feet. The world around Theo shimmered as he shaped it to his will, giving me plenty of warning of the spell he meant to use against me. I tore the energy from him, and he cried out in shock and fear.

They hurled wind at me, and lightning, tried to drown me in the rain. None of it touched me at all, unraveling before the sheer flood of power moving through me. I should have been cold in the soaking rain, but instead I burned from within. Steam rose from my skin.

I ignored them and ran for the spire of light only I could see. The very heart of the maelstrom.

Heat blazed through the scars on my arm. My coat and shirt turned to ash, the same blue-white light of the maelstrom pouring from the scars. Fire burned along my nerves; my breath was wind, my blood the sea, and my bones the earth which held it. I could see the thousands of flickers of life in the city and the ocean, feel the press of their feet on my streets, hear their laughter and taste their tears.

Miss Lester and Amelie had been right. Widdershins did indeed know its own.

My feet no longer touched the bridge, my body buoyed up by magic. I left off fighting the spells the Endicotts cast, and instead drank them down, absorbing their power into the vast sea that was myself and the city and maelstrom all at once.

They sought to destroy me. To destroy everything. I would not let it happen. I would not.

With all the howling power of the vortex backing my will, the earth spell responded as easily as breath. The bridge shattered into rubble, dragging my cousins down into the river with it. Fins cut the water, the river boiling with ketoi, and Fiona let out a startled scream. Then the water closed over her head, and she was gone.

Theo clung to a broken pier, his spectacles askew and his face masked with blood. "Even if you succeed here, this isn't over," he snarled. "Others will come. You'll be hunted like the monster you are."

"Let them try," I said.

Clawed hands grasped his shoulders and legs, and he screamed. The sound cut off abruptly.

Amidst the churn of ketoi and blood and shattered stone, Persephone broke the surface. She held Mother's body in her arms, limp and unmoving. For a moment, our eyes met. Then she dove beneath the water, carrying Mother with her, and was gone.

I hung suspended between water and sky, earth and cosmic fire. My clothes were charred and tattered from the arcane power, but my pocket watch floated free, still connected to the scraps of vest. Lightning arced on its surface and played around the chain.

The Endicotts were dead, but the wave they'd raised was almost on us now. I could hear its distant roar, like the growl of some great beast coming to feed upon us all. Magical energy had turned into physical force, which would grind on until it spent itself against the land.

Or unless something else took the energy from it first.

I could make myself a conduit between the power of the wave and the maelstrom. If I could feed the energy through me, the wave would dissipate.

And what would it do to me?

I didn't know. And it didn't really matter, anyway. There was no other choice.

I concentrated on the distant wave, feeling it as I felt everything in Widdershins, through my connection with the maelstrom. I closed my hand on the pocket watch, curling it to my chest, as if by protecting the picture inside I could protect Griffin as well.

Then I stretched out my scarred hand and drew the energy of the wave into me.

Arcane fire poured through me, but this time it burned. I screamed, back arching, and it seared through my very soul. I tried to feed it into the maelstrom, to ground myself, but it was too much, too fast. My heart stuttered in my chest; my mouth tasted of burning iron. My bones were hollow, veins nothing but conduits for the forces funneling through me. Even the air in my lungs turned to fire. I couldn't breathe, couldn't see, couldn't, couldn't—

The light went out. A moment later, icy water slammed into me, quenching the fire and closing over my head.

"Ival! Breathe, damn it, breathe!"

I opened my eyes. My legs still lay in the shallows of the river, but my shoulders rested against something warm. Figures leaned over me, silhouetted in the light from lanterns. For a moment, their identities escaped me, my mind still half expecting to feel the city around me like an extension of my own body, to see the arcane fire. Then I blinked, and everything came into focus again. "Griffin?" I mumbled. "Christine? I thought I told you to stay at the museum."

"Oh, thank God." Griffin clutched me to him. I returned the embrace, feeling as weak as a newborn.

"If you really thought we'd stay behind, while you risked your life, I'll—well, I'll be damned insulted." Christine scowled at me from Griffin's side. She was soaked the bone, and with a start, I realized she must have come into the river after me.

"Wh-what happened?" I managed to ask. "The wave—"

"Whatever the Endicotts were doing, you stopped it." Griffin leaned back and stroked my face. "God, you scared the hell out of me."

"Your wound—"

"Hurts like the very devil. I'll need help getting back to the motor car." He grimaced in pain. "Perhaps I'll just stay here the rest of the night, actually."

I managed to sit up, afraid to put any weight against his injured torso. "Persephone—she had Mother."

"I saw." Griffin shook his head. "When you left, I had an idea. I thought Stanford must surely have one of the summoning stones on him. It was in his pocket. We thought we could call the ketoi back and have them help you. We met Fenton on the way here, and he brought us as quickly as he could. Christine threw the stone in and the ketoi came. Persephone had Heliabel, but...I don't know if she was alive or not by then."

Persephone had dove down with her body. Taken her to the sea. But for burial or transformation, I didn't know. And the silent river offered me no answers.

A sob tore through me, and I couldn't hold it back. I wept for Mother, and Guinevere, and Emily, and maybe even for myself. Christine took my hand, and Griffin held me close, and we sat in silence on the riverbank while the black waters rolled out to the sea.

CHAPTER 27

TWO WEEKS LATER, I sat in my new office at the Ladysmith. The tall window behind me let in a flood of late afternoon light, which proved a welcome addition to the lamp on my desk. I puzzled through scraps of broken clay tablets, trying to discern the cuneiform stamped into them.

"Do you have an appointment, sir?" Miss Parkhurst's voice drifted from her desk just outside the door.

Rather than demand my resignation, the board and president seemed to regard me as something of a hero. Why, I hadn't the slightest idea—my own brother had threatened them, and I'd participated in damage to valuable museum property while thwarting his actions. Not to mention everyone had witnessed me using sorcery and heard a ketoi call me her brother. My reputation had gone from slightly eccentric scholar to hybrid monster-sorcerer in a single evening. It all seemed a bit out of bounds even for one of the library staff, let alone the Antiquities Department.

But they'd been quite insistent the next day I not only remain, but accept a new office and a personal secretary. Although bewildered, it wasn't an opportunity I'd pass up. Even though she wasn't the most senior member of the secretarial pool, I'd insisted quite strongly on Miss Parkhurst. Unfortunately, neither she nor my new office could keep Christine from barging in whenever she pleased, but perhaps it was to be expected.

"I don't need an appointment to see my own son!" Father

snapped.

I sighed. After our confrontation, I'd not expected him to ever speak to me again. But the events of Hallowe'en had come as a heavy blow. Stanford's betrayal, losing Mother...

I still saw that moment, every night when I closed my eyes: the knife sliding into Mother's chest. Her blood soaking the stones of the bridge.

Her still, white body in Persephone's arms, as my sister bore her away from me.

I rose and went to the door. "Thank you, Miss Parkhurst." I glanced at the clock. "It's almost five—why don't you go home for the evening?"

"Are you certain you don't need anything before I leave?" she asked. "Coffee? Or perhaps some tea? Or—"

"We're fine," I assured her. I didn't want anything to prolong this interview.

She flushed lightly. "If you're certain, Dr. Whyborne. Have a lovely evening."

"And you as well, Miss Parkhurst." I gestured to my office. "Come in, Father, please."

He'd never visited me at the museum before. He stopped just inside the office and looked around with a critical eye. "And you say this is an improvement?"

"Quite." I took my seat. It felt unspeakably odd for me to be the one sitting behind the desk, and him the supplicant.

"A reward, I suppose," he said, sinking into the chair across from me. "For...things."

All of Widdershins was rife with rumors about what had happened on the Front Street bridge. Not to mention the strange behavior of the ocean on Hallowe'en, the tide suddenly rushing out, ships spotting a great wave coming in...and then nothing but the ocean returning to normal with a slow sigh. Even so, the loss of the historic bridge was ascribed to damage from the freak wave.

The incident in the museum, however, had been too public to cover up, even with all the money and lawyers Father could summon. The official story claimed Stanford had gone completely mad and attacked the gathering with a gang of hired thugs dressed in Hallowe'en costumes. The gang had mysteriously escaped, but Stanford been apprehended by...well...me, unfortunately. Griffin had chased reporters off our walk several times after the story made the New York papers, although fortunately, interest died away quickly.

"How is Stanford?" I asked.

Father looked old. Up until Guinevere's death, his sixty-five years had hung only lightly upon him. In the last few weeks, however, every one of them seemed to have marked his face and body. His eyes were sunken, his back bowed, his clothes loose on his frame.

"I escorted him to the asylum in New York this morning," Father said. He shook his head slowly. "He seems to hold the two of us responsible for everything."

I couldn't say I was surprised. Stanford had never been one to take responsibility for anything. Hadn't he even blamed Guinevere for her own death?

In truth, he should be grateful to have escaped the hangman. He wasn't even being shut away in Danvers as a lunatic, but within a private hospital where he wouldn't face the sort of abuse that had left such deep wounds on Griffin.

But I doubted he would see it that way. And certainly it offered little comfort to Father.

"I'm sorry," I said at last, uncertain what else to say. Hard enough to know my brother had killed our sister; how much worse must it be for Father? To have his adored son turn on him as Stanford had? To discover his wife and children were descended from eldritch abominations, and the daughter he'd thought dead for years lived beneath the sea?

"Have you heard any news concerning your mother?" he asked, and the uncertainty in his voice was almost painful to hear. He'd always been so filled with vigor and conviction. The broken man in front of me seemed almost a cruel parody.

"No." I'd spoken with Persephone twice since Hallowe'en. Mother had still clung to the vestiges of life when Persephone found her. The ketoi had performed the transformation ritual just in time, but Mother had been left terribly weak, and had gone to the ketoi city to heal. The matriarchs had welcomed her, and confirmed Persephone's right to rule as chieftess. The new queen beneath the flood.

But I hadn't heard anything in days. The knife, the blood, played out again and again inside my skull, eroding hope. What if Mother had died after all? What if...

What if she hadn't, but she no longer wished to see me? I'd been part of the cage which had held her on land, hadn't I? What if, now that she was free and had Persephone, she didn't want me anymore?

"I walk the beach every night, though. I'm sure I'll hear more soon," I said firmly. Not that it would matter in Father's case. Whatever had happened to Mother, whatever choices she made, she was beyond his reach forever now.

He only nodded. Like me, he wore a black mourning band on his sleeve. Technically, the Whyborne family had suffered a series of tragedies: Guinevere dead from some unnamed illness, Stanford gone mad, and the reclusive Mrs. Whyborne killed by the shock of her children's fates. Black crape hung on the bell at both Whyborne House and the one I shared with Griffin, and we'd all suffered through a mock funeral in which an empty coffin had been interred in Mother's place. The more wild papers claimed our family to be under a curse, the source of which varied from my involvement in Christine's Egyptian expedition, to one of the objects on display during the private Hallowe'en tours.

"Is there anything I can do?" I asked.

Father seemed to take a grip on himself. He sat up straighter and met my eye. "I came to inform you the legal papers have been drawn up and signed. You're my sole heir now."

"I...what?" All the breath seemed to leave my lungs.

"I've settled a yearly sum on Guinevere's son," he went on, ignoring my shock. "Once he comes of age, of course. Earl Gravenwold will continue to raise him, none the wiser as to his true parentage. I thought it equitable to provide for the boy, since he's of our blood. I hinted the Endicott twins might have poisoned Guinevere, and warned the earl not to trust any of that clan with the boy."

We didn't know if the twins had wired England with the news about the American branch of the family before their deaths, but if they had, Guinevere's son would surely be in danger as a ketoi hybrid.

"Hopefully he will take the warning seriously," Father went on. "And of course, Stanford's sons will receive the same yearly sum, although their mother seems of the opinion they should never again have contact with any of us."

"You can't be serious," I finally found the breath to exclaim. "Not about the boys—about me."

"You're all I have left."

The words hung between us for a long time. "How sad for you," I said at last.

"Damn it, boy." His eyes flashed, a bit of the old fire showing. "I was wrong. Do you understand? I underestimated you. You stood against Blackbyrne, and the Eyes of Nodens, and even if I don't know what happened on the bridge on Hallowe'en, I know we're all still alive when we wouldn't have been otherwise. You've got as much courage as any soldier I fought beside on the battlefield, despite your... tendencies."

I'd dreamed of this moment, as a boy. Laid in bed, or hidden in the garden, and dreamed of hearing Father praise me instead of Stanford.

But those dreams had died a long time ago. "Thank you," I said.

"But the answer is no."

His brows snapped together in a scowl. "You don't know what I mean to ask."

"No, I won't take my place at Whyborne Railroad and Industries. No, I won't move to New York to learn the business. No, I won't even move back to Whyborne House, as befits my status as your heir." I folded my hands in front of me. "I will live with Griffin, just as we are now, and remain here at the museum. And if you cannot accept my decision, you may do with your fortune as you see fit. I'm sorry for all you've lost—all our family has lost. But I don't owe you my life to fill the gap left by Stanford's absence."

For a moment, he glared at me. Then his face crumpled, and he looked away. "You meant what you said that day, didn't you? You hate me."

He sounded bewildered, as if he couldn't understand how his actions had led to this point. No wonder Stanford had such trouble accepting responsibility; he mimicked Father in that as in so much else.

Father had lost, if not everything, almost everything. His wife, his eldest daughter. His beloved son. Only I remained, the despised, bookish son whom he'd never understood. And now I told him he couldn't even have me.

"No," I said at last. "I pity you."

"Save your pity." He took a deep breath. "Still, I expect you and Griffin for Thanksgiving."

It caught me off guard. "I...if you're sure."

"I'm sure." He rose to his feet. "It's what your mother would have wanted."

A few hours later, Griffin and I walked hand-in-hand along a deserted stretch of beach just outside of Widdershins. We carried a lantern, although the light from the full moon gleamed from wave crests and shells, so bright we hardly needed any other source of illumination.

I'd come here every night since Hallowe'en. Once the doctors declared Griffin's wound healed enough for exercise, he made a point to join me. Persephone had met me twice, but it had been more than a week since she'd last appeared. With so many nights of glimpsing nothing more than dolphins, I was starting to lose hope.

The November cold turned the wind raw, and we strolled bundled in our overcoats, hats pulled low and collars up in an attempt to protect our faces from the chill. As we walked, I told Griffin of my conversation with Father. When I finished, Griffin squeezed my hand.

"So. I'm sleeping with the heir to the Whyborne empire now."

"I suppose. Not that it makes much difference," I said. "No doubt Father and I will get into a quarrel over the Thanksgiving turkey. By Christmas, he'll have me disinherited again. He'll probably leave everything to charity, or throw it all into the bay. Or have every cent entombed with him, like some Egyptian pharaoh."

Griffin chuckled. "I wouldn't put it past him." Then his expression grew more serious. "I received a letter today."

"Oh?"

"One of my brothers has been located. He's mining gold in the Yukon." Griffin offered me an uncertain look. "I know such news must be painful for you, after everything. But I wanted you to know."

"I'm glad for you," I said, and meant it. "Of course, given what happened with Christine's sister and my own family, you realize your brother will turn out to be some sort of insane cannibal sorcerer."

"No doubt. But I'm willing to take the chance." He glanced out to sea, then gasped. "Look!"

Figures arose from amidst the waves, one after the other. Their orca-like skin gleamed in the moonlight, and the jewelry forming their only clothing glittered amidst the sea foam. Persephone, Stone Biter, and others I didn't know.

And one I did.

She walked into the shallows, the tendrils of her tentacle hair lashing idly. The sea had resculpted her body, pared away any curves still left behind by illness, and bleached her skin to white marked with swirls of dark blue. But even if her fingers bore claws and razor teeth lined her mouth, I knew her at once.

"Mother!" I cried, and ran to meet her. For the first time since Hallowe'en, since the moment she'd stabbed herself with Fiona's knife, I felt I could breathe again.

"Percival." The arms around me were strong, stronger than I remembered her ever being in my life. "Oh, Percival."

Tears burned my eyes, and her wet skin soaked my clothing, but I didn't care. "Persephone said..." My voice broke, and I had to catch myself before trying again. "She said they'd reached you in time. That the transformation would save you. Heal you of everything. But I-I was so afraid...and when weeks passed and you didn't come, I started to worry something had gone wrong."

"Shh." She stroked my hair gently, then pulled back to look up into my face. Her features were no longer entirely human, but her eyes hadn't changed at all. They were still my eyes, and Persephone's. "I'm sorry. It took longer than I wanted to regain my strength. But I did, and I'm here now."

I swallowed against the tightness in my throat. "I was afraid you didn't want anything to do with me any more."

"Why would you think such a thing?" She gripped my arms, claws digging into my coat. "You're my son and I love you. Nothing could ever change that."

"I know. I just..." I wiped my eyes. "Ignore my foolishness. Are you...are you happy beneath the sea?"

Her smile was one of the most beautiful things I'd ever seen, even lined with shark's teeth. "Happier than I've ever been." She took my hands in hers. "I'm free. Free to go where I wish, do what I wish. To swim beside dolphins and dive with whales. Or to gather in the House of the Matriarchs and listen to the old tales—such tales!" Her eyes shone. "They asked for our stories in return, so I told them about the grail, and Camelot, and the brave knight Percival. My sea name is Speaker of Stories."

I managed a smile of my own, even though it was tinged with sadness. "I'm so happy for you." And I was. She had a life she could never have ever dreamed of before. And yet I couldn't help but be sorry for myself. Never again would I sit in her room, discussing those same stories she now told to ketoi. Never would I knock on the door to Whyborne House, the gift of a new book tucked under my arm. No more Christmas dinners or quiet teas.

It was selfish of me, of course. There was no mistaking the joy in her eyes, the exhilaration. She'd left behind the confines of her sickroom in exchange for a new world, one of magic and mysteries none of us who belonged to the land could comprehend.

"I'm not gone, you know," she said, correctly interpreting my expression. But then, she'd always known me better than anyone except for Griffin. "I'll return every month by the light of the full moon."

It wouldn't be the same. But at least it would be something. "I'll wait for you here. Every month."

Her fingers tightened lightly on mine. "If you wished it, you could come to the sea. They've given you a sea name already."

"What is it?"

"Fire in His Blood."

The memory of my coat and shirt charring into ash against my skin haunted my dreams some nights. Widdershins lay quiescent, but like a dozing cat, it might wake again at any moment. "I see."

"Think about it," Mother urged. "You could swim beneath the waves. Taste the waters of every ocean, and be honored for the magic in our blood. Love who you wish without fear. Be free of all the constraints society has placed on you."

How strange that, in the end, the Endicotts and the ketoi both wished to offer me the same thing. A part of me wondered what it would be like, to cast off all shackles of humanity and swim beneath the waves. I'd have my sister with me, and my mother, and perhaps other family members I'd never imagined existed.

But no amount of freedom was worth giving up Griffin. "I can't," I said gently. "I'm sorry."

She nodded. Her hands slowly slipped from mine, leaving me grasping only empty air. "I know. But I wanted you to understand you had a choice."

"Mother..."

"Here." A pouch hung knotted into the mesh of her loincloth; she untied the strings and held it out to me. "I asked Persephone if I could be the one to give these to you."

Oh. Oh dear. When Persephone hadn't come for so long, my worry about Mother had driven everything else from my mind. I'd forgotten I'd even asked for anything.

The pouch lay heavy in my hand, water spreading slowly across my palm. "Thank you."

"You're welcome." She pressed her lips lightly against my cheek. "Now, go back to Griffin, before he starts to wonder if I mean to drag you away beneath the waves."

"Goodbye, Mother." I blinked away tears. "Thank you."

"No, my son." She smiled at me, a bit sadly. "Thank you."

Then she was gone, slipping away beneath the water. The rest of the ketoi vanished as well. Their fins broke the waves here and there as they returned to deeper water. And then one leapt like a dolphin, bright and laughing and full of joy, before she plunged back with the rest and disappeared beneath the ocean.

I turned from the sea, holding tight to the pouch in my hand. My clothing was soaked to the knee, my shoes full of seawater and sand, and I shivered as I rejoined Griffin.

"Are you all right, my dear?" he asked. The lantern light gleamed from unshed tears in his eyes.

My sister was dead, my brother locked in an asylum, and my mother turned into a shark-woman. It seemed likely the English branch of the Endicotts would hunt me down like a rabid beast.

But for everything I'd lost, I still had Christine's friendship and Griffin's love. "I am," I said, and meant it.

"I'm glad." He glanced at the pouch in my hand. "What did Heliabel—or perhaps I should say Speaker of Stories—give you?"

Nervousness turned my stomach sour. If it had been possible to conceal the pouch at this point, I might have done so, just to give myself a little more time to prepare. "I, er, that is, the second time I spoke to Persephone, while you were still recuperating, I asked her to...Damn it, I'm saying this completely wrong."

Griffin's expression turned worried, which was the last thing I wanted. "Is something amiss?"

"No! No." I took a deep breath and began to pick at the knots on the pouch. My heart felt like it might pound its way right through my ribs. "I couldn't stop thinking about what Persephone said, when she climbed through the window that night. Morning. Whatever. About us." Would the damned knots never come free? "About how things are different, for, well, people like us, among the ketoi."

"I have, too," he said, and I caught the wistfulness in his voice. "If I could join you beneath the waves..."

Finally the knots gave way. I upended the pouch and shook out the contents into my palm. A pair of heavy gold rings of ketoi make fell out. Each was set with a pearl—one black and the other white—framed by a protective sigil to either side. Innocuous enough; they could easily pass for those denoting membership in a club or society.

Griffin looked at them, then back up at me, his brows drawing together slightly. "Ival...?"

My hand shook with nerves, but I would do this properly. I went down on my knee in the sand. At least my trousers were already half-ruined. "Griffin, I...well. It's not the same as a church ceremony, I know, but would you consent to call yourself my husband?"

His emerald eyes were wide, his lips parted in surprise, but no sound came out.

Oh dear. Why had this ever seemed like a good idea? What was wrong with me? "You, er, don't have to," I stammered. "I—"

"Yes."

"Yes?" I repeated like a fool.

His eyes brimmed, and his smile turned tremulous. "Yes, yes, God, of course I will."

My vision wavered, and I blinked rapidly, letting the tears fall. My chest didn't seem to be big enough to contain my heart, or my face to contain my smile. "Then—then put out your hand."

He did so, and I took it in one of mine. "Griffin Flaherty, I promise to love, comfort, honor, and keep you, in sickness and in health, for as long as we both shall live."

I slipped the ring with the pearl onto his finger. It fit surprisingly well. "With this ring, I thee wed," I said.

A sound that was half-laugh and half-sob escaped him. I rose to my feet, and held out the other ring with the black pearl. "Would you care to...?"

He took my hand. "Percival Endicott Whyborne, I p-promise to love, comfort, honor, and keep you, in sickness and in health, for as long as we both shall live." He slid the ring onto my finger. "With this ring, I thee w-wed."

His voice cracked, and he pulled me into his arms. His mouth tasted of salt spray and tears. "I love you, Ival. So much."

"I love you too, Griffin."

We held each other for a long time, crying and laughing by turns. The gold band on my finger felt heavy and real, and I couldn't stop looking at it.

Eventually, Griffin leaned back from my embrace. His eyes were red, his smile brilliant. "We should probably leave," he said. "The tide is coming in. And we can celebrate more properly at home."

I pulled him closer for another kiss, to sustain us until we reached our door. Then, hand-in-hand, my husband and I turned to Widdershins and left the sea behind.

The adventures of Whyborne, Griffin, and Christine will continue in Hoarfrost (Whyborne & Griffin No. 6), *coming 2015.*

About The Author

Jordan L. Hawk grew up in North Carolina and forgot to ever leave. Childhood tales of mountain ghosts and mysterious creatures gave her a life-long love of things that go bump in the night. When she isn't writing, she brews her own beer and tries to keep her cats from destroying the house. Her best-selling Whyborne & Griffin series (beginning with *Widdershins*) can be found in print, ebook, and audiobook at Amazon and other online retailers.

If you're interested in receiving Jordan's newsletter and being the first to know when new books are released, plus getting sneak peeks at upcoming novels, please sign up at her website jordanlhawk.com

Made in the USA
Lexington, KY
30 June 2015